MURDER
ON THE
LEFT BANK

MURDER
ON THE
LEFT BANK

CARA
BLACK

**SOHO
CRIME**

Published by
Soho Press, Inc.
853 Broadway
New York, NY 10003

Library of Congress Cataloging-in-Publication Data

Black, Cara
Title: Murder on the Left Bank / Cara Black.
An Aimee Leduc investigation ; 18
ISBN 978-1-61695-927-2
eISBN 978-1-61695-928-9
1. Leduc, Aimee (Fictitious character)—Fiction. 2. Women private investigators—France—Paris—Fiction. I. Title

PS3552.L297 M875 2018 813'.54—dc23 2017055168

Printed in the United States of America

10 9 8 7 6 5 4 3 2 1

For the ghosts, near and far, and the poet of twilight

"We must push against a door to know that it is closed to us."
—Michel de Montaigne, sixteenth century

"We see only what we are ready to see . . . taught to see . . . and ignore everything that is not a part of our prejudices."
—Dr. Jean-Martin Charcot, nineteenth century

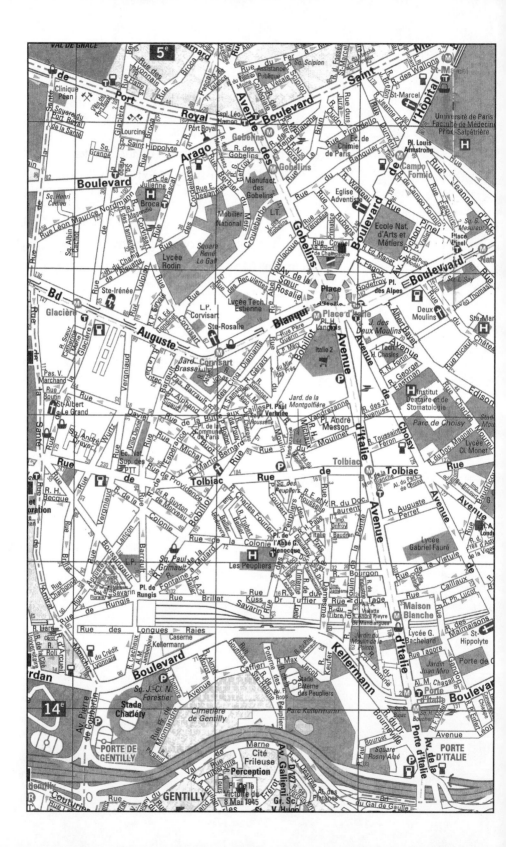

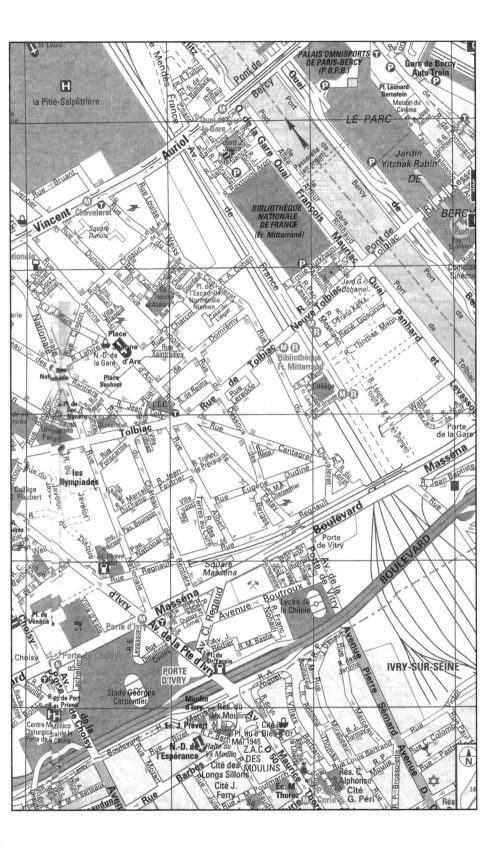

Paris • Early September 1999 • Friday

PALE AFTERNOON LIGHT filtered into Éric Besson's wood-paneled office as Monsieur Solomon untied the twine that bound together a bulging old notebook.

"We were prisoners together in a POW camp," Solomon said, wheezing, as the lawyer took hurried notes. "Stalag III-C, east of Berlin. Pierre saved my life." Another wheeze. "You understand why I did what I did."

Besson capped his pen. The effort of talking had cost Monsieur Solomon, who was in his eighties, and he reached for his oxygen mask. After several labored inhales, he grabbed Besson's arm with a crab-claw grip. "But Pierre's gone now," Solomon said. "It's all written in there: my confession, the amounts, dates. Years of entries."

Besson reached across his desk to take the notebook from the old man's shaking hands. He opened the well-worn volume to see columns of names and numbers, an accountant's tiny, perfect handwriting. He turned page after page, his eyes catching on names and franc amounts as it gradually dawned on him what he must be looking at.

Monsieur Solomon's rheumy brown eyes bored into the lawyer. "I'm dying. Get this to the right person."

Besson reached for his briefcase. "Tomorrow, first thing, I promise."

"*Non*, you must do it now."

A real pain, the old geezer. He'd waited fifty years to do the right thing, and now he couldn't wait one more day. "*Alors*, I'll keep your notebook in my safe. You don't have to worry—"

"Now," Monsieur Solomon interrupted. "This can't wait. I won't leave until you send a note to *la Procureure de la République*."

The old coot had barged into Éric Besson's office without an appointment—as well as anyone could barge with an oxygen machine. "My secretary's left already. I literally should be in court right now . . ."

Monsieur Solomon pointed a knobby arthritic finger toward the adjoining room. "Get that boy there, your helper. You trust him?"

"He's family, but—"

The old man stomped his shriveled leg. "If you can't trust family, then who? Send him."

Another bout of wheezing.

Worried that the old man would be carried out of his office on a stretcher—or worse, in a box—Besson stepped into the adjoining office, where Marcus was assembling a new chair. Marcus was Éric's sister's boy, a gangling, baby-faced eighteen-year-old with curly hair and the beginnings of a beard.

"Here's another job for you, Marcus," Besson said. "I need you to run this to *la Proc*."

"But I've got plans with Karine. A date."

Besson reached in his pocket for a wad of francs. "Do this, okay?"

Marcus glanced at his cell phone. "How long will it take?"

"Back and forth in a taxi, twenty minutes, that's all."

Besson shoved the old man's twine-bound notebook, its hand-written pages spilling out, into a plastic Monoprix shopping bag, knotted the plastic handles together, and zipped the sack into Marcus's backpack. "Go right away."

"Why can't it be tomorrow?"

Besson lowered his voice to a whisper. "Please, it's important, Marcus."

"Who is this old fart?"

"A friend of my mother's. Long story." The door buzzer sounded. Besson's colleague had arrived to pick him up for court in Meudon. "Marcus, just get this to *la Proc*. Tell her I sent you. Don't talk to anyone else. Don't meet anyone on the way except a taxi driver at the stand on the corner. *Comprends?*"

MARCUS, PERSPIRING, LOOSENED his collar as he shut his uncle's door and scanned Boulevard Arago. In the humid afternoon, a woman walked her schnauzer; a car radio blared news into the velvet air. No taxi at the stand.

Et voilà, Marcus would pocket the taxi fare and catch the bus. His uncle would never know. Marcus turned onto narrow rue Pascal and hurried through the dim tunnel created by the street that passed above it a block later. The tunnel echoed with his footsteps and with the rumbling of the cars passing overhead. The old notebook heavy in his backpack, he headed up the stairs to Boulevard de Port-Royal. Marcus was almost at the bus stop. He savored the thought of the money in his pocket.

His cell phone vibrated. His uncle. He ignored it.

Marcus scanned the sidewalk. Karine was standing near the bus stop and waved. Another call from his uncle. He ignored this one, too.

"You're late." A big pout on her red lips. He eyed her lace cami-sole top and hip-hugging jeans. "My friend's letting us use her place, remember?"

Marcus pulled her close. "We're going to a hotel. No attic room with bedbugs in the mattress today."

Karine shook her head. "On your allowance?"

He glanced at the time. "I've got to take care of a quick job first."

Karine's mascaraed eyes gleamed. "Why wait?"

What was the rush for the old fart—would an hour matter? "You're right. Meet me at the hotel on Cinq Diamants. Let me stash this first."

KARINE'S PERFUME FILLED the hotel room. Marcus laughed as he came up from under the duvet damp with their sweat. His laugh was cut short as a huge male arm caught him in a choke hold from behind. He gasped for air, tried to grab at the arm around his neck, but his wrists were yanked behind him, then flex-cuffed so tight the plastic cut his flesh. He was dragged off the bed and dropped facedown on the carpet.

The contents of his backpack rained down on his naked back. "Where is it?" a voice said.

Fear paralyzed him. He couldn't breathe.

A kick to his ribs. Then another. "Where did you put it? Tell me or I'll keep it up."

"I don't . . . know . . ."

"Of course you do. Where'd you hide it?"

All this over a stupid old notebook? But he couldn't fail his uncle. Maybe he could talk his way out of this, get this animal to untie him and then . . . what, jump out the window? What about Karine? "Let me up . . . and I'll . . ."

He coughed into the beige rug, his mouth furred from inhaling the dust and pilling. The flex-cuffs, slick with his blood, bit into his wrists like wire.

Karine was screaming . . . or was that him?

He couldn't see anything but beige and then the blindfold. His body was jerked up and slapped across the desk, the impact nearly snapping his spinal cord.

"I'll ask again. Where is it?"

"What do you want?" Marcus asked.

"Cut to the chase, kid. Then your fingernails will stay on . . ."

Paris • Late September 1999 • Monday Morning

HUMIDITY HOVERED IN the air, waiting for the drop in barometric pressure to drag Paris into autumn. A few leaves had turned and soon would carpet the cobbles yellow brown, red, and orange. It wouldn't be long before Aimée Leduc would have to break out her wool scarves. It was her first autumn as a mother, and for some reason, the changing temperature filled her with a sense of foreboding.

In Leduc Detective's office, Chloé squealed on the changing table while Aimée replaced her leaking diaper. Aimée had a meeting and wished her nanny would hurry up. She loved having her ten-month-old with her at the office in the mornings, but business was business; Aimée still had to earn their baguette and butter it, too.

Just then the frosted glass door buzzed open. Babette entered, accompanied by a wave of stale air from the landing. "*Désolée*, got held up by the Métro strike."

Another Métro strike. Tomorrow it would be nurses or bus drivers. September always brought the usual disruptions.

Behind Babette stood a tall man wearing a suit and dragging a rolling suitcase.

"This monsieur said he's here for a consultation," said Babette.

Consultation? No way—Aimée was on her way out the door to her emergency client meeting, and she still had an overdue proposal open on her laptop.

"Afraid not, monsieur," she said, wrangling Chloé's squirming, tiny feet through the leg holes of a onesie. "Today is completely booked."

"Forgive me for intruding, Aimée," said the man.

Aimée looked up. This time, she recognized his receding hairline. "Éric?"

It was Éric Besson, a thirtysomething intellectual property lawyer, buttoned-up and conscientious, the husband of the second cousin of Aimée's best friend, Martine. He looked as if he hadn't slept. Aimée had last seen Éric at one of Martine's huge family parties . . . a wedding, baptism—she couldn't remember.

"I hate dropping in," he said, his voice higher than she remembered, "wouldn't if it weren't important." Before she could ask if Martine had sent him, he'd wheeled his roller bag to her desk. "*Alors*, I'm catching a train to Brussels, giant court case. Please, can you give me five minutes?"

"Late night, eh?" She gestured to a chair. "Have a seat. Let me just finish a couple quick things."

Outfit accomplished, she quickly repacked the baby bag and kissed Chloé's warm pink cheeks. Babette waved Chloé's chubby hand as they headed out for *bébé* swim. Then Aimée opened her laptop, scanned her proposal's last paragraph, and hit SEND. "You've got my full attention."

Éric set a police homicide report on her late father's worn mahogany desk.

"What's this?" she asked, surprised. She sat back, felt a pressure in her chest. "*Non*, don't answer. You know I don't do criminal anymore."

Not since her father's death in the Place Vendôme explosion, when she'd inherited the agency and vowed from then on she'd do only computer security. That horrific day played in her mind: her father's melted glasses, his shoe . . .

Éric's anguished voice shook her from her reverie. "*Alors*, it's all my fault. I shouldn't have asked Marcus to do it. Never. I only wanted to help the old man. Now they're both dead."

Éric opened the folder and set it in front of her. Against her will, Aimée's gaze was drawn to the pages. A homicide investigation about a young man whose body had been discovered in the thirteenth arrondissement. In God's name, why was Éric showing her this?

"Should you even have a file like this?"

"I have a friend who got me a copy. The *flics* are writing off Marcus's murder as a drug deal gone wrong." Éric's shoulders heaved, and he covered his face. "He was only eighteen years old."

Aimée moved toward his chair and put her arm around him. "*Zut*, how did you get involved? You're an intellectual property attorney! This is a murder investigation."

"It involves you, too."

"*Moi?*" She doubted Éric had ever stretched the truth in his life. But there could always be a first time.

He wiped his tear-stained cheeks with the back of his hand. Glanced at his Rolex. "Please, Aimée, let me explain."

He seemed so shaken. She had to at least listen.

"I'm sorry, but it has to be quick. We both have places to be." As she spoke, she reached under the pile of files on her desk and pressed the button on the digital recorder hidden there. Standard procedure.

Éric wiped his eyes. Took a breath. "My mother grew up next door to a woman named Marie. They were best friends. Marie became a tapestry weaver, an *haute lissier*, at Gobelins."

Aimée suppressed her impatience.

"Marie married Léo Solomon, an accountant for the tapestry factory. He had been a POW in a German stalag. Marie and Léo were good friends of my parents. Last year, before my mother died, she told me Léo needed my help. She never explained, but I promised I

would help him if he ever came by my office. Two weeks ago, out of
the blue, Léo turned up, towing an oxygen tank. He was dying. Léo
had a secret and insisted the truth had to come out."

Aimée tried not to look at the time. "What does any of this
have to do with me?"

Éric's hands shook. "I'm getting there. Besides his work at
Gobelins, Léo also did accounting for his friend Pierre Espinasse,
who'd saved his life in the POW camp. Pierre had become a
policeman, as had three others they'd known in the camp. Pierre
was totally corrupt." He took a breath. "Early in the fifties Pierre
coerced Léo into funneling the officers' illegal kickbacks into
investments. Léo owed Pierre his life. But he always felt guilty
about helping them launder the money, and he kept a record of
everything, a notebook he filled with every detail of these investments for fifty years. Every person involved, every transaction."

"You saw this notebook?"

Éric's shoulders twitched. "It's a handwritten confession, with
fifty years of evidence to back it up. It names names—politicians,
ministers, business bigwigs, police . . . It's explosive."

Aimée nodded. She believed it. "You recognized these names?"

"Some. I made a few notes, but . . ." Éric's thick brows knit.
"Aimée, these *flics* taught at the police academy, knew your father."

Aimée felt a sinking in her stomach. On some level, had she
been expecting him to say that? The corrupt *flics* who'd killed her
father. "The Hand?"

Éric nodded. "That's what Léo Solomon called them."

Her hands were clenched so tightly her knuckles were white
against the desk. Her father's desk.

For almost thirty years, the Hand had diverted funds, taken
kickbacks, arranged cover-ups for ministers and politicians.
Libération had described the group as "endemic, institutional

corruption, top to toe" and *Le Monde* had called it a "deep-rooted protection racket run between police and government ministries." Aimée was the one who'd exposed them.

How could there be any remnant still running these schemes?

Her lips pursed. "I thought I'd taken care of them."

"According to Léo's confession, the Hand's morphed like a hydra. There are all kinds of business arms."

"But you have the notebook, written documentation. You can get it to *la Proc* and get it all sorted out. I still don't see what this has to do with me—"

"Your father's name was in there, Aimée."

Liar! she wanted to scream. Not her papa . . . no way did he ever take payoffs.

"From the little I read, I think he's implicated. I thought you should know."

"There's proof?" Her voice shook. Could she believe this? "*Alors*, I'm glad you told me—"

"*Non*, you're not." He stood, checked his phone. "The notebook was stolen. When Léo gave me the notebook, he wouldn't let me keep it in my safe. He insisted I send it directly to *la Proc*. Marcus, my sister's boy, was working for me, so I sent him as a courier."

He pointed to the homicide file.

"Marcus never showed up at the prosecutor's," he said. "Never answered his phone. Two days later his body was found."

Her blood ran cold. An eighteen-year-old boy murdered to cover up dirty police work? "You mean you think the Hand got to him? Didn't you say it was drug related?"

"The investigation claims Marcus was a druggie. A lie. Marcus was studying for his baccalaureate. Into girls, not drugs. He was on his way to meet his girlfriend, Karine, when I gave him Léo's package to take to *la Proc*. Karine has disappeared, too."

Convenient. "Did Marcus tell this girl, Karine, what was in the notebook?"

"Marcus didn't *know* what was in the notebook. He wouldn't have had time to look—he was to take it directly to *la Proc*. And no one knew where he was going; I gave him strict instructions. None of this was arranged in advance. But he was murdered on his way to deliver it."

Goosebumps rose on Aimée's arms.

"Maybe you can find out more about this Karine. Computer investigation, that's your expertise, *non?*"

He made it sound easy.

"It's not much, but all my notes are there. Please find her."

"Why should I get involved in any of this, Éric?"

"Your father was murdered by the Hand. I read in the papers about what you did. But is it really over, Aimée? A lot of people got 'retired,' and a lot of scandal got swept under the rug. Whitewashed. But Léo wrote it all down."

"And an old man's notebook is going to prove what? No doubt it's been destroyed by now anyway, *c'est ça?*"

"Please, Aimée. My sister asked me to give her son a part-time job, and instead I got him killed. All I'm asking you is to help me find Karine."

She hated missing-person cases, even if her *grand-père* had built Leduc Detective's reputation on them. Bile rose in Aimée's throat as she scanned the photocopied police report.

"You'll find her, Aimée?"

She had a baby to raise, a business to run, and a partner who'd shoot her if she took on any more cases. But Papa . . . Papa's name . . .

She nodded. "We keep this between us, Éric."

IF SHE DIDN'T hurry, she'd miss the whole computer security meeting. She stuck Éric Besson's materials in her secondhand
Vuitton bag. In her head she could already hear René, her partner,
saying, *Don't get involved*.

In the taxi, Aimée checked to make sure there was no lipstick
smudged on her teeth. Despite her sweating palms, she reapplied
mascara and paged through her notes. Checked there were no
teething biscuits hiding in the pocket of her vintage Lanvin
suit—a steal at the flea market.

Now she stood in a makeshift office on the ground floor of the
Bibliothèque François-Mitterrand. It reeked of fresh paint. Leduc
Detective had snagged the new *bibliothèque*'s contract, along with
a headache. This library had been President Mitterrand's baby,
although it was realized only after his death, and it had been riddled with technical glitches from day one. The ground it was built
on was cursed, the old timers said—it had once been the rail yard
where Jewish deportees' confiscated goods were packed and sent
on to the Reich.

The pink-faced, fiftysomething *fonctionnaire* threw a report on
the office desk. "*Mon Dieu*, network connection problems? Isn't
that what we hired you to iron out?"

"*Bien sûr*, monsieur, and we have," she said.

René Friant, all of four feet tall, took out a handkerchief to
wipe his wide brow. "However, subsequent problems have arisen."

"*Évidemment!*" the *fonctionnaire* snorted. "Eh, why has the
system crashed? What are you doing about it?"

René opened a file. "Our reports show an external system
caused the disruption."

"What does that mean, 'external'?"

As if they'd ever be able to make this clueless administrator
understand the inherent problems in the library's poorly designed

computer system. An old-school classicist, he'd proudly boasted he didn't own a computer himself. If the *fonctionnaire* didn't appreciate how complicated their job was, they'd lose this big contract.

Eyeing the tight suspenders he wore over his blue button-down, Aimée summoned a smile. "Let us show you how we've outlined the problem." Aimée prompted René with a meaningful look. René was much better at outlining complicated tech concepts for laypeople.

"We're here to help, monsieur." René beamed, exuding the famous Friant charm. "Let me explain."

Again wiping his brow with his handkerchief, René launched into his spiel.

Trying to keep her distracted mind from wandering back to Éric Besson and his missing notebook, Aimée surveyed the showpiece library, which had been open fewer than three years and plagued with catastrophes from day one. She knew it had been built not only without consulting technicians but also without consulting librarians. Mitterrand had dreamed of glass-windowed towers, which had looked breathtaking on the architectural plans but had ruined the books with direct sun exposure. The computer system crashed daily; students were unable to check out books; the librarians went on strike. The list went on.

"We've employed antivirus software to detect malware that's exploited your system's vulnerabilities," René was saying. He reached for his bottle of water. "We have automatic patching systems fixing that."

"You mean this service?" The *fonctionnaire* pointed to a report.

René nodded midgulp.

"*Exactement*," said Aimée, stepping in. "However, monsieur, you have to remember that software vulnerabilities aren't the most common attack vector."

"What do you mean by that?" The *fonctionnaire* plopped down on a large leather chair, which emitted a "puahh."

It sounded like a fart.

"The most common way hackers of all stripes break into networks is stealing passwords," she said. "Then they set up man-in-the-middle attacks to piggyback on legitimate log-ins and masquerade as authorized users."

The administrator rubbed his forehead. "So you're saying what exactly?"

"Credential stealing was how your network was penetrated," Aimée said, trying to keep her voice even. "With your permission, monsieur, we'll revamp your authentication systems with two-factor authentication, one-time passwords, physical tokens, and a bar code authentication."

Hydrated now, René took over again. "None of these measures is foolproof. But our firm will monitor constantly, detect attacks, and respond quickly to maintain your network security more effectively."

René handed the administrator a folder with Leduc Detective's logo on it.

"It's all in there," René said. A final dashing smile to close the deal. "We know you want the system humming efficiently. We want to help you achieve that."

Ten minutes later, a semipacified administrator signed off on their updated services proposal.

Outside, Aimée and René stood on the pedestrian walkway. Behind them loomed Bibliothèque François-Mitterrand's four glass towers and a forest of cranes over construction sites. Forlorn abandoned factories, covered in graffiti, stood semigutted amid the revitalization of the new Rive Gauche.

She noticed accusation in René's large green eyes. "You were winging it in there, Aimée."

"Let's get away from the relentless earthmovers."

At the quietest café they could find, Aimée gravitated to the counter and ordered a large mineral water. Only when she noticed René's wince of pain as he climbed up on the high stool did she remember how badly his hip dysplasia was acting up. *Merde.* Thoughtless.

Better to pretend she hadn't seen it.

But she couldn't.

"You all right?" she asked.

A snort. "Apart from having a partner who comes unprepared for a huge client meeting?"

"*Alors*, I did prepare! But you were *parfait. Comme d'habitude.* You got the deal done."

The Badoit, beaded with moisture, arrived. The waiter, in his long white apron, averted his gaze from René's short, dangling legs.

René's eyes flashed with anger. Instead of massaging his ego, her remark had had the opposite effect. "And you were late. Like always."

"*Desolée.*" She had to shift his mood. "*Très distingué,*" she said, pointing at René's new cocoa cream linen suit. René set the bar for dapper at any height.

"Don't think you can distract me like that."

"What do you mean?"

René pointed to the police report sticking out of her open bag, only half-obscured by baby wipes. "Why do I have a bad feeling that was what made you late?"

Great. Why did she always forget he read her like one of those sun-damaged books in the library? She'd thought she could get away with not even telling René about Éric's visit, had planned to dedicate a few online hours that afternoon to finding Karine. Or trying to, at least.

"We agreed when Chloé was born, Aimée. No cases beyond our workload and to always be up front and transparent with each other. And absolutely no criminal cases. Remember?"

"You're right." Up front and transparent? *Bon*, instead of lying to her partner, she'd give him an edited version. "Remember Éric Besson, the nerdy lawyer who is always at Martine's parties?"

René sipped his fizzing Badoit. "You mean the Dungeons and Dragons aficionado?"

René, an aficionado himself, never missed an opportunity to find fellow D&Ders. So far, a good sign.

"That one." She pointed to the police file. "So the poor guy blames himself for this kid's murder."

"How does it involve you?"

She hesitated. Bought time by downing her Badoit. The mineral water's sodium on her lips made her stomach growl. All she'd had to eat that day were the remnants of Chloé's yogurt and a crumbling teething biscuit she'd found in her bag. No time for breakfast.

"What aren't you telling me?"

She sighed, described haggard Éric Besson's visit, his begging her to find his murdered nephew's missing girlfriend. She left out the part about the notebook and her father.

"Terrible but not your problem, Aimée."

"Did I ask to get involved, René? Two hours digging and I'll find her."

"You agreed to help him and weren't going to tell me?"

Hurt filled his big green eyes.

"It's not like that, René. Éric needs help. You would have done the same, *non*?"

René's phone rang. Uncharacteristically, he answered it right away. "*Oui*. At two?" He glanced at his watch. Wiggled off the stool. "I'll make it."

He hung up and set down his phone to root in his linen jacket pocket for his car keys. A new girlfriend? Hot date?

She hoped it was that programmer she'd introduced him to the week before. Curious, she stole a glance at his phone. But at the top of the call list was a medical office. "Got a doctor's appointment, René?"

He paused. "Why do you say that?" He sounded more startled than annoyed.

"Psychic powers."

"You snooped," he said, glancing at the call list as he picked up his phone. "Allergies." He threw some francs on the counter. "Back at the office later."

And he'd gone.

Downstairs, she looked up the clinic's name in the old much-thumbed phone book in the phone bank by the WC. Back at the counter, she called the clinic.

"*Bonjour*, I'm looking for an allergy specialist—"

"Mademoiselle," interrupted a stiff voice, "this is a cardiac unit."

Aimée hung up. Talk about being up front and transparent. Why hadn't René told her?

SHE COULDN'T GET it out of her head as she rode the bus to the office. René's thirst, his perspiration, his bad temper. There'd probably be a simple explanation—maybe he'd just gone for a checkup. He'd be all right, wouldn't he?

She drummed her fingers on the bus seat as her call to his phone went to voice mail. Left a message. Next to her, a middle-aged woman was reading a recipe in *Femme Actuelle*. Aimée felt the hunger pangs. *Tripes à la mode de Caen* sounded good to her right then, and she hated tripe. She pushed the thought of food aside and tried to concentrate on the homicide report, which she shielded from prying eyes with an *ELLE* magazine. A breeze carried the smell of freshly watered greenery and musky foliage through the open window as the bus passed the Jardin des Plantes.

She'd need to multitask when she got to the office, try to squeeze in her search for Karine while she was implementing the Bibliothèque François-Mitterrand project. Finish it all in time to get home and give Chloé a bath.

As the bus crossed Pont de la Tournelle, Aimée turned a page. Read the horrific details about the discovery of Marcus's body when it was recovered in the rue Watt and let out a gasp.

"Those models. Too thin, eh?" The woman next to her nodded knowingly. "A scandal."

If only it were that.

STRUGGLING OUT OF the wire-cage elevator onto her office landing, Aimée hoisted her heavy Vuitton bag, which kept slipping off her shoulder, and punched in the door code. Leduc Detective's frosted glass door clicked open. In her rush, her Louboutins slipped on an envelope lying on the wood parquet.

She grabbed the door frame in time and righted herself. *Merde.* Someone must have slipped the envelope under her door. Another notice from the landlord attempting to hike up her rent?

She tossed the envelope on her desk, ground coffee beans, and brewed herself an espresso. The real thing—hopefully it would get rid of the bad taste left by the homicide report. Afternoon light—the hue of faded parchment—warmed her wrists as she powered up her computer.

The first sip of espresso, sweet and strong, was just hitting her as Maxence, their Québécois intern, entered. He was lugging a box of computer paper. Grinning, he dumped the paper in the corner and set a stack of mail on her desk.

"I'm making up hours, Aimée," he said, peering at her for approval through his long Beatle bangs. He wore a black turtleneck despite the September warmth. "René said it was a good time, with all the Y2K preparations and the *bibliothèque*'s issues. Shoot me anything you need updated."

"*Parfait.*" She'd off-load those mind-numbing report updates and tick that off her list. Already this afternoon looked more manageable. She downed the rest of her espresso and plugged in her phone to recharge.

But no sooner had she sat down than the phone started ringing. A seemingly endless parade of client calls—it wasn't until two hours later that she got back to Éric's notes on Marcus.

Éric had little information about Karine—he didn't know her last name, address, or school affiliation. Marcus had never told him how they'd met, where they hung out.

Great.

What Éric did know was that she lived in the housing towers in the thirteenth arrondissement and that she was of Cambodian origin. No wonder the *flics* couldn't find her. Who could without a name, a school? A Cambodian girl in the notorious block towers in *la petite Asie*, the area of the thirteenth often mistakenly referred to as Chinatown, where many of the inhabitants were of Southeast Asian heritage.

That information narrowed it down to what, thousands of possibilities? If Karine had been murdered, no corresponding bodies had appeared at the morgue. But as the saying went, "no one ever dies in Chinatown, left or right bank." Passports and IDs were sold and passed on.

And no one talked to the *flics*.

In the margin of the homicide report, someone had written in red pencil, *Find a grain of rice in that rice bowl?*

She listened to her recording of Éric's visit, replaying it to see if she could catch anything between the lines. Éric mentioned Marcus's mother, his own sister, but no additional information. Where was she, and what would she know? Aimée made a note to ask Éric.

Meanwhile, where had Marcus and Karine been headed on their date? A date meant what to an eighteen-year-old—a movie, a meal? In her student days—not so long ago—it was a jump under the sheets in the hours stolen from study group. Never at home, where you might run into family, or at a hotel, which cost money. In her case, she'd usually made use of a friend's place.

According to the investigation file, there were no reported fares from the taxi stand on Boulevard Arago the afternoon Marcus disappeared. Nor were there any young male passengers matching Marcus's description deposited at le Tribunal within an hour on either side of his departure. She studied the police note regarding Marcus's cell phone. They'd triangulated his last call location via the cell phone towers. A place to start. She put that on her follow-up list.

René always said, think of statistics as your friend. Using her newly won streamlined Bibliothèque François-Mitterrand portal access, Aimée started paging through census records she would otherwise be able to review only onsite. By law, French censuses didn't ask questions regarding ethnicity or religion, but they did gather information concerning one's country of birth. As of the 1990 census, there were almost eight thousand Cambodian-born Parisians, and close to half were former Cambodian citizens who had become naturalized as French.

She sat back. Drummed her pencil.

How could she find Karine?

MANY OF THE Cambodians in Paris had fled the Khmer Rouge's bloodbath. If Karine's parents had been part of that wave fleeing Pol Pot and emigrated in the seventies and Karine was Marcus's age, give or take—so born around 1981—she most likely was a French citizen. But no missing person report for her had been filed, according to these notes.

The single police line of inquiry to find Karine had been confined to the known Cambodian clubs and bars. The usual path flics investigated for call girls. It had turned up nothing. Aimée saw no link to vice—where had the idea that Karine worked the streets come from anyway?

Aimée put that aside. Would think about it later.

She'd widen the census search net, define new filters using a three-year age range and targeting the thirteenth arrondissement.

Two hundred and sixty Asian females, not one with the name Karine. Her parents might have registered her with a Cambodian name—but then how in the world would Aimée find her?

She scanned Éric's notes again. There was no mention of the flics' checking out the towers.

She combed through the homicide file. It showed a thorough investigation in some areas, in others only very cursory inquiry or no inquiry at all. That bothered her. A lot.

She glanced at Maxence, who was working on René's computer, headphones on.

She'd map out the little she knew. Things stood out if you put them down, her father always said.

The white dry-erase board was taken up by their project status updates, so she unrolled the butcher paper. Tacked up a sheet and got her markers out.

Karine
Background Cambodian, age and address unknown.
Date with Marcus—location unknown.

Marcus Gilet (nephew of Éric Besson)
Found in rue Watt in the thirteenth
Lived in the thirteenth above Besson's office on Blvd. Arago.

After a moment's thought, she added:

Léo Solomon
Gobelins accountant
Address unknown

Léo had been the one who'd started this, the one who'd worked for the Hand.

She pulled out a detailed street map of the thirteenth arrondissement and tacked it below. With her marker, she drew X's on the following locations: Éric Besson's office, the last ping from Marcus's phone, the tunnel in rue Watt where his body was found, and Gobelins, the tapestry factory where Léo Solomon had worked.

As strong as Éric's belief was that Marcus's murder was connected to the notebook, there was no proof.

Neither Marcus's wallet nor his phone had been recovered.

The handful of numbers the cell company had identified on Marcus's call record belonged to Éric, a tutor, and a cinema. Hadn't this kid had a life?

How had he arranged a date with Karine? Old-fashioned notes and letters? Smoke signals?

Or he'd had a burner phone for his private life. Aimée had at his age. Well, back then it had been a pager.

If such a phone had existed, the *flics* had found no trace of it. Too bad. Aimée could have called in a favor with her connection at France Télécom. Maybe she could have found Karine that way.

She rubbed her eyes, tired from staring at her screen all

afternoon. She needed to get out, breathe the air, and walk the cobbles—plus she had a burning desire to see the spot where Marcus's phone had last been pinged.

The last place he was seen alive? Maybe the girl had been seen, too?

If you didn't visit the crime location, it wouldn't be real to you, her father used to say. Go smell it, breathe it, until you get the feel of the place. Know it, and you'll have a better shot at knowing your victim.

She'd go on her way home. First, though, one last cross-check: she'd try to figure out if any of the 260 Asian females lived or had lived in the towers. The family might have moved, but it gave her a starting point.

It took longer than she'd hoped—there were four different addresses to check. Of the four women who lived in the towers, only one's name began with a K—a Kalianne. Aimée ran a name search; Kalianne came from the Khmer word meaning "little darling." A counterpart to the French Karine?

If Aimée were to call on the phone, it might panic the girl's family. Better to go in person.

But she needed more.

Benoît, the hunk she'd been seeing, taught Asian studies at the Sorbonne—almost as convenient as the fact that he lived across the courtyard from her. She liked Benoît's company as much as his cooking and his amazing skill under the duvet. But his phone went to voice mail; he and his sister, whose baby daughter, Gabrielle, shared childcare with Chloé, must still be away on their parents' anniversary trip. *Merde.* Aimée left a message.

With only an hour before Babette was off duty for the night, Aimée had to get moving.

Maxence took off his headphones as she grabbed her jean jacket and scarf. "I'm coding until René returns," he said.

Merde again. Why hadn't René returned her call?

"Anything else you need?" He grinned. "Always ready for a mission."

"Maybe you can see what you can learn about this older *mec* Léo Solomon." She copied down his details quickly for Maxence. "I'd like to find out all the firms he did accounting for."

Maxence loved a challenge. "On it."

LATE AFTERNOON WIND scattered red paper candy wrappers and blew them up against the stained concrete wall. Students, the after-school lycée loungers, hung out in front of the Asian grocers' shops. The faces reflected the quartier's diverse ethnic population.

Aimée felt conspicuous—her Lanvin suit pencil skirt, selected for the meeting at the *bibliothèque*, wasn't quite dressed down enough with an Indian scarf, jean jacket, and ballet flats. As the sole non-Asian in sight, she stood out.

She followed an old grandma with full shopping bags from Loo Frères, an Asian *supermarché*, into the tower's vestibule, holding the door for the old woman after she entered the door code.

The tower was a characterless reminder of seventies architecture. At least the elevator worked, even if its gears ground with juddering fits and starts. The ride gave Aimée time to polish up her story.

She got off on the fourteenth floor. The scuffed, once-green linoleum almost matched the greasy celadon concrete walls. She knocked on the apartment door—she was starting with Kalianne, whom she hoped would turn out to be Karine. No answer.

She listened for sounds—conversations, a *télé*, or a radio. Nothing. Cooking smells came from down the corridor.

She'd try the next address. This time she took the stairs. All the addresses she'd culled were in this building, thank God.

A girl of about twelve answered the door in yellow pajamas and pigtails. *"Oui?"*

"Would your sister Karine be here? Her school gave us permission to contact this address about the scholarship."

"My big sister?"

"Desolée, did I get her name wrong?"

"Well, they call her Camille at school. But now she lives in Toulouse with my aunt."

An older man came to the door. He wore an undershirt and scratched his chin. "What you want?"

Aimée vaguely described a scholarship for Cambodian students. He shook his head. "No kids in school except this one."

"What about the Cambodian families in this building? I'm looking for Kalianne, or maybe you know her as Karine. Do you know her?"

"Never heard of her."

She got basically the same answer at the other apartments. No one knew a thing. Or if they did, they kept quiet. Not that she blamed them if they covered up for their own. In their shoes, she might do the same.

Of the four Cambodian girls living in the tower who had come up in Aimée's search, Kalianne was the only one unaccounted for.

Back on the fourteenth floor, Aimée's calves ached, and there was still no answer to her knock. She pressed an ear to the door. The apartment on the other side was silent. Most likely everyone was at work.

She followed the smell of coriander, garlic, and chilies several doors down. Her stomach rumbled.

A woman in a lab coat answered Aimée's knock. Her brown hair was clipped up, and she wore latex gloves. Wonderful, spicy smells filled the apartment, which was jammed with teakwood furniture.

She took one look at Aimée. Shrugged. "I've already told the housing council, I'm here with permission to administer home treatment. Monsieur Khee is a housebound diabetic."

"*Alors*, it's not that," she said. "Sorry to take your time, but I'm desperate. I'm trying to reach the family in 1401. Their daughter's applied for a scholarship we're offering to Cambodian students. I wonder if Monsieur Khee can help me locate her, Karine or Kalianne—"

"He's just had a treatment. I don't think—"

"Who's there?" a man's voice demanded.

"*Attendez*," said the nurse. "I'll ask him."

By the time the nurse returned, Aimée was so hungry, all she could think about was whatever was cooking.

"Half-breed," the nurse said, "his words. Monsieur Khee asked if she would qualify."

Aimée was taken aback.

"The girl's part Cambodian, part French," said the nurse, looking embarrassed. "Is the scholarship only for full Cambodians?"

"We're not allowed to ask that question on our application forms," Aimée said carefully. "Does Monsieur Khee know how I can reach her?"

"He hasn't seen the family for a while. Several weeks. Heard they've moved out."

At about the time of Marcus's murder?

"A Fukienese family will move in. Monsieur Khee likes that. He's Fukienese."

"Does he have any idea where they went?"

"That's all he knew."

Nothing more to learn here. Yet she couldn't give up without finding something. The nurse had been more forthcoming than anyone else. "Do you treat any Cambodian patients?"

"Not since last year."

Monsieur Khee called from the back, "What's she want now?"

The nurse started to close the door.

"Isn't there any place where Cambodian kids in the building hang out?" Aimée said in a rush.

The nurse paused. "The Cambodian lycée kids stick together. It's all very segregated. Try Bánh Tân Tân, the pâtisserie. They hang out there."

"No hurry, Aimée," said a breathless Babette on the phone. "We just got back from the park. Dinner will take a while. Take your time."

A jewel, Babette. *Merci.*

Outside the building, Aimée felt eyes on her back. She pulled out a file, pretended to consult it, and headed in what she hoped was the right direction.

From the lycée loungers, she heard snickers as she went by. ". . . *la bureaucratie*, regulations . . ." Good, let them think she was a pencil-pushing *administratif* from social welfare. Nice cover. She'd use that more often.

She noticed how they nodded to a young man with short-cropped hair, gang tattoos on his neck.

Aimée smiled at the young Asian woman sweeping the candy wrappers and sodden leaves off the cracked pavement in front of Bánh Tân Tân, which specialized in Cambodian and Vietnamese pâtisserie. Scents of coconut milk and toasted sesame drifted from the shop's open door.

"*Bonjour*, my friend says you bake the best *boua loy*." Thank God the bright window held a photo display of sweets with their names written phonetically in large roman letters. "I hope you've got some left."

"*Bien sûr.*" The woman smiled. She was in her late twenties and had brown streaks in her black bob. "Our baker remarried; hence the Vietnamese name. But your friend was right—we're the best."

The shop's interior was adorned with red good luck banners, and gold-flecked lanterns—*exotisme* anchored by butter. A bright-colored shop inviting happiness, Aimée thought. Chloé would love it. "What's that?" Aimée pointed to what seemed like pastel sticky rice wrapped in banana-leaf bundles.

"Ah, that's for the Pchum Ben festival."

Aimée had to appear interested, keep the conversation going, and steer it toward Karine. "So it's a special festival tradition?"

"To feed the hungry ghosts," she said, smiling. "It's to honor our ancestors and relatives. *Alors*, in April, during our Cambodian New Year, there's a line out the door," she said, the lilting accent to her French tempered by glottal syllables.

"I believe it," said Aimée, taking in the trays of mostly Cambodian sweets, along with macaroons and rainbow gâteaux. "But I heard after school there's a rush."

"You missed it," she said.

"*Zut*, thought I'd see Karine."

No reaction. The young woman used aluminum tongs to pick up the sweets Aimée pointed out. An older woman wearing an apron brought a tray of fresh, hot, steaming buns. "My auntie just baked our sweet red bean specialty," the young woman said. "Like to try?"

At this rate, Aimée would buy up the shop. "Karine's told me how good they are." Stupid. Think of something smarter. "Give me two."

Again no reaction. Had she blown this? Made a fruitless trip to end up with only a mountain of sweet calories to bring home?

"Ah, stupid me," she said, frowning. "You'd know her as Kalianne. Her boyfriend, Marcus, works for my friend Éric. That's how

I know her." That sounded as awkward as she felt. But she was chasing a hunch.

Just then a woman rushed in flourishing a receipt. Pointed at a birthday cake with an inscription in green icing. An excited conversation in Khmer ensued.

Aimée noticed the wall behind the tall rolling dolly racks was covered in photos—snapshots of customers, young and old, eating the signature sweets.

"Help her. Go ahead." Aimée took one of the red bean confections off the tray and stepped back to study the wall. Starving, she wolfed down the pastry in two bites. Then another. The sweet bean paste stuck to her teeth, and she was already suffering a sugar high by the time she saw what she was looking for.

"I can ring you up now, mademoiselle," said the young woman, smiling.

"Call me Aimée. You're Lili, *non?*"

The young woman cleared her throat. "*Oui . . .*"

"Lili, you're here in the photo with Karine and Marcus." Aimée pointed to a smiling trio of Lili, squinting in the sun; a tall, curly-haired boy with the beginning of a beard; and a stunning half-Asian girl. Their names were written in pink marker underneath. "Where's Karine?"

Fear flashed in Lili's eyes. "How would I know?"

"We need to talk, Lili. Now."

"I'm working."

Lili plastered a smile on her face as the auntie brought in new hot trays of sweet bean buns. As Lili rang up Aimée's purchases, Aimée pulled the photo off the wall and stashed it in her pocket. Lili handed her a fragrant bag.

"Lili, it's talk to me or the *flics*. Got a preference?"

"You're some kind of what . . . undercover?"

Aimée shook her head. "*Pas de tout*. I want to help Karine. Get her out of some deep trouble. I'm the only one who can."

Lili looked around uneasily.

"If you don't talk to me, I'll be asking your auntie."

Lili hesitated, then wrote an address on the receipt. "Buy a ticket and go inside. Thirty minutes."

AIMÉE FOUND THE address behind the *mairie* of the thirteenth on Place d'Italie, a gargantuan Italianate Haussmann building.

The meeting place was a historic Haussmannian theater. Atop the façade she saw a sculptured frieze with the figures of Tragedy and the voluptuous goddess Comedy—attributed to a young Rodin.

Not the meeting point she'd expected.

Inside, she found an exhibition of vintage movie posters and a ticket booth.

"Film's started, mademoiselle. Would you like to wait for the next showing?"

A film buff, she hated arriving after a film began.

"*Non, merci*," she said. Bought a ticket.

It took a moment for Aimée's eyes to adjust to the darkness. She felt her way along the back of dark velvet seats. Only a few were occupied. The silhouetted heads were black blobs against the screen. The black-and-white silent film was accompanied by a pianist dramatizing the score.

Mon Dieu. She'd never seen a silent movie in a theater. The piano pulled the story along, punctuating, highlighting, rippling, and fading with an ever-changing tempo.

The iconic actress, Louise Brooks, had the biggest eyes. Black, fathomless. Her expressions spoke volumes. A curious radiance haloed her face—Aimée realized it must have come from the glow of a backlight.

Where was Lili? Had she given Aimée the slip and a bogus address?

"Ssss, here," a voice said.

Aimée found Lili in the last row.

She wedged herself into a seat. "Where's Karine, Lili?"

"I don't want trouble. *Compris?*" Lili's soft accent dangled on each syllable.

"*Bien sûr.* She's in danger."

"Me, too, if this gets back. And I don't see how it can't."

But she'd shown up. Must have something to say. "I'm a PI. Talk to me. It's safe."

"*Quoi?*"

"*Détective privé.* Marcus's uncle hired me." Not exactly a lie. "You know Marcus was murdered, *non*? And Karine is missing? The *flics* blame it on drugs, call Karine a hooker, but it's not true, is it?"

Lili stood. "*Non*, don't involve me, please." She disappeared into the shadows.

She'd blown it.

Aimée caught up with Lili under the exit sign, where she stood trembling against the burgundy velvet curtains. The piano music crescendoed.

"*Desolée*," Aimée said, rummaging through her brain to find the right words. "I'm trying to help Karine. Can you help me?"

Lili looked ready to bolt. "I don't know anything."

"You're afraid. I understand."

"Understand?" Her lips quivered. "How could you understand?"

"*Alors*, you're here. You want to help Karine. So do I." Aimée had to think of how to get through to this scared young woman. "Marcus was murdered, and Karine's in danger. Please tell me what you know. Please. I won't mention your name to the police."

"You think I worry about *les poulets?*"

The old term for police, since what was now the *préfecture* was once a medieval chicken market. Funny what stuck from centuries ago.

"Who then?"

"The ones with tattoos."

Aimée's mind went to the tattooed *mec* who the lycée students nodded to outside the high-rise. "A gang?"

Lili looked at Aimée as if she were a slice short of a baguette. "The Loo Frères *mecs*," she said.

"Loo Frères? You mean the Asian *supermarché?*"

"They're more than that. Big influencers, own many businesses, friends with the mayor. The Loo Frères sponsor the New Year parade, and their gang polices Chinatown. No one talks about anything. They make sure of it."

She opened the exit door to a slit of light in an alley.

Aimée grabbed her arm. "Please, when did you last see Karine?"

Lili hesitated. "They were supposed to borrow my place that afternoon. They went to a hotel instead. That's the last I heard. Karine doesn't answer her phone."

"That's helpful, Lili, more than you know. Write down Karine's number, and I'll try to trace it."

"I didn't keep it. Anyway, it's dead. I think Karine is, too."

"Or afraid and hiding from whoever killed Marcus."

Why wasn't there a flicker of hope in Lili's eyes? She knew something. Aimée let go of her arm.

"Where would she hide, Lili?"

"Her family left. I don't know."

Of course she knew. And now Aimée knew how to find out.

"I have to get back to work." Lili turned to leave.

"Wait, Lili! Which hotel?"

"Near Butte-aux-Cailles, a small one. On rue des Cinq

Diamants, I think." She paused. The sun's pale glow caught on her jade bracelet. "If you follow me or come around again, they'll know."

Aimée pressed a card into Lili's hand. She'd written Éric Besson's number on the back, too, in case. "Trust me. Call if you hear from Karine."

Lili stepped out, and the door closed behind her.

Aimée strolled back to the ticket booth. "The young woman who sat by me forgot this . . ."

Aimée showed the clerk a small agenda she'd bought and hadn't used yet.

"She's late twenties, Asian. I just thought you'd remember her." A shot in the dark.

"Oh, Lili," the clerk said. "She's our pianist for Wednesday matinees."

"This looks important—she might need it."

"That's so kind of you. She works at the pâtisserie Bánh Tân Tân. Leave it there. Or if she's already done for the day, I think she just lives upstairs above the bakery."

Aimée left the theater and called Maxence. "Ready for another mission?"

"Ready and waiting." Maxence's voice rose in excitement.

She told him to take petty cash for a taxi and mapped out his assignment. Then she rang Babette. "Will I still make bath time?"

"Chloé's asleep. Pooped out after bébé swim and the park."

Now Aimée felt guilty. "Can you stay a bit longer?"

After making arrangements with Babette, she headed for the hotel.

THE TWO-STAR HOTEL was the only hotel on rue des Cinq Diamants, the street of five diamonds. Aimée saw no trace of any diamonds. At least she'd snagged the photo from the pastry shop wall and could question the hotel staff about the trio.

The hotel staff consisted of a middle-aged woman with black roots showing in her dyed red hair, which was mostly covered by a hijab. She sat behind the tiny reception counter massaging her bare ankle. Arabic music played from a thirties-era Bakelite radio. For a two-star hotel, or even a five-star, the place's rectangular lobby looked spotless. A bottle of nail lacquer emitted a stringent alcohol aroma.

Aimée flashed her faux police ID.

"You're new," said the woman. "Haven't seen you before."

"*Brigade spéciales*, undercover," she said, making it up as she went along.

Without a murmur, the woman turned the *livre d'or*—the hotel register—around for Aimée to view. "Be my guest." A smile with several gold teeth.

Aimée flipped back to the date Marcus disappeared. Ran her chipped fingernails up the signatures. Found it.

"Do you recognize this couple?" Aimée covered Lili's face and showed the woman the photo from the pâtisserie wall of fame.

A nod.

"Can you tell me what you remember about them?"

"I do manicures. Professional. You want one?"

Was the woman offering her something else beside a manicure? Information?

Her nails definitely needed it. And she guessed this was the way to get this woman to talk. "How much?"

"Fifty francs," said the woman. "You choose the color. Extras are ten francs."

Aimée nodded and sat in the second chair in the small space behind the reception counter. "What kind of extras can I get?"

"I can tell you about how I clean rooms and how messy that one was."

Not a direct bribe from a policewoman. But a payment for information—*servis compris*. That worked.

"I'd like the extras," Aimée said. "All of them."

Aimée set her phone on her lap, putting aside her worry about Maxence and his mission, and focused on the woman, who introduced herself as Amal.

Amal's father-in-law's father had bought the hotel, which was still in the family. Perfect cooperation with the *flics*, *toujours*, but Aimée's was a new face. During the war, Amal's father-in-law's father had printed papers, documents, for Jews. Even once hid a family in the attic. Interesting, Aimée thought, that an Arab family had hidden a Jewish family.

She brought their conversation back to Marcus and Karine.

"The boy registered," Amal said. "The girl went up."

"Did anyone else go to their hotel room?"

"Not that I saw." She thought. "*Attendez*, I do remember a water pipe burst next door. The plumber's crew had to work in our courtyard."

Easy to slip inside.

"But you remember the couple well?" Aimée asked.

"So young. Sweet. Most of our clients are in their sixties, pensioners who live here." Amal sighed. "Laid off from the factories and nowhere else to live. My husband was a boy when they demolished the sugar refinery in the seventies. Such huge rats running up the streets, they paid him for every rat he caught."

Aimée suppressed a shiver.

More prodding got Amal talking about the room's condition. "A mess, completely torn up."

Had it been searched?

"May I see the room?" Aimée asked.

After the promise of more francs for this extra "extra," Amal agreed. As Aimée's Bordeaux-red fingernails dried, Amal led her across the small courtyard and up a switchback of stairs. This had probably once been a workers' hotel, simple and unadorned.

Number 210 held a double bed, a blue duvet, a reproduction painting of the Seine at night, a desk, and chair. Basic. Clean.

Aimée checked the desk—opened the drawers, ran her hands along the spindle legs—and behind the mirror's beveled edges. No dust. Doubted she'd find anything of value here—especially after two weeks, a thorough cleaning, and probably a police search. Just as she was about to give up, her index finger encountered something sticky. Alert, she got down on her hands and knees. But it was just a cobweb thread. Using her penlight, she searched under the bed. Not even a dust ball. Disappointed, almost dizzy, she stood again. She'd hoped to find something to make this worthwhile.

"Amal, did you see anything out of the ordinary that day? Hear noises?"

"L'amour." She shrugged. "They acted like rock stars . . . you know, tearing the room apart."

Nothing. What had Aimée expected after several weeks? She sat on the bed, scanned the room again. The view from the window overlooked rue des Cinq Diamants. Across from her was a graffiti mural by Miss Tyk, the rebel tagger who had achieved iconic status and was now a cause célèbre in the art world.

"We want no trouble," Amal said. "We keep a good name in the quartier—clean, discreet. If things get out of hand, our policy is tell the *flics*."

In a way, she had.

"*Merci*, Amal. We'll keep this between us. Great manicure."

Aimée handed her a card with an alias and the phone number for her answering service. "If you, or your family, remember anything else, give me a call."

MAXENCE'S CALL CAME as Aimée hiked up the steep cobbled street in Butte-aux-Cailles, "hill of quails." A maze, this hilltop neighborhood, like an eighteenth-century village, with some passages only wide enough for a cart.

"Reporting in on my surveillance mission, Aimée." Maxence's voice almost squeaked with excitement.

"*D'accord*, Maxence, see anything?"

Late-season yellow roses, swollen with their last blossoms, tumbled over a crumbling stone wall and perfumed the night air. Shadows from the streetlights filtered through the tree branches.

"Lili, the one you described, locked up the pâtisserie ten minutes ago. She entered a door around the corner at number fifty-three. A light's on now in the room above it."

"Anyone else?"

"Not yet. I'm standing in a doorway. Wait . . . A girl's gone in . . . Can't see her face . . . *Non*, now I can see. She looks half-Asian."

Karine.

What better place to hide than in Chinatown?

"I'm en route," she told Maxence.

She ran, waving at a taxi up at the corner.

MAXENCE HUDDLED IN the doorway. He was wearing a John Lennon cap and khaki fatigue jacket. "Should I call the *flics*?"

Catching her breath, Aimée panted, "The last ones to call."

She scanned the layout of the building and dimly lit, narrow street. A few men stood smoking by the closed hardware shop. She and Maxence couldn't stand here long before getting noticed.

"Call a taxi," she said, rummaging for the lock pick set she kept in her blush case, which was somewhere in the bowels of her bag. "Have it wait on the corner."

Maxence's eyes bulged.

"But first you'll shield me at the door, okay?"

With Maxence standing behind her, she started in on the lock of the door of the two-story building that backed the pâtisserie.

A scooter putted by, and Maxence jumped. Her fingers slipped. She took a deep breath. "Relax, Maxence," she said. Tried again, concentrating. After inserting the tension wrench, she jiggled the Z-shaped pick to move the pins. She heard the lock click. "Follow the plan, okay?"

Once inside, she shone her penlight beam through a musty corridor, followed it to a postage-stamp sized courtyard lined by garbage bins. Steamy vapor came from pipe vents from the bakery's oven.

She had to act quick. Another corridor ended in stairs up to the rooms over the bakery. Her collar stuck to her neck in the humidity. She listened for voices, heard a low murmur. For the second time, she used the tension wrench and jiggled the Z-shaped pick. Seconds later, she was inside.

Two women were standing in the stifling attic room, which was packed to the gills with hanging clothes and permeated by baking odors and cheap scent.

"Karine?" Aimée asked.

Karine, her cheeks hollower than they'd been in the photo, ran and crouched in the corner, looking terrorized. Lili grabbed a kitchen knife.

"Get out," said Lili. "I told you not to follow me."

Stupid again. Why had Aimée rushed this, put them on the defensive?

"Put the knife down, Lili." Aimée lifted her hands. Willed her voice to calm. "I'm unarmed. Won't touch either of you. Karine, I'm Aimée, a friend of Marcus's uncle Éric. He needs to know what happened."

Lili lowered the knife but didn't let go.

Karine looked ready to spring for the window.

"Karine, there's a taxi waiting at the corner. I'll get you to safety."

"She's better off here," Lili spat. "Whoever you really are."

"A detective, as I told you. Please try to understand. Marcus's uncle deserves to know what happened. And other people are in danger because of what was stolen."

"Who is in danger?" Karine demanded.

"There was very sensitive information in the book they stole. But you know that. Look, the police are claiming Marcus was a druggie and that you . . ." Aimée knelt down to look Karine in the eye. "They're claiming you're a prostitute."

"What?" said Karine.

"Look for yourself. It's here in the police report. Page six." As she took the police report from her bag, she pressed the ON button on her digital recorder as quietly as she could. She opened the folder and paged through so Karine and Lili could see. Aimée watched Lili from the corner of her eye. Saw her set down the knife. Took an inner breath of relief.

Karine's dark eyes narrowed in anger. "All lies. Marcus and I had been dating for a month."

"It smells like a cover-up," Aimée said. "The investigation's shoddy. Someone has another agenda."

"What do you mean, 'agenda'?" Lili asked.

"I'm guessing someone involved in the police investigation wants the notebook," Aimée said. "Do you know where it is?"

Karine's expression was unreadable. "What notebook?"

"Marcus promised his uncle he would deliver a notebook," Aimée said.

Karine shook her head. "I don't know anything about a notebook."

"Who came to the hotel room?"

Karine's jaw trembled. "I don't know." She burst into tears, mumbled something to Lili in what must have been Khmer.

"What? Tell me so I understand."

"Leave her alone," said Lili. "I told you, they rented a hotel room. All of a sudden someone came in . . . Karine hid under the covers but heard a man threatening Marcus."

Aimée turned to Karine. "You saw him, didn't you? Describe him."

"They drugged me. I came to as a taxi let me out at Parc de Choisy. I ran. Haven't stopped."

Karine was terrified; Aimée believed that much. But was Karine part of a setup? "Why didn't you come forward?"

A bitter laugh. "You're kidding, right? In our neighborhood, we don't go to the *flics*. It brings more trouble."

In every neighborhood, Aimée thought, but she kept her mouth shut. "You're putting your own life at risk, but that's your call," she said. "Where did the notebook go?"

Again, tears. "What notebook?"

Did she really not know? Aimée couldn't tell.

Karine rubbed her eyes. "The man kept asking, 'Where is it?' but I didn't know what he was talking about. Marcus was a big kid, always hiding things. He had all kinds of stashes."

"Stashes? Like drug stashes?" Had the kid sold dope after all? "Did he deal? Some kind of side business?"

"Marcus, drugs?" Karine said. Lili snorted, and Karine shook her head. "His uncle Éric spent a fortune on collectible fantasy merchandise, role-playing game things. Marcus pilfered stuff sometimes. His uncle never noticed. He'd hide it in the quartier—it was like a game to him. Then if his uncle didn't miss it, he'd sell it. There's a market for that, but it's so stupid."

"Where would he hide things?"

"I never knew or cared where."

"Then you owe Marcus's uncle the truth." Aimée pulled out her phone. "My job's done. You need to tell him."

Karine wiped her tears away and seemed to gather herself. "Wait, I need a cigarette." She stood, checking the pockets of her trench coat.

"Me, too," said Aimée, going to the door, wishing it weren't true. She needed to alert Maxence. She noticed a missed call from Babette on her phone. It was later than she'd realized. "I'll come outside with you."

But Karine didn't follow her. Lightening-quick, Karine dashed to the bathroom and slammed the door behind her. Aimée rushed after her, rattling the old door handle until it finally turned open. The window was open, and Karine was gone.

Footsteps raced over the adjoining roof. Aimée stuck her head out the window in time to see a flash of Karine's trench coat as she shimmied down a pipe to the courtyard.

"*Merde.*" She speed-dialed Maxence. "Karine's escaped out the bathroom window over the roof. She's wearing a trench coat." She hung up and faced Lili. "Where's she gone?"

"Like I'd tell you if I knew." Lili put her face in her hands.

Aimée surveyed the room more closely. A carryall and a handbag sat in the corner.

"Karine's just a kid," Lili said. She was crying. "She needed my help. She begged me to let her stay. Now look what you've done. I never should have trusted you."

Aimée had never wanted to get involved with this. Fed up

now, she wanted to forget this whole thing. Why should she keep trying to help a stubborn kid who wouldn't listen? She needed to get home; Babette was on overtime. What could she even find out now?

Where the notebook was.

Aimée grabbed the handbag and ran out of the apartment, down the stairs, and across the courtyard. Out in the narrow street, there was no sign of Maxence or Karine. Around the corner, she found Maxence sprawled on the cobbles, his face bleeding.

"Oh my God . . ." she said. "What happened?"

"I saw her!" Maxence said. "But she jumped on a scooter—it was waiting for her. Then someone tripped me."

She helped him up. "You all right?"

Maxence grinned despite the cut on his face. "Didn't get the license plate but caught a leopard tattoo on the scooter driver's arm." He noticed the handbag. "Hers?"

Aimée opened it to check. "She won't get far without it."

In the taxi, she called Éric's number.

"I found her, Éric," she said, thumbing through the handbag's contents: a thin coin purse, a wadded-up fifty-franc note, a Métro pass in plastic chained to the zipper handle. Makeup and cosmetic samples. Change of underwear. A leaflet in Khmer from a takeout.

No cell phone. No ID.

"Then I lost her," she said.

DEFLATED, AIMÉE STARED at the Seine from her balcony, wondering if she'd really tried hard enough to catch Karine.

Yet she'd made good on her word and then some. She'd tracked Karine down. Asked for the truth, tried to help and get her to safety.

Aimée hadn't been able to hold on to the girl. Or puncture her lies. Aimée's insides twisted knowing that Léo's notebook was gone. She hadn't known it existed yesterday, had had trouble believing it today, and now she was bereft at the thought that she'd never see it herself.

She'd wanted the notebook on the chance that it would reveal her father's connection to the Hand—a connection that had cost him his life. But the notebook incriminated a whole lot of other people. Looking at it from the other side, it was a veritable gold mine for blackmailing people.

A warble came over the *bébé* monitor, then a full-throated cry. Chloé.

A bad dream? Wet diaper?

Aimée waited, as it said to do in child-rearing guru Dr. Dolto's book, her bedside bible. Glanced at the clock and started a mental five-minute timer. After two minutes of nonstop crying, she couldn't stand it. Heated a bottle.

She looked out her kitchen window and saw a lone figure walking on the quai.

Ten minutes later, she'd changed Chloé's diaper, given her a bottle, and snuggled beside her on her own duvet. Miles Davis, her bichon frise, licked her toes as she sunk finally into blissful sleep.

Tuesday Morning

DAWN BROUGHT ANOTHER humid day with bruise-colored clouds hinting at showers. Chloé crawled on the bedroom floor with Miles Davis as Aimée peered through her armoire. Chloé had pulled herself up on one of the drawer handles of the claw-footed dresser. After a few lurching Frankenstein's-monster steps, Chloé plopped on her behind and cried out. She tried to pull on the drawer again, and this time it started to slide out.

Aimée managed a quick grab, catching the drawer halfway down. She heard a rip and looked to see a gaping hole in her silk Versace tunic from last year's January sales. At least it had been half-price.

She changed into a little black dress. Slid into black-toed Chanel sling backs. Meanwhile, Chloé had reached inside the open drawer, plucking Aimée's scarves out and waving them like colorful butterflies.

"Stealing *Maman*'s clothes already, *ma puce?*"

At the drawer's bottom lay the framed photo of baby Aimée in her christening dress, nestled in a woman's arms. The photo didn't even show the woman's face. Aimée's mother, Sydney, an American, had left when Aimée was eight years old. Sydney, a wanted fugitive on the World Watch List, had reappeared two months ago, wanting to meet her granddaughter, Chloé. Sydney had also wanted to warn Aimée about the Hand, implied that her daughter was naïve to believe the men who had killed Jean-Claude Leduc had gone away.

How had she known?

"*Bonjour,*" said Babette, coming into the bedroom. "You two are up early."

She swooped Chloé up in her arms and glanced at the photo in Aimée's hands.

"You rarely talk about your mother." Babette smiled. "It was so nice to see her with Chloé. You said she's traveling, but will I get to know her better?"

Would she? Aimée remembered how thin Sydney had looked. How she'd wanted to be allowed into their life.

Then left, as she always did.

ON THE QUAI, Aimée got into René's waiting marshmallow of a vintage Citroën DS. The controls had been customized for his height; it was his prized possession.

"Rough night?" he asked.

"Chloé woke up. She's been so good at sleeping through the night, but . . ." Suddenly, Aimée thought of the figure she'd seen on the quai in the night. She pulled down the visor, checked the mirror to see if anything looked suspicious. Buses. While she was looking in the mirror, she caught sight of the circles under her eyes and took out her Dior concealer. At this rate, she'd need to buy it wholesale.

"The Bibliothèque François-Mitterrand's system's an easy fix. I have a new program I'm going to install today. The *fonctionnaire* will think we're geniuses."

"Well, you are, René." He looked rested, smart as ever in a charcoal linen suit. "How are your allergies?"

If she hadn't been watching for it, she would have missed his surprised blink. "New medication, all fine."

Liar.

She was about to call him on it, but her phone trilled. A number she didn't know.

"*Oui?*" she said.

Horns, a rumbling like shaking trucks came over the line.

"Can you tell Marcus's uncle that . . . I'm sorry?"

"Karine?" Aimée recognized the soft voice despite the traffic noise. Be gentle—reel her in. Get her to meet. "*Ça va?* Are you okay, Karine?"

Aimée pushed the SPEAKERPHONE button so René could hear. Put her finger to her lips.

Pause. "Please, just let him know," Karine said.

Aimée figured Karine was scared, running out of places to hide, feeling guilty. Vulnerable.

"*Bien sûr,*" Aimée said. "Look, forgive me for bursting in on you at Lili's. Scaring you. My fault. I took your bag. You need it, *non?*" Talk fast. Don't give her time to think. "Where can I give it to you?"

René's green eyes widened.

Pause. More horns. "I've . . . got to go . . ." Karine said.

"*Zut,* Karine, I feel terrible. Please, let me return it."

Voices sounded in the background. Aimée pulled out René's large taxi driver map, opened it to the thirteenth arrondissement, and scanned. "Tell me where to meet you. Anywhere you like."

René pointed to rue de Tolbiac, mimed eating.

Aimée took his cue. "A resto?" she suggested. "Somewhere on rue de Tolbiac?"

Silence on the other end of the line.

"Or you pick a place, Karine."

"I can't."

Aimée couldn't let this opportunity slip away. "Please, Karine, you're in danger. You saw the homicide report. The *flics* won't help, but I will."

René blinked.

The shuffling sound of a hand muffling the phone. Crackling. "There's something I should tell you . . ." Karine said.

Had she come around, or was she in trouble?

"Good, Karine. Tell me and—"

"Tonight. We'll talk later."

The line went dead. *Merde.* Aimée hit the call back symbol. The phone rang and rang. No answer.

She couldn't place that background rumbling—a tunnel, a station? Not that it mattered. Karine was gone.

"That girl's terrified of something," said René, turning on his blinker.

He had that right. She remembered Maxence's description of the tattooed man whose scooter Karine had escaped on—a Loo Frères gang member?

"Weren't you going to tell me what happened with Karine?" He pulled onto Pont de Sully, one of the bridges connecting Ile Saint-Louis to the "Continent," as the locals said. "Or you figured I'd get it by osmosis?"

She'd gotten him bent out of shape again.

"*Desolée*, it's not like that," she said. "I need your help."

He shook his head. "Only when it's convenient, eh?"

So prickly. "Let me explain, René." Midway through her explanation of what had happened the night before, her phone buzzed again.

Without thinking, she hit answer. "Karine?"

"Eh? My office got broken into last night, Aimée." Éric Besson was shouting over traffic sounds in the background. What was it with people calling her from the middle of traffic? "Can you hear me, Aimée?"

Even René could hear.

"Horrible, Éric, I'm sorry," she said.

"I think someone is looking for Léo's notebook."

René jammed on the brakes as a bus cut in front of them on the quai des Célestins. Aimée put her hand on the dashboard. In the muggy heat, her little black dress was already stuck to the small of her back.

"But Éric, if Marcus was really murdered for the notebook, wouldn't his killers know that you don't have it?" she asked.

"Karine lied to you last night," he said, shouting. "She knows where it is. What if she's in cahoots with them?"

René raised an eyebrow. Mouthed, *Quoi?*

"I'm leaving court and taking an afternoon train back," Éric said.

Éric was overreacting.

"Can't your secretary deal with the break-in?" Aimée said. "Look, Karine just called me."

René pulled into a side street and parked.

"What did she say?" Éric asked.

"She's sorry, Éric. Told me to tell you."

"What good does that do?"

"She's scared. That's all I know."

"I need to talk to her. Please, make good on your promise, Aimée. Knowing you, you insisted on a rendezvous, *non?*"

"I'm not sure she'll turn up," she said, reluctant.

"*Bon*, I'm leaving court. I can't concentrate. All I want to know is what happened to Marcus," he said. "And the notebook."

She wondered if she should wash her hands of this.

René took the phone from her hand. "Éric, it's René. Aimée's in the car with me. Shouldn't you involve the *flics?*"

"You think I trust them, René?" Éric asked.

Click.

"HOW DO YOU get yourself into messes like this, Aimée?" René pulled out of his parking spot and honked at a car passing him. "Again and again?"

She snorted in disbelief. "René, did I ask Éric to come beg me for help? He was desperate, crying. Racked with guilt."

René downshifted at the roundabout. Frowned. "How's that your problem?"

Now it was.

"What's this about a notebook?"

René didn't miss a thing. So she told him.

"I can't back out, René." She'd decided. "I need to see this through to the end."

"C'est fou. You've got Chloé to think of. There are dangerous people involved in this, and you cannot put yourself in harm's way. Let me go in your place and meet Karine."

Sometimes René made her want to scream.

"Karine doesn't know you. You'll just frighten her off—she's already terrified." But she could use him for backup. And to talk sense into Éric. "Listen, I've got a plan."

ALL MORNING THEY worked at the newly painted *bibliothèque* office, until the fumes made René's eyes water too much. Then he dropped Aimée off to meet Martine for lunch.

Martine was smoking at a window table in the small bistro on rue Pascal. A local place run by two *mémés*, grandmas from Provence—one cooked and the other served and managed the superb wine list. Touches of Provençal-blue decor accented the dark wood and mirrors, which must have been there for a hundred years.

"*Et alors*, the usual?" Martine said after their customary *bisous* on each cheek.

Aimée nodded.

Martine stubbed out her cigarette and smiled at the granny, who came over to their table. The proprietor was casual chic with stylish white hair, a nautical-blue-striped top, and Jean-Paul Gaultier jeans.

Martine pointed to the prix fixe menu chalked on the *ardoise*. "*Deux, s'il vous plaît.*" As the granny left, Martine poured a rosé from a *pichet* into a glass.

"Did you invite me for lunch because you're going to ask me to babysit?" Martine's blonde-streaked hair highlighted her Sicilian tan. She glowed after her long August *vacances* with her squeeze, Gianni. Aimée felt happy for her. And a little jealous. But her best friend deserved this after a disastrous long-term relationship.

"*Pas de tout,*" said Aimée. "I know you'll babysit your god-daughter without any bribery. You brought what I asked for, *non?*"

Martine's fuchsia lips pouted as she pulled a file from her bag. An unpublished article Martine, a journalist, had written on the Bibliothèque François-Mitterrand's secret coffers. Juicy pickings for their further contract negotiations.

"*Merci.*" Aimée shoved Martine's file in her bag. "But there's something else. It's about Éric Besson."

"It's always something with you, Aimée. What's *le nerd* done?"

"Martine, you referred Éric to me, didn't you?"

"*Pas exactement.* I feel sorry for him, his horrific divorce, *c'est tout.*" Martine took a drag on her cigarette, expelled smoke. "He needed help finding something that had gone missing. I thought of you . . ."

Something that had gone missing?

Aimée dropped her fork. "He's dragged me into a murder investigation, Martine."

Martine sat up. She hadn't known. Now Aimée had her attention. "What happened?"

"It's not pretty."

Aimée related how Éric had shown up with a police report of Marcus's murder, the dodgy investigation, the names in Léo Solomon's notebook, and her search for Karine.

"First Karine climbed down a drainpipe to escape you, and now she's had a change of heart and wants to meet up? And you think she'll tell you the truth?" Martine put her napkin on her lap as the starter arrived, a *soupe au pistou* fragrant with garlic.

"Something has made her change her mind, but I don't know what, Martine."

"So where's this notebook?"

"Karine thought Marcus might have hidden it somewhere. Meanwhile, Éric's office got ransacked overnight."

"So you think the murderer's still looking?"

"Wouldn't Marcus have told his attacker where to find the notebook since his and Karine's lives were threatened?"

Martine didn't answer. Instead, she said, "But what does this all have to do with you? Be honest with me, Aimée. This is about your papa, *non*? That's why you're involved."

Aimée put down her spoon. Sipped the rosé, clean, delicate, and cold. No use hiding anything from her best friend. "Éric hooked me by telling me Papa was involved. How could I not listen? I think the implications are bigger than even Éric imagines."

"Bigger how?"

"Why kill a kid for information unless it's big stakes? I thought I chopped off the Hand, but it's grown back. Mutated into another generation." Aimée tore a slice off the baguette and wiped her soup bowl clean. "Or maybe some slick operator took over where the ousted guys left off. Who knows?"

"The Hand?" Martine thought. "You're going to find out. Is that it?"

How could she not at least try? What would her father want?

"With your help," Aimée said.

"Hold on. Don't drag me into this."

"*You* dragged *me* into this. Éric came to me because you told him to."

"Did not." Martine picked her thumb's cuticle, a nervous gesture that would have given away the fact that she was lying even if Aimée did not already know.

Martine had never been a good liar; Aimée had been lying for her since the lycée. For a moment, they were sixteen again, arguing about the lies Aimée had told Martine's mother to cover for Martine when she'd slept at her boyfriend's. It had been an easy ruse; Aimée had had no mother checking up on her. How deeply that had hurt—she would have given the world to have Martine's problem.

"Earth to Aimée," said Martine. "You there?"

She forced herself back to the present, gripped the thick cotton napkin, breathed the garlic-scented air. Martine was smiling and squeezing her arm. The storm had passed.

"Marcus's murder has been poorly handled, Martine. The whole police investigation's shoddy. They're writing him off as a drug dealer, although he never did drugs. That's proof to me that the *flics* are covering something up."

Martine reached for another cigarette. "So the autopsy confirms no toxic substances in his system?"

She hadn't verified that. Now that she thought about it, the autopsy hadn't been included in the homicide report. Strange.

But her friend Serge worked in pathology at the morgue. She'd follow up. "I don't think this is about drugs."

"*Alors*, Aimée, getting back to the Hand." Martine exhaled a plume of smoke. "Gianni's sister is a law professor in Rome. She's an expert in organized crime. According to her, the Italian mafia is completely modernized. It's not peasants carrying out vendettas or street thugs running gambling and drug rings."

"And you're saying what, Martine?"

"It's a new generation. Neapolitan Camorra and Calabrian 'Ndràngheta soldiers attend Oxford, Harvard, and Sciences Po. They come out trained professionals—lawyers, accountants, all clean. Then they run the family business." Pause. "You know, the Camorra's also called the Black Hand. Maybe their French counterpart isn't so different?"

Aimée's mind went back to Éric's words about the Hand morphing like a hydra.

"It only makes business sense for crime to change to remain viable. To modernize and incorporate new blood." Martine ground out her cigarette.

Aimée nodded. "You'll get a great story out of this, Martine."

"If there's what's called proof, Aimée." Martine winked. "Any editor worth their salt will require conclusive autopsy results, evidence that the notebook is real," said Martine. "Find me that, and I'll pitch an exclusive personal angle, blah blah blah."

When they finished lunch, Aimée paid with several crisp hundred-franc notes, hoping René had deposited the Bibliothèque François-Mitterrand's retainer and that the check had cleared. Client rich and cash poor, the curse of contractors, who were the last in line to get paid. Leduc Detective would need to line up more consulting gigs to cover the bills.

"Got a meeting at *Le Monde*," said Martine.

"*Merci* for the article."

After quick pecks on the cheeks, Martine jumped into a taxi.

Aimée used the window of time before her next client appointment to drop by Besson's office, only a block away. She hurried up rue Pascal to Boulevard Arago, the fault line where the Latin Quarter bled into the chic wedge of the thirteenth near Gobelins.

She met a blue-uniformed *flic* in front of Éric's building, a white-columned townhouse. Yellow crime scene tape drooped at the door.

"No entry, mademoiselle," he said.

"But I've got an appointment with *Maître* Besson," she lied. "Is there a problem?"

"Check with his assistant."

A petite, wire-thin redhead wearing a YSL black trouser suit consulted a PDA in her hand. Aimée lusted for the suit; if René were there, he would have lusted for the PDA. If only their clients paid on time.

"*Bonjour*, I'm Aimée Leduc."

"I figured," she said, giving Aimée's outfit an up and down.

Merde. Had she gotten out the stains from Chloé's apricot puree that morning? Did her dress not meet this woman's approval?

Did Aimée care?

"Éric Besson asked for my help."

"I heard," said the woman. For a moment, Aimée wondered if this proprietary assistant resented her. But then the woman added matter-of-factly, "I'm Gaëlle. Éric's in a tizzy. They didn't steal anything, from what I can tell. Someone opened the safe, but no documents were removed." She was still tapping on her PDA. "I'm trying to reschedule everything. A pain."

"So it was a professional job?"

"According to the *flics*. With Éric's mind on the divorce, this case in Brussels, and poor Marcus, it's hard to tell if he remembered to set the alarm."

More tapping.

Divorce? Aimée remembered that Martine had also mentioned that during lunch. Definitely not her business.

"So you knew Marcus, Gaëlle?"

The *flic* called to Gaëlle, who said to Aimée, "Look, I need to do a million things."

"I'll join you."

Before Gaëlle could throw up a roadblock, Aimée'd followed her past the uniform and into the black-and-white-marble-tiled foyer. The interior of Besson's office was exquisite: carved wood boiserie, Directoire furniture, sunlight streaming through floor-length windows that opened onto a private garden. The fingerprint technician was still busy dusting the room, leaving white powder traces on the walnut desk.

The oval inset in the high ceiling, bordered by sculpted garlands, made Aimée recall her one and only ballroom dance lesson, when she was fourteen, in a room just like this one. Feeling left-footed and awkward like now. Again on the Left Bank. Maybe this had been a ballroom once, she thought, noticing the double doors, the striations of the wood parquet floor, and the walk-in-sized stone fireplace.

The office breathed success. Serious success, with state-of-the-art computers and scanners. Good thing René wasn't there; he would drool.

Focus on the job, she reminded herself.

She asked Gaëlle, "Is there any chance this break-in could have something to do with Éric's divorce?"

"*Un peu* acrimonious, but why bother breaking in? There's nothing to steal when she's taking him to the cleaners already."

Wishful thinking on Aimée's part; she had been hoping she could convince herself the break-in wasn't related to the note-book. "Can you tell me about Léo Solomon's visit two weeks ago? Were you here that day?"

Gaëlle's thin brows creased. "I didn't even see him. Éric had me sending registered documents to the court in Meudon." Gaëlle's stylus paused on the PDA in her palm. "Éric's under such stress."

"What can you tell me about Marcus's parents?"

"*Tant pis.* Only a mother who's in the hospital. Éric's afraid to tell her the details."

Aimée blinked. "Details?" Didn't Marcus's mother know her son was a homicide victim? "How can I reach her?" She whipped out her Moleskine, ready to jot down his mother's info.

"You can't."

"I understand you feel protective, but—"

"I don't mean *you* can't reach her, mademoiselle. I mean, no one can. She's a paranoid schizophrenic."

There went that idea. Still, she pursued it until Gaëlle revealed the hospital's name.

Aimée had to get something concrete, though—something she could follow up on. "How well did you know Marcus?"

A shrug. "After school, he'd do odd jobs in the office."

"Would you call him secretive?"

Another shrug. "He talked about girls sometimes. And street art—he was really into it. He spent his money on collecting graf-fiti art. That's all."

"Did he mention a Karine? Perhaps bring her to the office?"

A shake of her head. "I didn't know him well. I mean, how interested is an eighteen-year-old in carrying on a conversation?"

In the corner, a fax groaned, spitting out pages. The wall safe behind Éric's desk, an easy target, looked ancient. White powder dusted that, too.

"You organized Marcus's work schedule?" Aimée asked.

"I do everything here. But it wasn't much of a schedule—he just hung around the office during business hours whenever he wasn't in class. He lived upstairs in the *chambre de bonne*. The *flics* went through it, too. Poor kid."

Aimée thanked her. She paused at the tall door. "Did you have his cell phone number?"

Gaëlle checked her PDA, then took a phone out of her pocket. "Shall I write it down? Don't know what good it will do . . ."

"Just checking."

Gaëlle started writing on a memo pad emblazoned BESSON ET FILS. "Which cell number do you need?"

Bingo. But this made Aimée wonder how Gaëlle would have both Marcus's numbers. Were they on a shared plan? A perk of Marcus's work? "Both, please."

Aimée left with the number she recognized as Marcus's and another she hoped would lead her to Karine.

AIMÉE RETRACED HER steps down rue Pascal, past the little bistro, timing Marcus's walk from the office to the point where his last cell phone call had been triangulated, under the Boulevard de Port-Royal, which formed a tunnel overhead. She stopped at the foot of the concrete steps that led up to it.

Four minutes. This was where Marcus had stood at 4:24 P.M.

She tried Marcus's second cell phone number. Dead.

She closed her eyes. Listened. Heard the rumbling of cars overhead on Boulevard de Port-Royal, the click of heels echoing in the tunnel, the rhythm of tires going through puddles. The chill in the tunnel sent goosebumps up her arms.

That rumbling overhead felt familiar. Had Karine called her from here?

Would Marcus have hidden the notebook somewhere between here and the Butte-aux-Cailles hotel? Did Karine think so, too? But where?

Aimée scanned the area. Old buildings, full of history. Her phone alarm trilled, and she remembered life goes on. She had another business meeting to get to.

But whatever had happened here had changed Marcus's course. Ended his life.

Tuesday Afternoon

THE FEAR OF a computer meltdown in the new millennium got people twitchy. Aimée's afternoon appointment was a client who was nervous about possible Y2K system malfunctions. Or complete and total chaos, as some doomsayers predicted.

Nice to have a client meeting that ended with a hefty retainer. For once.

Pay up front—her new mantra.

Pigeons cooed from the eaves as she parked her scooter near Leduc Detective. A violent rain shower had left the pavement slick and sparkling in the afternoon light. Freshened the air.

In the office, quiet with René working at the *bibliothèque*, she kicked off her Chanel sling backs and relished the smooth wood floor under her bare feet. The chandelier's crystals fractured the light into rainbows, reflecting on the age-patinaed mirror—Chloé loved that.

Aimée could do this. Manage her business, help out Éric Besson, and be a good *maman*. Couldn't she?

She'd ignore the cold unease that crept over her when she thought of the Hand. The Hand had engineered the explosion that had killed her father—she knew that. Would proof of his collusion in their dirty dealings matter? Matter enough for her to risk opening that basket of deadly snakes?

But if the Hand was still running the show, wouldn't her father want her to deal with it?

She pushed those thoughts aside and got to work running virus scans, returning client calls. Noticing only an hour later Maxence's folder labeled LÉO SOLOMON.

Brilliant. More information.

First, though, she took the time to try to reach Marcus's mother, an Eve Gilet, at the clinic whose name Gaëlle had given her. Madame Gilet, Aimée was told, was a patient there, *oui*, but did not take calls or visits. Family would be notified at the appropriate time for making contact.

Translation: Eve Gilet resided in a locked down secure facility—either a zombie from shock treatments or under severe sedation.

Next Aimée tried her contact at France Télécom. With some luck, he'd be able to get her the call log from Marcus's second cell phone number. But he'd left for the day. Great. She left him a message telling him to call her.

François, whom she'd traded favors with before, had been a classmate of hers at the lycée. She couldn't butter him up—or sweeten her request. Just remind him of what he owed her.

A minute later he called her back. Thank God.

"What do you want now, Aimée?" said François.

"I'd think you'd be happier to hear from me, François," she said. "Didn't I run that credit check on your sister's fiancé? Find the back taxes he owed and foreclosure history?"

"For which she still hasn't forgiven me," he said. "Continues to remind me the hotel won't refund her wedding reception deposit."

"I'd call that averting disaster."

"Wish she saw it that way." She heard a phone ring in the background. "Make it quick."

She gave him the new number Gaëlle had furnished. "I need that number's call log ASAP."

"You're kidding, right? I'm heading out the door. Tomorrow."

"Aren't you always complaining your union wants you racking up overtime? Here's your chance."

By the time he agreed, she was running late for her next meeting.

SHE STUFFED MAXENCE'S folder on Léo Solomon in her bag to read later, set the daily surveillance scans, and locked the office. Serge, her pathologist friend, was waiting for her at the café. This would be a quick meeting; she'd get home in time to play rubber duckies with Chloé. She'd have a work-over-dinner session with René, and then tonight she'd get the truth from Karine.

She hoped.

SERGE, WHOM SHE'D known since her year of premed, sat at the outdoor table of the *très moderne* café, les Docks, a Métro hop from Serge's office at the morgue. The thick black frames on his glasses matched his thick black hair and trimmed beard. He glanced at his watch.

"What's so important, Aimée? Got to pick up the twins."

"Your wife away?"

"Her girlfriend weekend."

"But it's Tuesday."

Cigarette smoke drifted from the couple at the next table. Aimée wished she hadn't quit. Again.

"They took advantage of a midweek rate for a thalassotherapy spa package in Saint-Malo," said Serge. "I just go with the program."

A docile husband ruled by a wife he loved and a gorgon of a mother-in-law. Aimée had never seen him so happy.

She set down the homicide report. "Marcus Gilet."

"Who's he?"

"An eighteen-year-old whose body was discovered in early September on rue Watt."

"Sounds like that Léo Malet crime story. They always dump bodies there. Notorious."

She hadn't known. "*Vraiment?* You mean some gangland drop point?"

"*C'est la tradition.* A spooky tunnel. A badge of honor for a hood's first murder."

She shivered. Gruesome. "An old-school initiation?"

"Something like that. Still do it today."

If Marcus was murdered in the hotel room, as Karine had seemed to indicate, why go the distance to rue Watt to dump the body? "Do me a big favor. I need a copy of his autopsy."

"Not my 'client.' I was away at a conference in Marseille. Lots of murders there."

"But you can pull it up on the computer, Serge."

The cigarette smoldered in the ashtray at the next table. She wished she didn't want to reach over and grab it. When would the desire to smoke go away?

"As if it's that easy," said Serge. "You know the transcription process. Then there's the pathologist's report . . ."

Sea gulls waddled by, emitting high-pitched cries and scrabbling over bread crumbs. Downriver the smokestacks of the incineration-recycling plant near Ivry belched white.

"Here we are about to enter the twenty-first century, and the morgue technology has barely made it to the twentieth," Serge was saying. "Madame Lelong, our transcriber, uses a typewriter because she says she doesn't believe in computers . . . takes her time. Plus, it's not like I can just—"

"Of course you can. You do it all the time."

"What's this Marcus Gilet to you?"

Algae scents rose from the Seine's quai. She took a sip of espresso, needing the hot sweet jolt. "I need proof there weren't drugs in his system."

"Answer the question, and I might think about helping."

She gave a brief recounting of how she'd gotten involved in looking into Marcus's death.

"It's difficult to rush a report order. So much red tape. And our budget's tightened."

She needed his help.

"Make a call, Serge."

He sipped his espresso. Shrugged and glanced at the time. The river police Zodiac boat cruised by, trailed by a spreading V of foam.

"The last time you helped me on the sly, didn't you end up with a new office?" Aimée said.

He'd inadvertently nailed a fugitive war criminal in the process of running her report.

Serge sighed. She knew that sigh. Now the negotiations began. He'd extract a favor in return. "I'm horrible with costumes, Aimée. It's the twins' preschool play . . ."

And she knew anything about costumes? On second thought, school plays loomed in Chloé's future. Serge's twin boys were only a few years older. "What kinds of costumes?"

"Honeybees."

Might as well. She had a friend who worked in the costume and prop department at the opera and might be able to help.

Ironing out the twins' costume details took longer than Serge's phone conversation with his colleague at the morgue.

"No go," said Serge. His thick black brows knit together. "My colleague can't find Gilet's autopsy."

"He can't find it as in it's not yet entered into the system?" said Aimée. "Or it's misfiled? Under something on someone's desk?"

"We're not that sloppy." Pause. "Usually." Serge looked worried.

"You mean the autopsy got lost on purpose."

"Let me check tomorrow morning, Aimée," said Serge, grabbing his briefcase. "I'll comb the system, okay?"

"Can someone disappear an autopsy report?"

"Sounds like paranoia, Aimée."

She didn't think so.

BATH TIME OVER and rubber duckies put aside, Aimée rocked Chloé to sleep in her arms. Chloé's sweet soapy fragrance and the smell of the fresh cotton sheets lulled Aimée into sleepiness. She wished she could join her daughter. So tired, yet she had work to do.

With Chloé's sleeping whistles in her ears, Aimée tiptoed down the hallway, clicked on the baby monitor, and fed Miles Davis.

"Almost out of horsemeat, fur ball."

Miles Davis's white ears poked up in attention. He cocked his head toward her suitcase-sized fridge.

"You think there's a bit left in the freezer?"

His tail wagged nonstop. She bent and ruffled the fur around his collar.

"Smart boy."

RENÉ ARRIVED WITH takeout—Lebanese from a place near the Panthéon. No word from Karine. Worried, Aimée wondered if the scared young girl would call.

When Aimée was midway through a kebab, an alert beeped on

her laptop. She checked. Thank God, François had come through and emailed her Marcus's cell phone log.

Only a handful of numbers, none of them the number Karine had called her from earlier. Most likely that had been a pay phone.

She showed René.

"Didn't you say the *flics'* report already contained a cell phone log?" he asked.

"It's for Marcus's other phone."

"Eh, how did you find that?"

"I didn't. Gaëlle, Éric's assistant, gave me Marcus's other number."

René shook his head. "How would she have that if Marcus kept it secret?"

"A shared plan? I don't know. All I know is, she handles the bills. But look, René; no activity since the day he was murdered."

"*Et alors*, that's two weeks ago. Even if Karine's number's here, that doesn't mean she'll still have that phone."

"Only one way to find out."

She punched in the number of the last call made. Hoped it was Karine's. Ringing, ringing, ringing.

Then she tried the three other numbers. Same thing. Disappointed, she sat down cross-legged on the recamier. Her thoughts went back to the tunnel where Marcus's last call had been triangulated. She scrolled through the call log on her own phone and matched up one set of digits with the call log for Marcus's second phone: Éric's number, which had called Marcus's phone twice.

Still, that got her nowhere. How could she get in touch with Karine?

"Face it, Aimée. Karine's not calling."

"What if she can't?"

René set down his kebab skewer. She saw him slip Miles Davis a minted lamb chunk with his other hand.

"You've done what you can," he said. He wiped his hands on his linen napkin—her grandfather had found the set at auction. "We've got to finish this, remember?"

René had his laptop out, a *bibliothèque* file open.

Aimée's phone trilled.

A number from Marcus's second phone. Hopeful, she nodded to René.

"*Oui?*" she answered.

"You called. Who's this?"

She recognized the glottal syllables, the lilting accent. Lili.

"Lili, it's Aimée Leduc. Can I talk to Karine? She's there, right?"

A sob escaped Lili. "Not anymore."

"What happened?"

"Someone followed her."

Aimée's pulse skipped. "Where'd she go, Lili? Please tell me. I can help her."

Lili sucked in her breath. "She said she wanted to talk to you."

"About what?"

"I don't know."

Great. But maybe she really didn't know. "Help me out, Lili." Calm. Aimée needed to stay calm, control the conversation. Try to. "Where would Karine go? Can you think of friends, you know, people she knew from school or—"

"There's an old painter . . ." Lili clammed up.

"Go on, Lili."

"I'm not . . . sure, but he's Cambodian. An avant-garde painter with an atelier . . ."

"Where, Lili?"

"Cité fleurie . . . but maybe I shouldn't have told you."

"You're right to tell me. She's your friend, and you want to protect her. So do I."

Lili hung up. Aimée figured she'd gotten as much as she could. She took out her map and searched for Cité fleurie.

"Aimée, just tell Éric Besson," René said. "Let him take it from there. You don't have to be involved anymore."

"Who knows if Karine's there? Say she is and he appears; she'd run like a scared rabbit. Lili said Karine was followed."

But it was true she needed to tell Éric.

On the third ring, he answered. His voice sounded distant, as if it were underwater. "So you're meeting Karine now?"

"No guarantees, Éric, but I might know where she is."

"Where?"

"Cité fleurie. I'll call you if she's there. Someone has been following her."

"What do you mean?"

"Later." She hung up and nodded to René. Punched in her concierge's number—Madame Cachou had agreed to babysit. Three minutes later, dressed in motorcycle jacket, black leather pants, and high-tops, Aimée met the older woman at the door.

"Will you be long?" Madame Cachou carried her laptop case with her. Madame Cachou wrote "romances"—more like steamy erotica, in Aimée's opinion. The sideline earned her more than her salary as a concierge.

"Doubt it."

RENÉ SANDWICHED THE Citroën between two camionettes near La Santé, the last prison in Paris. Dark, high stone walls loomed in the fading twilight. They passed the adjacent Square Cadiou, a park lost in a fog of foliage, and came to the Cité fleurie gate.

A Digicode. Great. Aimée's penlight revealed names next to a buzzer. Phan sounded Cambodian, at least Asian, so she buzzed it. Silence apart from the muted chirp of crickets. What if Karine was crashing there and was afraid to answer?

Aimée buzzed another atelier.

"Who's that?" said a tired man's voice.

"*Desolée*, it's the materials for Monsieur Phan," she said, plucking a reason for buzzing out of the air. "I'm dropping them off, and he doesn't answer . . ."

"At this time of night?"

"Tell me about it, monsieur," she said. "Important delivery, he said, and now no answer . . ."

"Atelier 417."

The gate clicked open.

THEY WALKED INTO gardens that surrounded clusters of two-story timber-frame white stucco maisonettes with north-facing windows. Greenery and plants everywhere. The uneven paver walkway led through courtyard after sculpture-laden courtyard. A place for munchkins—this would be fairyland for Chloé.

"What's this place besides being the land time forgot?" said René, slipping on wet ginkgo leaves.

Aimée pointed to a plaque by the narrow path—names of artists who'd worked in ateliers here: Gauguin, Modigliani, and Rodin, among others. Another related how a free German library with anti-Nazi books was pillaged during the German Occupation.

She scanned the walkway for the atelier number. Wanted to keep out of sight of the man who'd buzzed them in.

"You sure about this, Aimée?" René whispered.

Not at all. "It's a place to try, René."

"*C'est privé*. People live here, too."

"Got a better idea?"

A strange place for Karine to crash—a historic artists enclave—but secluded. In the shadows, only a few lights showed behind drawn curtains.

Toward the enclave's rear, the timbered ateliers gave off an abandoned air, leaves strewn around the doorways.

"*C'est là-bas.*" René pointed to atelier 417, which lay in shadows. The minute he knocked, the wood door creaked open, yielding on to darkness.

A bad feeling danced up Aimée's spine. The chilly breeze carried the fragrance of night-flowering jasmine and cat piss. "Wait, René."

"*Allô?*" he called. "Karine?" He'd hit the light, flooding the narrow studio and revealing a large skylight over a collage piece on an easel. Canvasses were propped against the wall. Fabric scraps, metal bits, half-squeezed pigment tubes, and Spackle brushes were scattered on a bench. As if they'd been tossed haphazard or rooted through.

She noted the paint-speckled wooden floor, a thin mattress covered by a blanket in the corner.

No Karine. Only an aluminum pot on a hot plate. Touched the rim. "It's still warm, René."

Too late. If she'd been here, she'd gone. Had Lili warned her? But why?

Nervous, Aimée dialed Lili. No answer.

Then she tried Éric's number—to stop him from making a fruitless trip. Heard a faint answering ring.

Merde! He'd come already.

Holding her phone, she followed the ringing sound outside to where tree branches formed a tunnellike overhang. Then she couldn't hear it anymore. Beyond, an eerie clump of shadows turned out to be an elongated Giacometti-style sculpture of sprouting metal pipe.

"They call this art?" she heard René mutter.

"Éric?" Aimée called. She punched in his number again. Heard the ringing. "This way."

And then Aimée didn't hear the ringing phone anymore. Just leaves rustling in the wind. She paused, her eyes catching on a small scrap of light-colored fabric hanging in the branches, glinting in the night. And then she heard a scream.

Tuesday, Late Evening

THE GARDEN HAD ended at a wall. Footsteps crashed in the dark underbrush. Aimée shined her penlight, revealing red smears streaking the glossy leaves.

Blood. Her knees trembled. Whose blood?

Aimée heard a high-pitched whine of a cat in heat and then René's shout: "Over here!"

Had René found Éric?

She forged ahead, continuing along the wall until she came to a woman's slumped figure.

Aimée stumbled, caught herself. "Karine?"

Karine's glassy-eyed stare reflected in Aimée's penlight beam. The tarnished, paint-spattered handle of a pair of scissors protruded from Karine's neck.

"*Mon Dieu*," said René.

Aimée struggled to take in what she saw. Karine still wore the trench coat she had been wearing when she fled down the drainpipe. She was barefoot, pink nail polish on her toes.

René stepped back, shaking.

Aimée bent down, fought the reflex to pull the scissors from Karine's neck. Clinical objectivity took over, her premed training kicking in, and she reached for Karine's wrist.

No pulse.

Still warm. "René, come here."

No answer. Where had he gone?

"René?"

Her heart jumped. Was Karine's killer still here?

She rooted in her bag for her Swiss Army knife, flicked it open. Shadows moved in the rustling branches.

Her heart pounded. Where had René gone? Where was Éric? Would they find him next, his throat slit?

Branches snapped. A moan. Good God, had René been hurt?

She found her way through a thicket.

"Aimée?" René leaned on the wall, heaving. His jacket pocket had been ripped off.

René, a black belt, could defend himself. But he looked shaken. "Are you okay? What happened?"

René whispered. "I heard someone climbing over the wall."

Aimée looked to see blood smears trailing up the stone.

"Karine's killer . . . escaped over the wall?" Aimée's words caught in her mouth, dry as sandpaper. She struggled to make sense of this. What felt like minutes or maybe hours passed in what could have only been seconds. "Who was it?"

"Too dark; couldn't see."

A light went on in the studio behind them. Voices.

"I'm calling the *flics* . . ." said René.

Aimée shook her head. "What if it's a setup?"

Realization dawned in René's eyes. He'd heard Éric's phone ring, too. "Did Éric set us up?"

How could that make sense? Or was he a victim here, too? "Why would he? Éric couldn't have had anything to do with Marcus's murder." Could he have? Éric Besson was one of the most ethical, straight-shooting people Aimée had ever met. And his grief had seemed so genuine. "Karine wanted to tell me something."

Aimée edged along the path, René behind her.

"And the murderer shut Karine up before she could talk."

They'd reached the end of the wall. "No one's here."

Voices were approaching. A shout.

No time to figure more out now. They had to get out of here. "I saw a gate," Aimée said. "Quick."

"Aimée, we've got to tell the *flics*. I can't walk away from a murder."

"Stick around and be accused of it?"

"This feels wrong."

"Nothing's right about this, René. Got any other ideas?"

The gate was locked.

"Climb. Hurry," she said.

"Not my style, Aimée."

Was he worried about his linen suit? It was already ripped. But given René's four-foot height, he'd never make it over the high wall. *Merde*, what could she do?

Lift him up? She bent down. "Stand on my back. Or will you call Madame Cachou, tell her we're suspects in a holding cell and we'll need her to stay with Chloé overnight?"

After René scrambled up to the wall ledge and dropped to the other side, she hoisted herself up. Found purchase and seconds later made it over the top. She landed on a crumbling planter, and her foot twisted. *Merde*.

Keep going. They were in another garden, wild and unkempt. The grass had been trampled. Were they following the murderer's escape?

Didn't matter right then. Hobbling behind René, she made for a rusted gate that yielded on to a rolling lawn. It belonged to a school in a former mansion, glassed-in terraces overlooking a grassy slope. Every minute counted.

All of a sudden she was drenched in cold water. In her shock, Aimée slipped.

"Think you'll rob us again tonight?" Silhouetted in the light of a second-floor room, a woman holding a pail called down to them, "The *flics* are already coming."

A siren wailed in the distance.

"Great, and we're fleeing a murder scene," René huffed.

Aimée grabbed René's arm and ducked into the shadows. Her ankle hurt. Her cold, wet jacket hung heavy on her shoulders. If only they could make it to the next street. To the Métro—or get to the car.

She pointed to a decrepit ladder lying sideways by a gardening shed. René needed no further prompting. He leaned it up against the wall separating the yard from the grassy park of Square Cadiou. He climbed up first, then reached down to help her. Her weight broke the last rung. A sharp pain shot up her already throbbing ankle.

Sirens wailed closer. Shoving down the pain, she scrambled over the wall and landed on damp mulched grass, wrenching her shoulder. Gasped in pain.

What next? All they needed was a shining spotlight, and they'd be caught fleeing a murder scene. Aimée could see René's parked Citroën over the hedge in front of them.

Right where they'd started from.

Police cars had pulled up, blue lights flashing and reflecting on the trees. Forget crossing the grass with the *flics* out front.

A walled walkway running between the school and apartments led out of Square Cadiou to the next street. No doubt it had a locked gate, but she'd worry about that if they made it that far.

"Hurry, René, that way." They hobbled through the back of dark Square Cadiou, disturbing night birds, who fluttered noisily in alarm. Great.

"We should just tell them the truth," René said. "Help them investigate."

"Never in a blue moon." The *flics* hated her. She'd exposed corruption in the "family," gotten her godfather, Commissaire Morbier, shot. Once family, always family—they would never forgive her, an ex-cop's daughter, for betraying the family. Even if they'd betrayed her father by drumming him out of the force.

Right then she was spit on the soles of their shoes.

She pulled her key ring out and fumbled with the old keys. She picked an ancient one she'd stolen from Morbier years ago and copied when he wasn't looking—one of the master postal and park keys.

It worked.

Music and laughter drifted from a lit passage. People spilled out onto the narrow street, smoking and drinking.

"Mingle, René," she said, trying not to wince as she punched the number for a Taxi Bleu into her cell phone.

An artistic crowd—what Aimée had taken for a party turned out to be a *vernissage*, a gallery opening.

"They call this art?" René complained as they waited under a plastic palm.

"I heard you the first time, René," she said, helping them both to wine from a copper tray. She smelled of damp grass, and her shoulder was pounding with pain. "It's called found art; I told you." From the corner of her eye, she watched for a taxi. Her heart skipped. Two blue uniforms were coming up the street.

"Dumpster diving and slapping junk together, more like it," he said. "Even graffiti's art now. Don't forget—tomorrow night we're giving the award at Demy's art foundation."

Demy's art foundation was their pro bono account. It showcased street and graffiti art and was championed by the Socialist mayor of the arrondissement. "You'll meet Xavier, the mover and shaker," said René, nervous, gulping down the wine. "Gets things done. He's brilliant."

The two uniforms were making their way through the crowd.

"So how do you know the artist?" asked a rail-thin man, a culture-vulture type wearing a black jumpsuit and frameless designer glasses. Aimée hated questions like that—scrolled through a mental list of go-to stock answers.

"We're neighbors," she said, smiling. "Delighted to be invited and see what goes on in the atelier."

"I didn't think she knew anyone here yet," he said, curious. "Why are you all wet?"

Before he could grill her further, the taxi pulled up.

"Excuse us, monsieur. Have to go. Come on, René."

"In a taxi?" the thin man asked. "I thought you were neighbors."

"Theater tickets," Aimée said. "Adieu."

"*L'Institut du Monde Arabe, s'il vous plaît,*" Aimée told the taxi driver, a *mec* with a cigarette and cap.

René shot her a look. Mouthed, *Why?*

She put a finger to her lips. Taxi fares and locations were logged. They'd walk from there.

She overtipped the taxi driver, hoping in his pleasant surprise he'd remember little about his passengers.

Ile Saint-Louis's globe lights shimmered on the dark, moving Seine. The warm air couldn't dry her jacket, which stuck to her neck. Once the taxi had pulled away, she and René crossed the Pont de Sully.

"I need to go back and pick up my car." René looked nervous.

She imagined his *classique* Citroën DS parked on the boulevard swarming with police cars. "Not a good idea. Wait till tomorrow," she said, limping as discreetly as possible.

On the streets of Ile Saint-Louis, the restaurants were closing. She nodded to the patron of her local café and dipped inside. Emerged a moment later with a bag of ice. Leaned on René's shoulder to take off her high-tops. Damned cobblestones.

"Are you okay?" René asked.

"After I get home, I will be."

She'd ice her ankle, get her shoulder fixed, and figure out what happened.

IN THE SALON, she thrust a wad of francs in Madame Cachou's hands to forestall any questions and ushered the older woman out the door.

In Chloé's room, Aimée breathed in her *bébé's* scent, talcum powder, freshly laundered crib sheets, and sweet baby's breath. Felt her cool brow and kissed that rosebud mouth.

Aimée discarded her wet clothes, donned *après-ski* silk thermals, and wrapped herself up in her father's old bathrobe.

The salon's chandelier sent a soft glow over the freshly folded piles of baby clothes. Miles Davis had curled up with René.

"I can't understand what happened, Aimée," said René. His laptop was already open in front of him. "We heard Éric's phone ring. He was there. But then that poor girl, those scissors sticking out of her neck . . ." René shook his head. "Éric is such a geek. I'd never have thought he could go to such lengths."

She popped two Doliprane for her shoulder and sat down, putting the ice on her swelling ankle. She felt the cold and numbness taking over.

René was typing angrily. "Can you believe Éric could make up that whole story, pull you into it to disguise the fact that he murdered his nephew?"

She couldn't.

"This poor Karine." He sighed. "It doesn't make sense. Too convoluted."

She agreed. It didn't add up. "I don't think Éric killed her. Lili said Karine was being followed."

"Okay," René said, "so what? A serial killer with scissors?"

She pulled out her phone. "Let's ask Éric."

The call went to voice mail.

She was tired, and her shoulder throbbed. She couldn't lift her arm. Impossible to ignore the signs of a dislocated shoulder anymore—or to ignore the pain. She poured herself a double shot of her grandfather's old brandy. Knew that she had to pop her shoulder back in. "René, can you help me? Please?"

Alarmed, he looked up from his laptop.

"Stand on the sofa, René."

"I hate this," he said, making a face.

"Not more than I do," she said, gritting her teeth as she lay on the floor. "Take my wrist, support my elbow, and lift it vertically toward the ceiling. Keep the upward traction and gently rotate, okay?"

René did as she'd instructed.

"Ow . . . Wait, my muscles need to relax."

René took a deep breath. Waited.

"Now, again."

She fought through the searing pain. "Once more, René."

She almost passed out from the white-hot pain, and it felt as if her arm were being wrenched off. Pop.

The shooting sparks of heat subsided; her shoulder slumped.

After several minutes she felt some relief, thank God. She put the ice pack on her shoulder, hoping tomorrow it would hold.

René took a slug of brandy. "I can't believe what I just did. Or that I ran away from a murder scene."

As the pain cleared, Aimée's mind returned to the sight of the scissors sticking out of Karine's neck. A horrifying image. And behind it, something was niggling at the back of Aimée's mind. She sat up.

Papa.

"René, I remember Papa telling me about a case from the seventies, a woman murdered in a Marais sewing factory with scissors in her neck."

"You're saying . . . a copycat?" René put his drink down and picked up his laptop again, tapping away furiously at the keyboard.

"The *flics* suspected one of the factory workers. Or maybe a jealous husband."

"*Voilà.*" René's voice rose in excitement. "I found it—1975. It was her lover—killed her over some jewelry he wanted for his new mistress. He escaped to Venezuela, no extradition."

She remembered now. "My father said the killer threw suspicion on the victim's husband. Some rivalry in the factory. The *flics* took the bait, and the murderer got away."

She pushed the ice up higher on her shoulder.

René stroked Miles Davis, who'd rolled on his back. "So twenty years later he's back? Grabs the artist's scissors from the atelier?"

Far-fetched, but she considered it for a minute. "But that has nothing to do with Marcus's murder."

Her phone trilled.

Éric Besson's number showed.

Aimée answered. "Where are you, Éric?"

"Leaving. You must listen." In the background she could hear announcements on a loudspeaker.

"Did you set me up?"

"*Quoi?* I found that poor girl . . . dead. Horrible." His voice dropped. "He saw me."

"Who?"

"I couldn't see his face. He said, 'You're next,' and was gone over the wall."

"Rows thirteen through twenty-four boarding now," Aimée heard. Éric was at the airport. Escaping again.

"I'm afraid, Aimée."

"You're an attorney. You must know someone who can help."

"Find Léo's notebook."

"*Moi?* Two people have already been killed for this notebook. Even Karine didn't know where it was."

"We're boarding now, monsieur . . ." a voice said.

Aimée heard Besson suck in his breath. "I'm going dark. You won't hear from me for a while. If the notebook still exists, no one's safe until you find it. Including you."

Wednesday Morning

OCHRE LIGHT STREAMED on the kitchen floor tiles, promising a mixed weather day—rain and sun. René was perched next to Chloé's high chair, shuffling flash cards in his lap, while Babette finished up the laundry. René, nervous to go out in the street in case the police were still looking for them, had slept on the recamier.

Benoît hadn't returned Aimée's call. Was it over between them? Had she misread his signals? She couldn't worry about that now.

"How are you feeling, Aimée?" René asked.

"I'm all right."

The swelling of her shoulder had gone down, leaving a blue-purple bruise. The good news was she had the full, extended range of motion of her arm. Her ankle was another story. Forget her black-tipped Chanel sling backs. Her red Converse high-tops, which hurt to lace up, at least gave her ankle support.

Chloé gurgled, intent on licking her fingers, which were sticky with mashed pear.

"We're off to the park," said Babette. "Give Maman a bisou."

Chloé offered Aimée a pear-scented cheek.

"Later, ma puce," she said.

René slipped the flash cards into his pocket and opened his briefcase.

"*Alors*, René, enough with the flash cards," Aimée said. "Chloé doesn't need to learn quantum physics right now."

René started to protest.

"Or Cantonese or colors."

She opened her laptop on the table. "I did some thinking last night." Her fingers clicked over the keyboard as she pulled up flight information. "*Regardes, René*. Last night Éric was either at Orly boarding the AF to Toulouse or Brussels, or if he had his passport on him, he might have boarded the Morocco flight at CDG."

René looked up, his green eyes big. "There's nothing else to do here, Aimée. Leave it alone."

"Poor Karine . . ." Her insides churned. "How can I? I have to find that notebook."

"The notebook's gone."

She popped more Doliprane. "There's one person who knows about the Hand."

"Then isn't it time you ask him and be done with this?"

Wednesday, Noon

AIMÉE COULD DO this. She really could. Suck up her pride and see if her suspicions panned out. Beg her godfather, the *ex-commissaire*, for help.

Put aside her guilt for getting him shot.

Her thoughts looped, like a stuck record, replaying last night over and over: Karine's open, vacant eyes; the scissors' worn handle protruding from her neck; the rustling, wet leaves; Éric's phone ringing.

She had to find this notebook.

Weaving her scooter along the boulevard, she made her way past the police hospital that was treating her godfather, Morbier. Not five minutes before she was threading her way into a narrow winding warren, once part of the village Saint-Marcel, which had become part of Paris in 1860. Finally into a slanting cobbled lane lined by two- and three-story houses and metal-scrollwork fences, up which climbed the last roses of the season. These *petite maisons* on Square des Peupliers had been gentrified by bobos eager to live as close as possible to the center of Paris. Until earlier in the century, these houses had belonged to factory workers. Before them, Aimée could imagine tanners and dyers living here near rue du Moulin des Prés, where a long-gone mill once stood on la Bièvre, the ancient and underground still-flowing river. By 1912, it had become so polluted that it was covered over.

Reminders of its rural past dotted the thirteenth arrondissement: artist ateliers in small lanes, steep cobbled streets, ivy and flowering creepers adding charm to even the old factories and warehouses. Approaching postcard pretty. Yet time marched on in the thirteenth, and only a few blocks away from this pocket, developers were building new commercial zones.

Number 37 was a little jewel of a *maison*. Morbier, a dyed-in-the-wool Socialist, here?

She parked her scooter. Took a deep breath.

She opened the scraping gate, buzzed. No answer. Dumb. Why hadn't she called first?

A slate-grey cat slinked around her legs, rubbing its velvet fur against her shin, then nudged the front door open.

Since when did a *flic* keep a door unlocked?

The house was full of the scent of baking apples. Delicious. Her eyes became accustomed to the bright light from overhead skylights, revealing an open floor plan and graphite Scandi-style furniture. What she imagined had once been a configuration of tiny rooms had been opened up. *Très à la mode* in a minimalist modern way.

Morbier's temporary new digs—a friend's sublet with no stairs. The proximity to the police hospital made it ideal.

A spoon clattered on the polished toffee wood floor in the kitchen area. "*Merde!*"

"Someone's in a good mood," she said.

Morbier, ex–police *commissaire*, sat in a wheelchair, his legs covered by a mohair blanket, old plaid wool *charentaise* slippers peeking out beneath. The dark circles under his basset hound eyes were even more pronounced than when she'd last seen him; stone-white hair curled thick and long over his collar.

She bit her lip, suppressing a gasp. How he'd aged since her hospital visit two months ago, after she'd gotten him shot. The awkward visit had been an attempt at reconciliation and had left so much unsaid.

"So look what the cat dragged in," he said. If he was surprised to see her, he didn't show it. "Took your time, Leduc."

Before him stood a bowl on a wood chopping block. Above it hung copper lights strung through a wire sculpture that resembled the mobile over Chloé's crib. No doubt *this* one qualified as *l'art abstrait.*

"*Bonjour* to you, too, Morbier," Aimée said.

"Where's Chloé?"

"Enjoying the park with Babette, then *bébé* swim," she said, noting the slump of disappointment in his shoulders.

"Jeanne said she ran into you at the pool, and you said you'd drop by."

But not today. Jeanne, his squeeze, meant well, but Aimée hadn't been ready for that yet. She fought down her guilt. Should she keep this visit light, pretend it was just social? Work up the courage to ask the hard questions later?

"How do you feel?" she said.

"I know you're not here to visit," he said, reading her face. "Word gets around, eh?"

Ashamed and unsure of what he meant, she sucked in her breath. He shot her a knowing look. She couldn't tell if it was sadness or resignation in his sharp brown eyes. Or both.

"You're looking for Léo Solomon's missing notebook, Leduc," said Morbier.

This *poor me* charade—of course he knew about the notebook. Was he behind this somehow? The snake.

She picked up the enamel spoon from the floor, wishing it were a knife she could stab into the chopping block. Instead she slammed it in the stainless-steel sink. He started. Good. It felt good to put him off-balance for once. But she regretted it right away—so childish.

"How would you know about the notebook," she said, "unless you're involved, too?"

"That weak-chinned lawyer Besson called me. I told him to leave you out of it." A sigh. "*Et alors*, he didn't. Knowing you, you can't leave it alone."

If Besson had called Morbier, it was because his name was in the notebook . . . wasn't it? From the blue bowl on the chopping block, she plucked a leftover apple slice, popped it in her mouth. Chewed furiously at the tangy sweetness.

"And you, Morbier? I doubt you're leaving it alone."

A snort. "Look at me. What can I do? A discredited old invalid."

Liar. She could sense that his nerves were taut as a wire. His razor-sharp mind was intact and scheming.

"Quit playing sorry for yourself, Morbier. Sounds like your kind of party; get the balloons and show up. Confront your old cronies."

"Get real, Leduc. They're all gone."

"Not from what I heard," she said, guessing.

Morbier handed her ground coffee beans. "Make us espresso."

"*Attends*. Caffeine with your heart condition?"

"*Décaféiné's* all I drink, on the Nazi's orders." He noticed her blink. "The German doctor who installed my defibrillator. Now I'm *bionique*."

The stainless-steel Italian espresso maker steamed on the cooktop. Buttery aromas drifted from the state-of-the-art oven, which had no visible dials and was almost invisible among the cabinets. "Take the tart out before it burns, Leduc."

Clenching mitts, Aimée withdrew a bubbling tarte tatin from

the oven. She salivated. She was reminded of her grandfather Claude's Sunday desserts, how her grinning father would wipe the sticky bits from the corner of her mouth.

Morbier poured the espresso into two cups, then pulled a laptop from under his mohair blanket. "Let the tart cool."

Morbier with a laptop? Baking? Wonders never ceased. "Gone tech savvy in your retirement, eh? Next you'll be writing your memoir."

"You overestimate me, Leduc. What else can I do with a useless body?"

He wouldn't pull her in with that one.

"That notebook's history. Gone," said Morbier. "No doubt it was nothing but chicken scratch anyway, with the old man's Alzheimer's."

"Morbier, Besson didn't say anything about Alzheimer's—just the man's guilty confession as he was dying. And he read the entries. Wouldn't have taken it seriously otherwise." She paused, trying to banish the image of Karine's staring eyes and bloody neck, another innocent life lost over whatever was in this note-book. "I have to find it."

Morbier's hand stilled on the handle of his demitasse.

"Aimée, look at me." His eyes bored into hers. "It's better you leave this alone."

"Not after last night." Her ankle hurt. To relieve the pressure, she leaned on the kitchen island. "First we strike a deal—you tell me about Pierre Espinasse, the *flic* who saved Léo Solomon's life in the POW camp and what he had to do with the Hand. Then—"

"Who?"

Was he playing dumb? She doubted that. Was this too-ancient history?

But she didn't have time to waste. Had a meeting in an hour, then had to pick Chloé up at the pool. She'd give him some-thing and get something in return. It always worked like that with Morbier.

"*Bon*, I'll tell you the little I know," she said. "Then it's your turn. I need your insight."

"That's what you're calling it now?"

"Please, Morbier. We share, okay? Deal?"

Morbier sipped his espresso. The mobile-like sculpture rotated in the warm wind, making a soft shushing sound. Greenish light slanted in from the windows on to the garden.

He excelled at the waiting game. But she had places to go.

When he didn't answer, she swallowed. Hard.

She noticed the old cookbook open on the counter, notes in the margins with dates and comments—*burnt, undercooked*. Had he been testing this recipe every day in hopes that she'd . . . ?

"And I'll bring Chloé by after *bébé* swim tomorrow for a slice," she said.

He blinked.

"I'll take that as a *yes, we have a deal*," she said. "Last night, Besson's nephew's girlfriend was murdered in Cité fleurie."

"And you know this how?"

She told him; spared no horrific details, outlined her specula-tions.

"So the murderer forced the information about the notebook out of her, then shut her up." Morbier's thick brows knit. "Or the girl knew nothing, but the murderer tied up loose ends and is still on the hunt for the notebook?"

Aimée nodded. She didn't think Karine had been lying to her about not knowing where the notebook was. But who could say what information the killer might have extracted with threat of violence? "She said she had something to tell me, Morbier."

"Either way, right now you've got *rien*."

He may have retired his uniform, but he was all *flic*.

"Besson's terrified," Aimée said. "Called from the airport—chances are he skipped the country."

"But you don't think he stabbed the girl, do you?"

She shook her head. "Your turn, Morbier."

"*Moi?* You've just gotten the benefit of my 'insight.'"

"I want to know about this Pierre whom Léo owed." A knot formed in her stomach. She had to hear the truth. Part of her wanted to know, and another part didn't. "All those things you've never told me about your colleagues in the Hand."

A pause. "Get me a coffee."

"Or maybe I should throw it in your face."

Had she really said that?

"Wouldn't be the first time," said Morbier. A long, drawn-out sigh. "How many times have I pulled your ass out of the fire, Leduc?"

"And demanded payback each time."

She hated herself for reverting to her childhood, to her ten-year-old self. Her neck flushed. She had almost stamped her foot. Why couldn't she act grown-up for once?

"You're right." Morbier's voice came out a whisper.

If she hadn't been paying attention, she would have missed the muscle twitching in his neck. The spasm in his fingers.

Guilt flooded her. She'd put a bullet in his chest. Landed him in this wheelchair.

Her tongue thickened in her dry mouth. She fought to speak. To again say she was sorry. No words came out.

"No need to throw a tantrum or storm out, as usual." Morbier gave another deep sigh. "I hoped just this once you'd listen."

The overhead sculpture turned again.

"That's all the help you're going to be?" Aimée said. "Warning me off?"

No answer. She wouldn't get anything more from him.

She glanced at her Tintin watch. "I've got a meeting."

"There's something you should know, Leduc. Give me five minutes."

Something got to her—maybe guilt, sadness, the aroma of butter, or all three. Aimée nodded.

Morbier shoved two Limoges dessert plates and a filigreed silver pie server at her. "Invert the tart, and get serving."

Go off her diet? The caramelized apple tarte oozed butter and sugar. Would add a kilo to her hips.

"Think you'll bribe me with this?" she said.

"I can try," he said as Aimée sliced the tart. After a moment he said, "Vauban, a *flic* on robbery detail, was a go-between for a gang. For ten years, I couldn't get anything to stick on his greasy back."

"What's Vauban got to do with Pierre and the Hand?" she said. The first forkful tasted like heaven.

"Vauban graduated to brokering deals with big-timers," said Morbier. "Whoever he worked for was hands off. Protected. Unseen. Files went missing."

"Files went missing?"

She swallowed. Couldn't eat anymore.

"Listen, Leduc. Vauban got caught and *la Proc* figured out how to nail him. Everything would have come out: his connections, the links, the money trail." He paused. "Vauban *fell* under a bus two days ago."

Her insides curdled. "You're saying he was killed."

He lifted his palm and spread his thick fingers with their nicotine-stained nails. She realized he hadn't smoked a cigarette the whole time she'd been here.

"The Hand, Leduc."

There it was—confirmation.

"After the can of worms you opened, they're cleaning house," he said. "No one's safe or protected anymore. The notebook would nail a lot of coffins."

"Yours, too." A white lie here. "Éric said your name was in it. And Papa's."

"It's complicated, Leduc."

All of a sudden the kitchen seemed to close in around her—the heat, the butter smells, the prickle of the mohair blanket brushing her leg.

She wanted to tell him she felt afraid. Scared as her ten-year-old self had been when she'd gotten lost on that field trip to the Louvre.

"Eh?" Morbier set down his fork.

Had she said what she'd been thinking out loud?

She noticed he'd dug his fingernails into his palm, leaving pink half-moon crescents. Poor Morbier—after a long career, crippled and out of the action, yearning to score one last goal.

"Give me names," she said.

"As I said, it's complicated, Leduc. People like your father and me never knew the top level. You know, these are the people who got your father killed. One of them, I never found out who, heard your father was quitting the Hand and set up his hit. I heard the rumor, tried to warn him, got there too late. Now it's time for you to leave it alone."

Like hell.

His mouth hardened. "You're not hearing me, Leduc. Let me handle it. Just cooperate; lay low. Très simple."

She wasn't going to get anything else out of him today or maybe ever. Frustrated, she made a show of looking at her Tintin watch again and stood to leave.

"You think I blame you for my being put out to pasture," Morbier said suddenly. "For making me an invalid. After the havoc you wreaked exposing the corruption."

Her entire body tensed.

"I'm an old dog, around too long," he said, his voice low. "I know you did what you had to do."

And those were the truest and sincerest words he had said since she arrived.

The retro-modernistic clock on the wall ticked out the time. And hers was running out.

"I understand," said Morbier.

A petite woman with a long braid looped around her head swept into the room, hanging up her bag. "Naughty boy," she said in a thick accent. The clomping of her chunky clogs was as menacing as her stern look. "You're impossible."

"Meet *le dragon*," said Morbier, shutting his laptop.

"I'm Rasa, his physiotherapist," she said. Clucked disapprovingly. "How could you let him eat this?"

Morbier grinned. "Maybe I'll have a smoke, too . . ."

"Not if you want to live, *chéri*."

In a fluid move, the muscular therapist whisked the laptop away and released the wheelchair brake.

Morbier sighed. "Torture time."

With a snort, Rasa wheeled him into a back part of the house. "Think about it," Morbier threw over his shoulder. "We'll talk when you bring Chloé by."

Like Aimée would hold off until then? She shouldered her bag, waited until she heard a door close, then opened Morbier's laptop.

He was still logged in. Her lucky day. She'd have to work quick. She pulled up his emails. A quick glance showed one email from an encrypted *police judiciaire* account. Wasn't that still intranet, accessible to only the OPJ on-site? Had Morbier somehow kept his access to his old account? Whatever the source, it didn't matter. She forwarded the email to her proxy account and checked his browsing history. Took a screenshot and emailed that to herself, too.

The clunk of clogs was coming down the hall. The therapist. She hit several keys, erasing her last actions, closed the laptop, and thirty seconds later was out the door.

AIMÉE WAITED IN traffic on rue de Tolbiac, trying not to breathe the tepid air drifting from the Métro on her right. Riding her scooter, she'd make it to the Bibliothèque François-Mitterrand meeting in time. Just.

René called.

"I'm en route," she said. "On time." For once.

"No need," said René. "The *fonctionnaire* postponed the meeting to later this afternoon. A good thing. Means I'll have more of a report ready, and he'll see progress."

A stroke of luck. That gave her time. Time she could use to investigate Léo Solomon before meeting her nanny at the pool.

Her father always said, never assume; find out. Take it step by step—legwork paid off.

She'd start with Gobelins, the tapestry factory where Léo had worked. She had caught mention of the place during her hurried look at Morbier's emails.

The light changed. "Got to go," she told René.

THE NIGHT BEFORE, she'd tried reading Maxence's file on Léo Solomon. So far, mostly background. Her ankle had throbbed, and when she had fallen asleep, it had seemed like only minutes before Chloé woke her up at dawn.

Léo Solomon, a young accountant, had married Marie, an apprentice weaver, after the war. They'd worked and lived on the Gobelins premises until just a few years ago. According to Besson, all that time Léo had been amassing entries in his notebook.

She made a quick call to Maxence as she was gunning up broad Avenue d'Italie. The September weather, unpredictable like the strikes and demonstrations, made her glad she'd stuck her warm wool scarf in her bag. Thank God it hadn't rained yet. Clouds blotted out the sun, and a rising wind whipped her ankles.

Maxence answered on the second ring, but with the street bustle and horns, she couldn't catch everything he said.

"Léo Solomon's will . . ." he was saying. ". . . latest news." The rest was lost in the blare of a car horn.

She pulled over. Caught whiffs of garlic from a pho noodle hole-in-the-wall. Her phone in one hand, she used the other to pull her leather jacket on. Her sore shoulder protested as she extended her arm.

"Léo Solomon's will what? Tell me that again, Maxence."

"I checked the legal notices, given that his will would have gone to probate or be in process by now."

"If you say so."

Smart. The kid had thought big picture. Why hadn't she?

"His estate left bequests to a range of charities," Maxence said. "Including a nice sum to Gobelins in his wife Marie's name."

Overhead the leafy chestnut tree branches rustled; a bicycle bell tingled. She thumbed open her red Moleskine to an empty page, found a kohl eye pencil, the first thing at hand to write with. Maybe it was time to upgrade to a PDA.

"How long ago did Marie pass away?" Aimée asked. "Any more details?"

After scribbling notes, she thanked him and hung up. Revved her scooter and took off.

TEN MINUTES LATER, she'd parked her scooter, knotted her scarf, applied Chanel red in the reflection of a storefront window, and come up with a story.

La Manufacture des Gobelins's brick and stone façade, fronted by an ornate gold-tipped gate, evoked royal grandeur. But it had originally been a dye works, founded by a fifteenth-century dyer where la Bièvre, the river, used to run. Gobelins's name stuck even after the factory became renowned for making tapestries for the king, then later for Napoleon, and now for the *république*.

A museum and studios thrived in this centuries-old complex where tapestries were still loom-woven by hand in the traditional style. Pieces took years to make. Who'd have that patience? Aimée wondered, eyeing a château-sized piece through a window.

No time for culture. On her left a crow perched on the statue of Le Brun, painter to Louis XIV, in the center of the courtyard. The painter's bronze shoulders were splattered with cream pigeon droppings.

Instead of entering the museum's door, she unhooked the red velvet barrier rope and hurried across the cobbles to the *gardien* loge by the gate.

From inside the loge came the faint sound of a woman's sobbing. Hesitant, Aimée stepped forward.

"He came again. Demanding to see me at work. But he'll never leave his wife. Why can't he understand it's over?"

A lovelorn concierge spilling her heart out on the phone.

Aimée hated to intrude. She knocked on the half-open door, the glass warm against her knuckles.

"*Excusez-moi,*" she said. "I'm looking for *le patron.*"

Sunlight streamed in through the mullioned window, splashing across a desk strewn with a crossword magazine, some mail, and a demitasse with coffee dregs in the bottom. Security procedures were taped to the stone walls. A young woman looked up, holding a cell phone, and wiped her swollen eyes, leaving blue and green smudges on her hands. Her hair was piled in a bun, her frame muscular.

"Madame Livarot?" She sniffled, getting businesslike. "You have an appointment?"

Aimée would soft-pedal. "I assume so. I'm delivering her documents."

Aimée set down a card from her business file. For a fake legal firm, convenient for such occasions. The young woman's red eyes didn't blink. Uninterested, she blew her nose. Aimée saw a badge on the desk with the name Olivia visible under a wad of wet tissues.

"Leave the documents here," the woman said.

"Only in person, my boss said." Aimée checked her Tintin watch.

An expulsion of air. A shrug. "I'm not supposed to let anyone in. The concierge took a break."

Looked like a long one.

"You take security seriously, I understand, but I'm pressed for time." Aimée's gaze had caught on the directory on the wall: ATE-LIER HAUTE LISSE, CHAPELLE, ATELIER DE TEINTURE, CANTINE, SALLES DE COURS DESSIN ET HISTORIQUE DE L'ART FORMATION, MAISONS. She'd had no idea this place was so huge, a functioning artisanal haven. "Madame Livarot's in the *atelier haute lisse* section?"

Olivia, Aimée assumed from the badge, hesitated, then nodded. "Don't say I let you in. She's particular. Second courtyard, behind the garden on the left. You can't miss it. It's the oldest building here."

"*Merci.*"

OLDEST? HOW COULD she tell in this centuries-old enclave? Aimée felt as if she'd stepped into the past or found herself suddenly in a country hamlet. Butterflies stopped among the beds of orange peonies. Several young men in blue work coats walked past a medieval covered well; they were carrying wooden poles, and Aimée heard the tap-tapping of a hammer. The past come alive.

She picked her way over the worn cobbles, battling the dull ache in her ankle. Beyond the garden, she spotted the mustard-colored *atelier haute lisse* tapestry studio, rectangular and vaulted. It reminded her of a village washhouse. In the *entrée*, glass cases displayed polished wooden bobbins, ivory tamping combs, old scissors, vials of madder root and indigo leaves for dyes. She caught a faint aroma of fresh linen, which reminded her of the old laundry that had been on Ile Saint-Louis when she was a little girl. That scent was undercut by a deeper note—what did it remind her of? The dark scarlet tannin dregs left in a glass of Burgundy?

A tour group clustered around a guide sporting a Ministry of Culture badge, blocking her way.

"Please, no talking to the *hautes lissiers*, the weavers," the guide said. "Concentration is required, and on this tour, we respect their craft."

Great.

"Gobelins was first established in the fifteenth century. In 1662, the crown purchased the tapestry workshops. The first royal director was Le Brun, Louis XIV's court painter, who, with the king's confidence, directed an array of craftsmen—tapestry weavers, bronze workers, gold- and silversmiths who supplied objects for the royal residences and produced diplomatic gifts." The guide's drone almost put Aimée to sleep. "After 1699, it produced only tapestries. In 1826, Gobelins switched from the low- to the high-warp technique, unlike the Aubusson tapestry factory. Yet now, as in the past, the techniques follow guild statutes that originated in the Middle Ages."

Aimée tried to make her way forward. However, there was no way through this group of provincial seniors with bad sun hats, who hung on the guide's every word.

"As you'll see, the weaver sits behind the loom and works on the back of the tapestry with the daylight coming in on the other side so she can follow the design," said the guide. "You'll see some of the fifteen looms used by thirty weavers. The factory produces six or seven tapestries a year."

Heads shook in awe at the fact that so much time was spent on a single tapestry. And Aimée was spending too much time with this tour group. She edged forward past a senior with a cane.

The guide gave her a sharp look. "The office shouldn't have allowed latecomers. We're on a schedule."

Aimée had no intention of going on a tour. Or dealing with this uptight woman. Aimée excused herself, shoving her way through the group. "I'm not on the tour. I'm expected at Madame Livarot's office."

Aimée could tell the guide was itching to exert her authority. "Office? You're in her office." The guide opened the atelier doors and spread her arms to take in the tall, cavernous studio, light filled and bursting with color. A row of almost ceiling-high looms stretched down the room. The incandescent, multihued spools of shimmering silk thread blurred Aimée's vision.

The guide's group had moved on.

But the hushed whoosh and click of the looms took Aimée's breath away. She was riveted. The rhythmic, smooth sliding; the nimble knotting motions—they were hypnotic to watch. The weavers were working on a piece that stretched all the way to the ceiling. She watched bits of color appearing as the weavers wove and threaded, how the design emerged from a pattern in front of her eyes.

"Madame Livarot's by the window." A middle-aged woman with a chopstick holding up her hair spoke to Aimée. She jutted her chin toward a corner, her hands busy, never stopping their work on her loom.

Aimée made her feet move, approached the older woman hunched at what appeared to be a slanted architect's desk. Pastel chalks, rulers, and scissors filled a workbox. "*C'est magique.*"

Aimée hadn't meant to say that.

"You're here why, mademoiselle?" The woman hadn't looked up from the pastel drawing with attached colored thread swatches in front of her. The no-nonsense tone brought Aimée back to earth.

"Madame Livarot," she said, "it has to do with the Solomons."

The wrinkled face looked up at her. Expressionless. Deep, hollowed eyes, long chin—the woman could have been fifty, but she could also have been seventy years old.

"The walls have ears." Madame Livarot's calloused finger pointed outside. "Beyond Cour Colbert at the *chapelle.*"

AIMÉE TOOK CARE as she crossed the cobbles, avoiding the deep grooves between them. The last thing she needed was to aggravate her sprained ankle.

At the *chapelle's* worm-eaten doors, Madame Livarot directed her past a sign that said ATELIER DE TEINTURE. Aimée winced as she mounted the steep, winding stone steps. They followed a hallway to what appeared to be a medieval add-on—a jumble of odd corners, hairpin turns, and wood-beamed ceilings.

Aimée caught her breath as they stopped in an airy mullion-windowed room overlooking a courtyard. Large round vats and boilers the size of washing machines were set into stucco counters. The acidic odors reminded her of the old *teinturerie*, the fabric dyer's, near her lycée, long gone now.

"The dyers are on strike. Typical," said Madame Livarot, closing a shutter. "No ears here."

Dyers went on strike? Aimée had had no idea. But it was September.

Skeins of drying silk and yarn hung from wooden bars over the dye vats, vibrant from pigments—now synthetic, formerly made of ground minerals, plants, and insects. The studio reminded her of that premakeover château kitchen she'd seen in *Elle Decor*. This was definitely a "before" medieval. Hadn't changed much in five hundred years, she figured, except for the gas lines.

Madame Livarot turned to face her. "Who are you, mademoiselle?"

She wondered that herself sometimes. "I'm Aimée Leduc," she said. She'd debated whether to tell the truth. She sensed talking to a private detective wouldn't sit well with this woman. But Aimée needed information.

She flashed her PI card. "Éric Besson, the son of Marie Solomon's best friend, hired me." Stretching the truth. "How well did you know the Solomons?"

"You're the second one asking today."

She felt a chill. The killer was looking for Léo's notebook.

"But as I told him," said Madame Livarot, "I run the weaving studio. I have nothing to do with the accounting department."

"Who was asking?" Aimée said. "It's important. Can you describe him?"

Madame Livarot's eyes narrowed. "Why is that your business?"

"Léo Solomon kept records that have gone missing—"

"I asked how that concerns you."

Aimée would get nothing if she didn't explain.

Outside the window, a blue jay swooped over the courtyard. Aimée moved closer to the woman. "The day before he died, Léo went to Éric Besson for help—"

"I haven't seen Éric since he was a pimply adolescent," she interrupted. "Marie and Léo treated him like a son."

Like a son? Éric hadn't mentioned they were that close.

"Then you know Léo trusted him," Aimée said. "Léo asked Éric to take sensitive information to a magistrate." She kept her gaze on the door. "Éric's nephew, who was acting as courier, was murdered en route. The information Léo was desperate to get to the magistrate is missing."

Madame Livarot waved dismissively. "Léo's records are kept in accounting."

The woman was holding something back.

"Léo kept double books," Aimée guessed, "records of his sideline accounting business. But you'd know that."

"Would I? You're making crazy allegations."

"Last night a young woman, Éric's nephew's girlfriend, was murdered in Cité fleurie."

The woman blinked. "What's that got to do with anything?"

"She was with Éric's nephew when he was murdered. Before she was killed, she'd told me the notebook was hidden somewhere in the quartier." Another guess.

Aimée paused, suddenly remembering the scissors protruding

from Karine's neck. She'd seen scissors on Madame Livarot's desk
. . . and everywhere in the atelier.

"You could be in danger if you know anything about what Léo's
notebook contains," Aimée continued. "Or if the killer thinks
you do."

"All I know is that Léo's estate was donated to charity in
Marie's name."

"Guilt money?"

"I don't understand what you mean. Léo never embezzled from
the Gobelins. We'd have known."

He wouldn't have had to if he worked for the Hand. "Maybe he
used his position here to cover for other businesses—"

"That's not the man I knew," Madame Livarot interrupted,
her tone raised. "Or the man Marie spent her life with." Madame
Livarot moved to the next window and pointed to the wing across
from it. "Marie and Léo lived there from the end of the war until
a few years ago, even after she retired in her seventies. A perk of
being a *fonctionnaire* and for her years of service. Couldn't happen
now."

Aimée thought of her own accountant: detail oriented, always
erring on the side of caution, always keeping backups. What if
Léo really had made a duplicate record of his dealings?

That ancient building where he'd lived had to be riddled with
cellars. Maybe there was an old trunk in storage. She took her red
Moleskine from her bag. Jotted down a rough sketch of the courtyard, where pigeons were fighting for scattered hunks of bread
under a sign that said, DON'T FEED THE PIGEONS.

"When did you last see Léo?" Aimée asked.

Madame Livarot's eyes were faraway. "It was sad. He was just a
shell of his old self, on oxygen. Marie died only six months ago.
I'm surprised he lasted as long as he did without her."

"So you saw him just before he died?"

"Maybe a week, *non*, a few days before. He'd come to explain his bequest in Marie's name. Theirs was a love story."

Madame Livarot was leaning against a vat under a row of hanging silk skeins, peacock blues and greens. Her lip trembled. "I worked at Marie's side for fifteen years. She was a true artisan with an eye for color. Such technique, yet with a touch of whimsy. Léo was a good man. Worshipped the ground she walked on." Tears brimmed in the woman's eyes. "I don't believe he was dishonest. Why would he be? He had all he wanted here—his Marie, a civil servant's salary, and a home in this village."

"Sometimes good men do bad things for a good reason," said Aimée. "Or at least think they do."

"What do you mean?"

Aimée could see in Madame Livarot's eyes that she had hit on something. "Please help me. Who was the man who came to talk to you today?"

"I don't know."

"Didn't he give you his name?"

"When he started asking questions, I just told him to speak to accounting."

"How long ago?"

"Maybe an hour ago."

"Can you describe his hair color, clothes? Was he tall or short? His walk, voice?"

Madame Livarot looked away. Shrugged.

Frustrated, Aimée didn't know how else to prod this woman. "Come on now. Wouldn't an artist notice details?"

Her face crumpled, like the face of a child whose *glace* had been taken away for bad behavior. "I don't . . . see things like that. But I can draw."

Aimée thumbed past her to-do lists to a blank page in her Moleskine. Handed the notebook and a pencil to Madame Livarot. "Can you show me?"

While she waited, Aimée watched the pigeons in the courtyard below. Even more had flocked to the bread; the courtyard was swarmed. She thought she caught movement—a black leather sleeve? Her antenna up, she watched the courtyard like a hawk until the scratching of Madame Livarot's pencil stopped.

"Best I can do, but it gives the idea."

Madame Livarot's quick pencil sketch, professional and photographic in detail, depicted a *mec* in jeans with narrow shoulders, short hair, a squashed nose, and narrow, piggy eyes. It was the work of a real artist. The man in the drawing was somehow familiar.

Aimée looked back out the window at the man in the courtyard feeding the pigeons.

Compared.

"You mean him?"

Madame Livarot nodded.

If Aimée didn't hurry, he'd get away.

"Stay away from the window," she said, tearing a sheet out of the Moleskine and scribbling her number down. "The *mec's* more than trouble. You're in danger. And call me so we can talk more about Léo." Aimée hiked her bag up on her sore shoulder. She'd have to back-burner checking out Léo's old place.

Madame Livarot's eyes widened. "Where are you going?"

"To catch him before he disappears."

Aimée ran into the warren of hallways, searching for the stairs to take her down and into the courtyard. An older woman, carrying an armful of fabric, was blocking her way.

"*Excusez-moi, madame.* Which way to the courtyard?" Aimée asked.

"There are three."

Aimée tried to remember some detail. "I mean the one with the sundial. You can see it from the dye works."

"You're a new intern?"

Why did this woman want to chat? Vital time was passing. "I'm in a hurry, madame." She spied an exit sign behind the woman. "*Excusez-moi.*"

The woman didn't move. Her eyes narrowed. "I've never seen you before. Only employees are allowed in here. Who are you?"

"In the scheme of life? To be determined."

Aimée squeezed around the woman—difficult in the tiny corridor—then barreled out the door.

The courtyard was deserted apart from the pigeons.

Had he sensed he'd been seen?

Or . . .

She heard a gate give a little scrape—as if someone was trying to close it quietly. No time for subtleties. She took off down a gravel path, past hanging clematis vines and a drooping willow, and shoved the gate open. Bursting through, she grabbed the man's leather-clad arms. Shoved him up against the stone wall. Came face-to-face with a leering grin.

"Been a while, Aimée," he said.

Her stomach wrenched. The undercover vice *flic*, Cyril Cromach, who'd arrested her cousin Sebastien back in his using days. Cyril had been masquerading as a punk rocker—or had it been a goth?—the last time she'd seen him. She wanted to hit him.

"Not long enough," she said, stepping back and catching her breath.

"What's your angle here?" he said, pulling his scrawny blond ponytail out of his leather jacket collar. Crooked nose, big jaw, and piggy eyes—she should have recognized him from Madame

Livarot's sketch. He was large shouldered but shorter than Aimée.

"You first," she said. Her ankle throbbed.

"It's a paycheck." Cyril shrugged. That *n'importe quoi* attitude she remembered from when he'd locked up her cousin. As if he gave a rat's ass. "I contract out. Freelance PI."

So he'd left the police force. Had he told her he was a PI to build camaraderie? It hadn't worked.

"Who signs the check, Cyril?"

"*Et alors*, it's your turn to tell me what you're doing here," he said.

"Spill, and I might pretend I never caught you."

Fat chance of that.

"*Vraiment?*" His eyes flicked back and forth along rue Berbier du Mets. Nervous? Waiting for someone? The trees were changing color—pale green to light orange and autumnal yellow.

She tried again. "Who's your employer?" The scumbag could be working for anyone. Might even be . . . a hit man? One never knew.

"What's it to you?"

"You know how curious I get," she said, wishing her ankle didn't hurt. "Like I've got time for this, Cyril. You're the primary suspect in the case now."

"What case? What are you going on about?"

Greasy then and slimy now. "The murder investigation, that's what I mean."

"You're crazy."

Her gaze caught on the blue and white barreling down the street. Thank God—Madame Livarot had called the police.

"Good luck explaining that to the *flics*."

The police car pulled up with screeching brakes. Just as one *flic* pushed Cyril against the wall, a Gobelins security guard ran out from the gate.

"That's her," he said. Pointed at Aimée. "She's the one."

"What do you mean?" Before she had time to react, her arms were pulled behind her back, and she was pushed up against the wall next to Cyril. She suppressed a groan as her tender shoulder was wrenched. "What's going on? Look, this man's—"

Her wrists were cuffed, she was patted down, and the phone was pulled out of her pocket. Panic seized her. Calm, try to calm down.

"There's a mix-up," she said. "It's him you want. I've got to pick up my baby."

The next thing she knew she was in the back seat of the police car. No Cyril.

The rat.

"You're making a big mistake," she said, ready to kick the driver's seat. Scream.

"I'm sure you'll tell us all about it at the *commissariat*."

AIMÉE SAT IN a dank green interrogation room on a stiff chair bolted to the floor. The place was designed to make anyone feel like a criminal.

Her dress was stiff with dried perspiration. The chill goose-pimpled her bare legs. Wrong day not to wear stockings.

"*Bon.*" The *flic* seated across from her glanced at a report. He was in his late forties, rough stubble shading his plump cheeks after an all-night shift. He smelled like *a flic*—cigarettes, spilled coffee, and too-strong freshly applied Paco Rabanne cologne. Greying chest hair peeked out over his shirt, which was flecked with tobacco. A real fashion plate edging toward retirement.

His phone rang. For a full five minutes, he spoke, turning away without even an *excusez-moi*. He was giving her the "treatment," what *flics* did to unnerve a suspect. Talk about professional. She almost snorted.

Had Cyril the rat set her up? Or was this about running from a murder the night before?

The *flic* hung up and rescanned the report.

She uncrossed her legs and stood. "Since you haven't even offered me coffee—"

"Cool your *bazketz*," he said. Slang for basketball shoes. Lazy and affected—she hated that.

"They're high-tops."

"Sit down."

"Why am I here?"

"There's a complaint you were illegally in a ministry building. Trespassing."

"So a squad car pulls up to arrest me, a visitor at the tapestry factory?" she said, sitting down. "I had a meeting with Madame Livarot, who's in charge of the weaving atelier. You should be talking to her."

"Thanks for telling me my job."

Anytime, she almost shot back. Instead she bit her tongue.

"You're about to be charged with assault."

Her mouth dropped open. "Assault on whom?"

"Monsieur Cyril Cromach has filed a complaint against you."

She shook her head in disbelief. That wimp, that limp-wristed coward. "You've got to be kidding me. You have no evidence. My father was a *flic*—"

"I'm aware of that, Mademoiselle Leduc. You've got quite a reputation."

She should have known that was what this was about. Exactly why she hadn't gone to the police for help the night before. "*Tant pis*. Cyril is the one you should be investigating, not me. He was trying to flee the scene after illegally—"

"Actually, he's a hired employee of a Madame de Frontenac," the *flic* said, consulting his report, "who states he was the victim of a violent assault while attempting to perform his paid duties."

A violent assault—catching his sleeve and pushing him against the wall? She should have punched him when she'd had the chance. "Who's Madame de Frontenac?"

"That's not pertinent to this investigation."

Great.

SHE PACED IN the *commissariat*'s holding cage while she waited in line for processing. Could things get worse? And it wasn't even three.

Priority one, she needed to reach her nanny—who had an exam that afternoon—and arrange care for Chloé. Number two—warn René he'd need to cover the meeting. *Merde.* She'd make them look unprofessional by not showing up. When would Madame Livarot talk to the *flics* and straighten out the story? How soon could Aimée get the hell out of there?

The old clock's minute hand moved with maddening slowness. Her makeup had congealed. The smell of fear and unwashed bodies was always the same in the *commissariat*.

She was one of them now. The heated corridor made her perspire in places she hadn't even known she could sweat from—the creases of her elbows, behind her knees, behind her ears. In the winter, of course, the heat wouldn't be working, and the place would be glacial.

How could her afternoon have gone so upside down?

Cyril, the liar, would have to prove assault, wouldn't he?

Her gut instinct was to call Morbier. But he couldn't rescue her anymore.

She needed a lawyer.

No phone. No bag. Stuck.

She was still waiting for her one phone call; the station had gotten busy. Yelling demonstrators filled the corridor, hauled in from a hospital workers' strike at Place d'Italie. Who knew how long it would be until things settled down?

She had to get out of there. Now.

"Either charge me, or let me go," she said to the female at the admitting desk.

"Your name?"

"Leduc, Aimée."

"All in good time."

"I've been here two hours," she said, stretching the truth.

"Sit down and wait your turn."

"I want to make a phone call."

"Good news. You're third on the list."

This was ridiculous, unfair, and so wrong. Who was behind it? It stank like an overripe reblochon.

Wednesday Afternoon

THE RECEIVER OF the public phone was greasy in Aimée's hand as she slotted in coins. She dialed Babette's cell phone number.

Brrrrng. Brrrnng. No answer.

Her knuckles whitened clutching the phone.

Answer. Please answer. She only had one call.

"*Allô?*" Finally. Aimée heard splashes, children's voices.

"Babette, it's Aimée."

"What's this number? I almost didn't answer. Anyway, we're just about to get in the pool. Chloé's excited . . ." Babette chattered on, and Aimée felt a pang hearing her daughter's happy squeals in the background.

"Babette," Aimée interrupted, "this is important. Ask Noémi to take Chloé home after *bébé* swim, okay?" Aimée and Noémi, another mother, sometimes took their daughters to the park together after swim class. They had babysat for each other before.

"Working late this afternoon?"

"Long story. And I don't know when I'll get released."

"Released?"

The time left on her franc ticked away.

"I'm on a pay phone," Aimée said. "Can't talk long."

"But Noémi didn't bring her baby to the pool today." Pause. Gurgles. "I've got my exam this afternoon, Aimée."

Of course she did. She'd asked to get off early this afternoon a month ago.

"Can you reschedule?" Aimée asked.

"It's a make-up exam. They won't give me another chance."

Bad to worse.

"I need a lawyer," Aimée said. "You're my only phone call." How embarrassing to have to confess this to her babysitter. "Could you please ask René to call our lawyer? I'm at the *commissariat* at Place d'Italie."

René might not answer. The *bibliothèque* meeting was in a few minutes.

Babette gasped. "Are you all right, Aimée?"

"I will be when I know Chloé's taken care of . . ."

"Don't worry. Noémi just came in. There's always plan B, remember?"

"But what if—"

The phone had clicked off.

She looked at the *flic* standing nearby, who motioned her to sit back down.

Wednesday, Late Afternoon

RENÉ ALWAYS THOUGHT Charvet's sixth-floor shirt-tailoring salon on Place Vendôme resembled a men's club. Exclusive, with an expensive hush—all it was missing was cigars. René had dropped by when the Bibliothèque François-Mitterrand meeting had been postponed—again—on the off chance they'd be able to squeeze him in between scheduled appointments. Now he stood on the fitting stool, his right arm extended for measurement. The crisp smell of custom-woven Egyptian cotton filled the wood-paneled room. The deep honey light of the late afternoon slanted across the hundreds of fabric bolts and the pale blue paper shirt patterns.

Chantal, the fitter, took a straight pin from her magnetic bracelet and tsked. "Monsieur Friant, I'll need to remeasure your shoulders."

He'd gained more muscle mass from all the working out he'd been doing, and it would cost him. This lightweight chambray needed to be a perfect fit for the wedding. Not his wedding, although he'd often fantasized about his own wedding suit—it was a classmate from his Sorbonne days getting married.

"Your goddaughter must be so big now," Chantal said. "Will she attend?"

"*Bien sûr*, she's the flower girl."

Chloé, almost eleven months, could totter and climb already, and she showed a fascination with numbers—René attributed that to innate mathematical ability. He'd start coding lessons as soon as she could sit still.

"You've decided on this chambray, Monsieur Friant?"

René nodded. "Perfect for a late September reception."

His gaze caught on the grooms' sample photo album on the table. The open photo spread showed a just-married couple, poised on church steps, framed by smiling well-wishers and bouquet-holding attendants. The perfect wedding. In his mind, the man in the picture dissolved and was replaced by him, René, somehow taller in a morning coat . . . The bride was Aimée, leggy, big-eyed, sporting René's family diamond ring. Chloé stood between them, his daughter, Aimée's perfume mingling with the flowers, her hair catching in his, their kiss . . .

A sharp prick of a pin brought him back to reality.

"*Pardonnez-moi*, Monsieur Friant. Try to stay still. We want to get a precise fit."

Back to the sad truth—he was just Aimée's best friend at the end of the evening. As he always would be.

His phone buzzed on the table.

Chantal's eyebrows rose. "You know our policy, Monsieur Friant." Absolutely no calls during custom fittings.

A surreptitious glance at his cell phone revealed Maxence's cell phone number on the screen. Maxence knew not to disturb him. If he'd told him once . . .

"Of course," said René.

His phone buzzed again. Maxence. What could the emergency be now? René groaned inside. Another server glitch at the Bibliothèque François-Mitterrand? A problem with a Y2K-program model?

"Can you bend the rules?" he asked.

"Monsieur Friant, if I let you move so you can answer, the preciseness of the measurement will be ruined."

"Could you answer for me and put it on speakerphone?" he said. "It's work—"

The buzzing stopped.

Chantal sighed as she tucked a fold in one of the four layers of fabric composing the collar.

The phone buzzed again. Chantal made a face. This time, she lifted the phone from the table, pressed ANSWER, and put the call on speakerphone.

"René, I'm on the Métro. Aimée's nanny is trying to reach you." The call was cutting out, but René recognized the angst in Maxence's voice.

"Is something wrong with Chloé?" René asked.

"Aimée's at the . . ." The line clicked.

René felt sweat forming on his neck. "Where?"

"She needs a lawyer . . . *commissariat* at Place d'Italie."

A click. The line went dead.

His mind raced. Aimée was in jail. What if Karine's murder the previous night had been a trap, a setup? He hadn't been able to convince Aimée to come forward.

Coward. If only he'd insisted.

"*Desolé*, Chantal, it's an emergency."

Chantal, wide-eyed, nodded. "*Bien sûr.*"

He struggled out of the sleeve around one of his arms. Tried to not wince at the pinpricks. "We'll reschedule the fitting."

He reached into his coat pocket and grabbed his prescription. Downed one pill with a swig of water from the bottle he carried. He couldn't forget his medicine.

Wednesday, Late Afternoon

AT THE GRILLED storage locker window, Aimée signed for her belongings—her leather jacket, her bag, the Tintin watch her father had given her so many years ago.

Her palms damp, she called René.

"I'm out. You're a lifesaver, René," she said, breathless. "Still in the meeting? Shall I come?"

She thought she should take a shower to get the smell of sweat and fear off her.

"Thank God," said René. "You had me worried. The lawyer called and filled me in. What's this about an assault?"

"A total fabrication," she said. "Never mind."

"*Alors*, the meeting's winding down," he whispered. "We'll talk later."

"I'll make this right." She'd put too much on his shoulders, and now she was missing a big meeting. She'd let him down. He'd lay into her later for sticking her nose where it didn't belong, and he'd be right.

"Just don't forget tonight's the reception—we're giving the award. And you're meeting the media *mec*, Xavier, fundraiser extraordinaire." Pause. "You will make it, *non?*"

Merde. She'd forgotten. The reception and award ceremony at the graffiti art foundation.

"... and Chloé ..." René was saying.

She'd clean forgotten her daughter after she'd talked to Babette. What kind of mother was she? She had to check with Noémi.

"See you later, René."

She hung up, feeling terrible. But it wasn't as if she'd been able to do anything locked in a holding cell without phone access.

Breathe, she reminded herself.

Babette's phone went to voice mail. Of course, she couldn't answer during an exam.

Noémi answered on the first ring. "Aimée, ça va?"

"Fine." Squeals and banging. "Is that Chloé making all that noise?"

"Happy as a clam with garlic. Did you know you have a drummer?"

Relief spread through her. But what must Noémi think of her being arrested and held at the commissariat? "There was a huge misunderstanding, Noémi. I'm sorry to take advantage like this—"

"Pas de problème," interrupted Noémi. "Take care of what you need to do; get legal counsel . . . Come by, and if we're not here, we're at the park across the street. You know the one I mean."

"You're a jewel, Noémi. Merci."

"You'd do the same for me," she said, "and I might ask you for help next week."

"Guaranteed!"

After they'd set a pickup time, Aimée's mind turned to the next problem—the award ceremony that night. How could she wangle this?

She'd think about it later.

Outside on Boulevard de l'Hôpital, she breathed in the afternoon air. She needed a shower.

Avocat Dillion grinned as she shook his hand.

"Merci," she said.

His white teeth highlighted his South of France bronze tan. Another distant relation of Martine's, he specialized in criminal law. "You do get into trouble, Mademoiselle Leduc."

No doubt that meant a hefty check.

"I don't understand how they could hold me," she said.

She had her suspicions but wanted his expensive opinion and advice. After all, she'd be paying for it.

With Cyril now in the mix—nosing around for Léo Solomon's notebook—she wondered if he had anything to do with Karine's murder. She wouldn't put it past him.

"Cyril Cromach decided not to press assault charges," said *Avocat* Dillion. "That's a good thing. But he won't answer my calls. I'd say someone wanted you out of commission."

A shiver traveled up her arms. "Out of commission? Can you explain?"

"Someone wanted to keep you out of the way a few hours. I'd speculate Cyril fabricated the incident, then dropped it once he'd done what whoever was paying him wanted him to do without your interference. Take it as a warning to watch your toes." He looked behind him. "And I never said that."

"So you've done that kind of thing, too, *non*? That's why you know what happened."

"Not I, mademoiselle, *bien sûr*. But let's just say I've seen it done. It's a delaying tactic. Unethical."

"I think . . ." Should she tell him? "Do you have fifteen minutes?"

ON THE PLACE d'Italie roundabout, they stood at the bustling *café tabac* counter among old-timers and matrons buying Loto tickets and Pernods. Keeping her voice lowered, she gave him an edited version of what she knew. Cigarette smoke spiraled to the nicotine-yellow ceiling. She wished she had a Nicorette patch.

After listening, *Avocat* Dillion downed his espresso. "I think you're omitting a few details."

"If you look at Marcus Gilet's homicide report," she said, "you'll see what a shoddy job the investigating cops did, blaming his murder on drugs, claiming his girlfriend was a prostitute."

If he was surprised by anything he'd heard, he didn't show it. Or even ask her how she knew anything. He didn't want to know. "If the *flics* are treating this as the homicide of a druggie and his trick-turning girlfriend . . . they don't put much energy into those."

"It's a cover-up."

"Easy to say. The autopsy will clear up the drug accusation," he said. "That's the first call."

"Meanwhile, I'm in the way. An irritant to shuffle aside, as you said."

"You're important enough if they pulled a stunt like this. My advice?" he said as he threw down several francs. "Stay under the radar. And keep me on your speed dial."

Nagging thoughts followed her all the way to her scooter still parked by the Gobelins. How could she get out of the Hand's cross hairs?

Heat shimmered on the ivy dripping down the vanilla-colored brick.

Despite Morbier's so-called retirement, the old fox was still connected. She remembered what he'd told her about Vauban— thrown under a bus, supposedly assassinated by the Hand. A group of people who protected one another and their interests.

Who was left now?

Only one way to find out.

She parked at Bibliothèque Marguerite Durand, a modernistic affair of chrome and glass on the corner of bustling rue de Tolbiac. She got online via an alias account. Didn't want this on her home or office computer. Aimée pulled up Morbier's search history and that email she'd forwarded to herself. Sucked in her breath. Let it out with a whistle.

Morbier's web search history revealed articles on the 1989 murder of a petty thief, Charles Siganne, and of his family. Siganne and his wife and two young children were victims of a gruesome stabbing in their apartment near Porte d'Ivry in the thirteenth. It had been during Aimée's premed year—she remembered the horrific family murder detailed in *Le Parisien*, the sensational head-lines. The perpetrator had never been caught. Soon afterward, there was a bloodbath in a rival gang of Siganne's, a slaughter of two members and their entire families—attributed to a revenge spree, although that was never proven. It had been a notorious gang war.

She opened the email, in which Morbier's contact at the *pré-fecture* updated him on Vauban's upcoming trial, even going so far as to cut and paste supposedly secure *in-house* intranet com-munications. How Morbier managed to get people to . . . *Zut*, no time to think about that now. Not the point. The email was part of what must have been a running email exchange—elliptical and hard to comprehend. If only she'd forwarded more.

Passing of the torch . . . take-over by the fixer? No one's sure. He contracted out to Vauban. The fixer leaves no loose ends or witnesses.

Her eyes gravitated to the references to the "fixer" employed by "the big fish."

Vauban's meeting la Proc. *Talk to him. Tell Dandin. We've got to keep our story straight.*

Dandin . . . had she heard that name before Morbier's email?

She thought back to her father's time—those Friday night poker games at the kitchen table. Of course. Now she remembered Dandin's cauliflower ears. He'd worked in robbery detail, too. She searched the police database she'd uploaded on the quiet. Nothing on him. Retired, maybe? Still, no one threw away records.

This smelled riper than yesterday's fish.

But right then she had to pick up Chloé.

THE STREETS OF Cité florale, where Noémi lived, were named for the flowers that blossomed in this fragrant pocket—rues des Orchidées, des Iris, des Glycines. Birds fluttered in the jasmine vines, the only disturbance in the quiet cobbled streets of two-story houses—built on a former meadow unable to support any taller buildings. Many were painted in turquoises, yellows, and pinks. Like a village, Aimée thought.

She punched in the code. Her index finger came back sticky, smelling of Carambar, a sweet she had loved as a child, and the gate buzzed open. She winced at the shriek of the green metal gate over the stone. In the matchbox-sized garden, Aimée passed Noémi's bicycle, her lemon tree in a pot, a table and chairs, and chopped firewood piled under her winding metal stairs. Noémi, a textile artist and a single *maman* like Aimée, lived in a second-floor studio apartment with work space below. They had become immediate friends when they'd met at the pool—and their babies had, too. Noémi's ex, a bigwig at the Mobilier National, was a real thorn in her side over custody. Aimée sympathized; dealing with Melac, Chloé's biological father, had been difficult, although Aimée had eventually allowed him to put his name on Chloé's birth certificate.

Come to think of it, Melac's new job brought him to Paris once a month, and he owed her babysitting. Aimée made a mental note to get in touch with him.

Noémi answered the door, petite in her paint-spattered shirt and zebra-striped leggings, the phone crooked between her shoulder and ear. She pecked Aimée's cheeks. Her brow was creased in frustration, anger, or worry; Aimée couldn't tell.

The girls crawled on the wood floor under the graphics that plastered the brick walls. Noémi's *bébé*, Elodie, a chestnut-haired button of cute, looked so much like Chloé they could have been siblings. They were only a month apart.

Noémi mouthed, *My ex*, then twirled her finger by her forehead—*Crazy*. Aimée nodded. Poor Noémi. Time to get out of her hair.

Aimée grabbed Chloé's diaper bag, swept her up, and planted kisses on her pink cheeks. Inhaled her warm, sweet scent.

Aimée held up Chloé's chubby fist to make it wave goodbye.

Merci, à demain, Aimée mouthed.

Aimée set Chloé in the scooter car seat especially designed by her godfather, René. Chloé kicked in glee; she loved riding on the scooter. Her strawberry-pink helmet, not so much.

Aimée collapsed Chloé's stroller and bungeed it to the rack, also custom crafted by René. They took off, winding through Cité florale as the wind fluttered the plane-tree leaves over them.

Her phone rang. René. She glanced at the time.

Mon Dieu, she's forgotten.

Blown it again. He'd shoot her.

Wednesday Evening

THE RECEPTION WAS held in the nineteenth-century two-story *maison de maître* in Square Héloïse et Abélard. This *maison* was a village vestige that had once been a *commerçant's* country house, now smack-dab in the sprawling thirteenth arrondissement, not far from the Bibliothèque François-Mitterrand. The building had been renamed la Maison des Cinq Sens and now functioned as a community center, a preschool, and an art exhibition venue.

René reached for a limoncello.

"*C'est très cool, non?*" breathed the pink-haired graffiti artist next to him.

If only the concoction in the frosted jam glass met one's expectations of an Italian aperitif, René thought. He managed a grin. But the artist had vanished in a whiff of spray paint fumes. Where was Aimée?

Amid the throbbing beat of techno music and laughter, René felt a hot suffocating in his lungs. He hated crowds. Wished he hadn't agreed to present this award. Wished Aimée were there.

He couldn't even see over the tables laden with wine, Chinese spring rolls, and honey-drenched Algerian sweets. The hosts had tried to reflect the diverse quartier in their catering. The reception celebrated graffiti supernovas Jef Aérosol and Miss Tyk, and other tag artists were tagging the walls with "masterpieces" that would be up for the art foundation award. A new world to René. His friend Demy said art was most vibrant before it went mainstream. René remembered when, not so long ago, they used to jail kids caught tagging.

As René edged through a forest of suits, his phone rang. Aimée. About time.

"Tell me you're here and I just can't see you," he said, fuming.

Pounding techno all but drowned out her voice. "René . . . a problem . . ."

Now? But when wasn't there a problem?

"Show your face for ten minutes." He had to shout over the din. "It's important. You've got to meet these people—make a good impression. Xavier is going to be an important business contact. You promised." Caught himself before he yelled, *I got you out of jail for this.*

Loud laughter drowned out much of her reply. ". . . scooter . . . as soon as Madame Cachou . . ." Then he heard a click.

He hoped to God, as he rummaged for notes in his linen jacket pockets, she'd make it in time. No way would he stand on top of a table trying to make himself seen and heard.

Finally he made out Demy's familiar face in a corner. As René worked his way over, he kept telling himself he was fine with who he was, didn't feel lost in a large crowd. The smallest person there.

The dwarf.

"Impressive, Demy, great job," said René, clasping the shy man's hand with his free one.

"*Merci*, René. Your support means a lot," said Demy, breaking into a smile. He leaned on a cane, his young face at odds with the grey at his temples. Soft-spoken Demy ran the nonprofit, which was committed to urban art movements, with the support of the arrondissement's progressive mayor. Demy had convinced René to get Leduc Detective involved by donating website design, maintenance, and security. "It's young artists' means of expression. Let's give it value, not treat it like crime." Demy, who had grown up in foster care, had told René over beers that he'd gotten into trouble as a kid and come out of it through an art program. René, in a way, identified with Demy, a self-made player. It wasn't because he was a cripple—it was that he was different.

"Where's Aimée?" Demy asked.

The crowd jostled, surging to watch an artist named Jellesse tag a wall, and someone knocked René's drink. Limoncello splashed over his handmade Charvet shirt.

Ruined.

Wednesday Evening

AIMÉE JOINED THE applause as René presented the award.

She then found a flute of champagne and him in that order.

"Nice speech," she said.

His large green eyes popped. "Nice outfit."

She'd worn her cowboy boots and a denim jacket over a black liquid sequin mini accessorized with a slouchy Céline boho bag. Given the outfits here, it was a good thing she'd left the couture in her armoire. Thank God she'd had time after Chloé's bath to shower and re-ice her ankle.

"In case you hadn't noticed"—René pointed—"that's our boss at the Bibliothèque François-Mitterrand, with some fellow Ministry of Culture people. These could be our people."

She groaned.

"Smile until it hurts," he said. "At least your sequins will grab their attention."

Show time. But first, a kiss for Demy on each cheek. His friendly face flushed from the champagne, he tugged her into his conversation. "I finally get to introduce you to Xavier, the *éminence grise* of fundraising."

She turned to a man with dark blond hair, a chiseled chin, and a lopsided grin. He grasped her hand, shaking it. He wore a pinstripe suit, polished shoes, and a whiff of something expensive.

"Demy's asked me to join the art foundation board," he said

with a self-deprecating grin. She caught how he swallowed his
e's—*un vrai Parisien*. "Few would accuse me of being an art con-
noisseur, but I have been known to milk a few pockets for this
foundation."

"Quit with the modesty, Xavier," said Demy. "You're a power-
house. We've got two exhibitions of *art courant* lined up at the
ministry courtesy of you."

By that time she'd registered that the charm she attributed to
Xavier's smile—no doubt it was a smile—was due to maxillofacial
nerve damage. Textbook case, like one she'd seen in her year of
premed.

She grinned back. "According to my partner, René, you're the
one who turned Demy's foundation around."

He returned her grin with a shrug. "And your website got
Demy's foundation noticed."

She averted her gaze from the smooth white scar that ran from
his chin to the corner of his lower lip, causing a slight downturn.

"Car accident," he said, reading her thoughts; everyone must
have had the same question upon meeting him. "They got me
into rehab right away; otherwise I would have a frozen jaw."

She lifted her palm, showing him the burn scar in the shape of
the door handle that had been on her father's smoldering van that
morning of the explosion in Place Vendôme.

"We kind of match," she said. "Lucky the tendon wasn't damaged." She never showed anybody. But Xavier had been so direct
with her. "My father . . . I couldn't save him. I was too late."

"When did it happen?" Xavier asked.

The pain welled up. "Feels like yesterday, but almost ten years
ago."

Had she really said that aloud?

A look of discomfort flitted across his eyes. Why had she

brought up something deeply personal at a business-oriented art reception? Embarrassed, she realized she had to steer the conversation back toward the art foundation.

But he'd gripped her hand. "I'm so sorry." His blue eyes were full of understanding. "Fathers leave all kinds of scars." She felt lost in a shared pain.

René tugged her arm. A reminder that it was time to schmooze.

She and Xavier exchanged cards. The reception passed in a blur of introductions. When she left for her appointment, she didn't see Xavier in the crowd anymore.

MARTIN SAT IN Le Drugstore on the Champs-Élysées on the last banquette in the rear, where he kept "office" hours from midnight until dawn. He was steps away from "his" public pay phone—more of a relic every day—in the lavatory downstairs. Martin operated without a cell phone. Or business cards.

Martin's contacts were legendary, even if you didn't approve of his methods. He knew the players, from street gangs to ministries, and got results no one else did. Even the *flics* consulted him, and a "hands-off" attitude reigned at *la préfecture*. He used no computer, left no paper trail—all word of mouth. If you wanted to know the skinny on a gang in Barbès or get the word out about a hit, Martin was your man. A conduit who brokered deals, hooked up connections, made introductions—for a fee.

And he'd once been Aimée's father's informer. So valuable her father had gotten Martin's prison sentence reduced. She didn't know how or why.

Martin had never forgotten what he owed Jean-Claude Leduc. "Mademoiselle Aimée, motherhood becomes you."

He clasped her hands between his knobby fingers as she slid into his booth. The skin at the backs of her knees stuck on the red leather seat. Like always. Trying to scooch down, she felt like the awkward eleven-year-old she'd been when she first came here with her father. Her sequins crackled, and she tugged her mini down.

Martin's dove-grey pompadour, large tortoiseshell glasses, and tanned, leathery face made him look like an eccentric uncle who'd come straight from a 1970s Cannes Film Festival. Despite his appearance, his information didn't come cheap.

The back dining room was deserted apart from the waiter, a man with dyed-black hair and a widow's peak who'd been here as long as Aimée could remember.

"The usual?" Martin asked.

Aimée nodded, returning his squeeze.

"*Un chocolat chaud pour la mademoiselle.*" He waved. "It's *un peu pressé . . .*"

"*Immédiatement,*" said the waiter, slipping his crossword puzzle into a pocket under his ankle-hugging white apron.

Martin slid a package across the marble tabletop. The signature Galeries Lafayette box. "I'm sorry the . . . *l'hoodie*—is that what you say?—didn't fit Chloé. This should."

"*Mais non,* Martin, you shouldn't . . ."

"But I want to. What other ten-month-old can I spoil? You have new pictures?"

She rustled through her bag and found a recent photo with Miles Davis. Chloé was feeding him a strawberry.

"Ah, *quelle beauté.* She's got her grandpa's dimples." Martin took the photo, briefly held it to his heart. "Not a day goes by I don't think of him. As always, I'm having the mass said for him in November. You should bring Mademoiselle Chloé."

Aimée nodded. She'd never gone to Martin's mass. Maybe it was time.

"Papa is why I'm here, Martin."

He leaned back as the waiter appeared and set down Aimée's steaming *chocolat chaud*, which was accompanied by a dollop of crème on top and a slim rectangle of dark chocolate on the saucer.

Aimée sipped the piping hot chocolate through the cold crème. Savored how it ran down her throat, thick and rich as velvet. Perfect.

Martin leaned forward and, with a fatherly swipe, wiped her chocolate mustache with his napkin. "You haven't changed. I've been doing that since you weren't much older than Chloé."

Quite a bit older than that, but Martin liked to exaggerate.

"I'm still curious, too, Martin. Curious why a certain Monsieur Vauban's *accident* shut down an inquiry investigating the Hand. Why a dead man's missing notebook caused two murders."

Martin lit a cigarette from the one still smoldering in the Ricard ashtray.

"So not a social call, Mademoiselle Aimée." These were working hours for him. "You know, I'm semiretired."

Not by a long stretch.

"It's a young man's game now," he said. "Not for old dogs like me."

He always said that.

"Morbier's an old dog, and he's in the middle of it," Aimée said.

"Ah, that old *salopard*."

"The Hand's still alive, Martin."

The light from the wall sconces reflected back on Martin's lenses. She couldn't see his eyes, read what was in them.

He inhaled. The smoke spiraled up to the gold-inlaid ceiling. "Not my area of . . . let's say . . . knowledge."

Like she believed that?

She briefly sketched the story of Léo Solomon's missing

notebook, the murders of Marcus and Karine, and Pierre, Leo's friend who might have been involved with the Hand.

"*Et alors*, Mademoiselle Aimée, I'm an old man."

That was all he could say?

"Don't be modest, Martin. Your connections are impeccable." At least better than anyone else's she knew of. "Please, can't you nose around?"

He puffed.

She gathered mocha foam on her index finger and licked it. "If I'm just paranoid and reading too much into this"—of course, she wasn't after two murders—"I need to know. Can you help me?"

She slid the envelope with the check she'd prepared toward him. This was business.

He pushed it back. "For you and your papa's granddaughter, anything. A little mademoiselle who has his dimples."

So he would help.

"One more thing, Martin. Who is the Hand's fixer?"

"Ah, that's something else." Martin looked up as the waiter signaled him. "My next appointment's here." But the waiter leaned and whispered in Martin's ear. "My appointment's detained. I have a few minutes."

"Have babysitter, will listen." Aimée's phone vibrated. She let it go to voice mail.

He pushed the red leather-bound menu to the side. Inhaled, then blew a smoke ring. "He's anonymous. The best ones are."

"But what have you heard, Martin?" she said. "And don't say you don't know the rumors."

A shrug. "Some say it's Charles Siganne."

Hadn't she caught Morbier nosing around the Internet about that horrific murder? "*Attends*, I remember, but Siganne's long dead."

"*Bien sûr.* Urban myths spring up when nobody knows the truth."

"Do you?"

Martin tapped ashes into the Ricard ashtray. "I'm not entranced by myths. Or ghosts who strike and then evaporate."

"How can I get in touch with him, the fixer?"

"You can't. He gets in touch with you. And that, Mademoiselle Aimée, you don't want."

Aimée's phone rang again. Madame Cachou. Trouble?

This time Aimée answered.

AIMÉE IDLED HER scooter on Pont Marie, watching the furred yellow light coming from her Ile Saint-Louis apartment window, the parked cars on the quai in front, the regulars walking their dogs, who watered the trees in the streetlights' glow.

Madame Cachou answered Aimée's call on the first ring. "About time, Aimée. There's a *mec* just sitting there in a car. A Peugeot," she said, her voice quivering with excitement or fear— Aimée figured both. "I saw him when I walked Miles Davis on the quai before I came over to babysit. He's still there."

Aimée scanned the quai lit by streetlights for a Peugeot. "At your nine o'clock?"

"Is that spy talk?"

"*Alors,* it's the only Peugeot," said Aimée.

"What should I do?"

"Stay away from the window. Check Chloé. Stay with her."

Aimée hung up. She revved the scooter, took the long way around the Ile Saint-Louis, parking her scooter by the island's only garage, where it lived most of the time, the damned temperamental machine. Pulled on a cap; took a side street, then another; and went through the small door that opened to a courtyard from which she could get into another courtyard and then into hers.

What if that rat Cyril was surveilling her apartment? If she confronted him again, would he cry wolf? Did she care?

She stood under the pear tree in her courtyard thinking. She should do it. Show him and whoever employed him they couldn't intimidate her.

After setting her cowboy boots under the pear tree and tugging down her sequin mini, she opened her Swiss Army knife in her jean jacket pocket, gripping it tight. With her left hand, she buzzed the massive door. It clicked, and she pushed it open with her good shoulder and crossed the cobbles barefoot, staying in the shadows under the linden trees. She hunched down behind the Peugeot, listened. No conversation. Only acrid cigarette smoke.

She took a breath. Popped up beside the driver's half-rolled-down window.

"Why don't you tell me who's put you up to this?" she said.

But it wasn't Cyril. The *mec*, who had long, curly salt-and-pepper hair and the red-veined nose of a drinker, stabbed out his cigarette in the car's ashtray. He didn't even look up. His meaty hand reached for a phone on the dashboard.

"No, you don't—" she said.

"Better you speak to the boss." He looked too big for the car, all shoulders and thighs. Like a turtle stuck in a box.

Wary, she nodded. It seemed too easy. Was the creep just a go-between? Had they counted on her doing this?

"Who's your boss?" she asked.

"I think you know."

A frisson traveled her spine.

"Someone wants to talk to you," he said, then handed her the clamshell flip phone.

"Took your time noticing, Leduc," said Morbier. "Chloé had a good day?"

She wanted to slap him.

"I'd have felt better if I'd known a big *mec* in a Peugeot was sur-veilling my place," she said. "I almost kicked him where it hurts."

Pause.

"Why? I told you I'd take care of things. Frans owes me a favor."

Another call came in on her phone. Melac. She let it go to voice mail. She'd deal with him later. If ever, the way she was feeling right then.

"Why did you go behind my back?" she said. "I don't mind help if I know about it."

"Said I'd handle it, didn't I? We just didn't want schedules to conflict."

Handle it? Talk about treating her like a child!

"But, Morbier . . ."

He'd clicked off.

Why did she feel cornered instead of safe?

Thursday Morning

WAITING OUTSIDE ON quai de la Rapée in front of the red-orange brick morgue, Aimée got a call from Serge, who told her to meet him at the side door—the staff entrance.

When she arrived, Serge's brow was creased in worry.

"What's wrong?" she asked.

"What's right?" He glanced behind him. "I shouldn't be doing this."

"Can't you copy the autopsy report and just—"

"You don't understand. It's under lock and key."

"That's not normal procedure. Why?"

"There's something fishy; that's why." Serge took a deep breath. "I don't like it. The pathologist who performed the autopsy is a friend of mine, but he's gone to Rouen. We've only got a ten-minute window. Hurry."

He thrust a packet containing a long white lab coat, a white cap, and white plastic boots at her. "Put this on, and let me do the talking."

The white plastic boots came up to midcalf, like the kind the fishmongers wore at *poissonneries*. She pulled on the cap, buttoned the lab coat, and followed Serge.

They passed the cadaver room with its aluminum slabs, the refrigeration room, the toxicology lab and offices, making their way to the rear-bay double doors. Serge took a clipboard from the

IN slot, held it under his arm. Seconds later they'd exited to the body-receiving platform. Serge hopped down, and Aimée followed suit. He waved to the technicians, dressed just like Aimée, who were hosing down the concrete in the back.

Aimée stifled a shiver.

Serge jerked his thumb toward a blue van, the cadaver pickup vehicle, and Aimée got into the passenger seat.

With keys he pulled from his pocket, he started the van and shifted into first. He pressed a remote device that opened the metal gate, and they were driving over the Pont d'Austerlitz. The breeze from the Seine below couldn't mask the pungent odors emanating from the gurney racks in the back. "Don't tell me we're on a pickup call," she said.

"The walls have ears."

The second time she'd heard that in two days.

"Look under the seat."

Her fingers felt pâtisserie wrappers, a wad of chewed gum, then a manila envelope.

She opened it to find Marcus Gilet's autopsy report.

"Why wasn't this in his homicide file?" she asked.

"That's the problem."

"What do you mean?"

While Aimée scanned the report, Serge turned off Boulevard de l'Hôpital into the grounds of Pitié-Salpêtrière Hospital, the largest hospital in Paris, sprawling over a good chunk of the thirteenth arrondissement. He pulled up under a chestnut tree. Set the parking brake but kept the engine idling.

"Toxicology indicates he was clean, no drugs in his system," said Aimée. The plastic boots were cutting into her calves. "But what's this . . . Marfan?"

Serge checked his phone. "Keep reading. I copied as much as

I could. Got the most important pages. I'll explain after you look at the photos."

Black-and-white photos of Marcus's corpse provided gruesome viewing. The Y incision from his pelvic bone to his shoulders was stitched in rough black thread. The baby face she'd seen in the photo from the pâtisserie had taken on the gauntness of death. "Just a kid. So sad."

"You're not looking close enough, Aimée. Hurry. I've got to get back ASAP."

"*Zut* . . . his fingernail's gone." She gasped. "That wasn't in the police report. He was tortured? But here it says the cause of death was cardiac arrest."

"Marcus exhibited the classic physical traits of Marfan syndrome—tall, thin build, long arms and legs, thin fingers, slight curvature of the spine, concave chest, crowded teeth, and flat feet."

"*Et alors?*"

"So of course the pathologist tested him for Marfan syndrome, which as you know, is usually diagnosed in adolescence."

She didn't. Hadn't gotten that far in med school. Something Serge always forgot. She took out her digital camera, photographed each page as he went on.

"The biggest threat of Marfan syndrome is damage to the aorta—it's weak and can tear, causing a heart attack. The danger ratchets up with surging adrenalin. Would make sense."

"What would make sense?"

Serge sighed. Scanned the rearview mirror. "A heart attack. Torture elevates stress levels."

Aimée cringed. Pictured the hotel room. Had Marcus been tortured there?

"Why wouldn't this kid give up the notebook under torture?" she asked.

"Maybe he didn't have time," said Serge.

"So you're saying he died quickly?"

Serge took a breath. "My guess? After his first fingernail got pliered out."

Her gut said Marcus had died with his secret.

"I've got to get back," said Serge.

She wedged her feet out of the boots, folded the lab coat, and left it on the seat. "Why would this autopsy have been removed from the files?"

"You didn't hear this from me, but someone's taken a bribe. Makes me sick. It's wrong. That's why I showed you. But I'll deny it if I have to."

"Who?"

"Someone with enough influence to have this kept in the drawer. The body's slated for cremation."

"Then I need to move fast." She opened the door, glad to get out of the van and away from its pungent odors.

Serge released the parking brake. "Be careful, Aimée."

SHE WALKED, TURNING things over in her mind. Marcus's autopsy proved he'd been tortured; he hadn't died of a drug overdose. Yet how could she use it?

All this ruminating, but what now?

She found herself in one of Pitié-Salpêtrière Hospital's courtyards. Under an alley of chestnut tree branches, she tried calling Martine. Voice mail.

What was her next step? How did any of this get her closer to finding the notebook?

Frustrated, she wanted to kick somebody. Settled on gravel. And realized she was lost. One dilapidated old wing looked like another. This place had been built over an ancient gunpowder factory—hence the name, from saltpeter. By the French Revolution, the Salpêtrière hospice had been home to the mentally disabled, the criminally insane, epileptics, paupers, and prostitutes who had been cleared off the streets of Paris.

Aimée tried to orient herself using the gravel path. Her frustration increased as she passed the Quartier des Folles, where a plaque on the wall described its nineteenth-century use: six hundred "hysterical" women were kept in cells, led on chains outdoors once a day for a "hygiene" regimen of fresh air. Like animals, she thought, disgusted. The women had been used as experimental subjects for Dr. Charcot, whose stable of research patients evolved into the notorious Parisian asylum for the insane and incurables. By hypnosis, Dr. Charcot induced hysteria attacks in women before crowds that gathered for his "Tuesday Lectures." He'd even experimented with electroshock therapy. She shuddered. The Napoleon of the neuroses and the father of modern neurology, who counted Sigmund Freud and La Tourette among his students.

Among the notable patients who'd been treated here more recently was Princess Diana, whose heart the doctors couldn't revive after her infamous car crash.

Poor Marcus. His fragile heart had given out on him. Besson needed to know what happened to his nephew.

Éric Besson's number went to a recording: "You've reached an unrecognized number."

Reason told her a successful attorney with clients, in the middle of a case, wouldn't have totally abandoned his business. His assistant, Gaëlle, would know where he was hiding.

AIMÉE HAILED A taxi on Boulevard Saint-Marcel. The short ride took forever due to a teachers' demonstration that had closed off Place d'Italie. Stupid of her. Every Parisian knew to take the Métro or bike in September.

She reached Besson's office perspiring and hoping the morgue van's cloying odor hadn't permeated her clothes.

Before she could press the buzzer, the door clicked open, and Aimée slid in behind the person leaving. From the black-and-white marbled foyer, she could hear Gaëlle soothing a client on the phone. The door to the office was open, and Aimée entered the suite. The fax machine was spewing paper, and the door leading to the next office was also standing open. No voices audible except Gaëlle's.

"*Bonjour, Gaëlle.* I need to speak with Éric."

"He's away on business. Sorry, I don't have any other information."

Not if those faxes from a hotel in Brussels were anything to go by. "Marcus died from a heart attack while he was being tortured, not from a drug overdose."

Gaëlle's phone slipped from her hand, clattered onto her desk. Her lips trembled faintly. "I don't understand."

Aimée had to get Gaëlle on her side. "He was tortured for Léo's notebook. Whoever did it pulled out his fingernails."

She gasped. Knocked over the vase of jonquils on her desk.

"Tragic. He had an underlying heart condition—Marfan syndrome—and his weak heart gave out under torture before he revealed the notebook's location. A senseless loss. The scariest part is that his autopsy report has been suppressed."

Gaëlle nervously wiped up the water from the vase with a tissue, threw the flowers in a bin. "That's illegal. No one can suppress an autopsy. It's a public document."

"Moot point. It's been suppressed. But I got this copy." She showed Gaëlle the digital photos of the autopsy report. "Éric should be demanding the original and exposing the problems with the police investigation."

Uneasy, Gaëlle said, "You mean there's a cover-up?"

Took her enough time.

"I need to talk with Éric. He needs to stop Marcus's cremation before it's too late." Aimée handed Gaëlle a card. "Have him ring me on this number. I'll call him back on an encrypted line."

A HOT, FUSTY Métro ride took Aimée back to Leduc Detective. Her mind spun as she pondered the lengths to which someone had gone to camouflage the cause of Marcus's death.

Her ankle tingled. So much work to catch up on today, and the morning almost gone. Prioritize. She'd done her part, tried to relay the message about Marcus's autopsy to Besson. He could handle it from there, she reasoned. He was an attorney; his family was well connected. Not her job to pursue this further.

Fat chance. She couldn't give up until Martine wrote the article to expose the corruption. Couldn't give up until she found out how her father really was involved. *Merde!* Couldn't give up until she found this damn notebook.

She shivered, knowing that Besson had been right. No one would be safe until the notebook was recovered.

"THAT'S NOT THE point, Aimée," said René, working on two screens at his desk at Leduc Detective. He was all revved up about the autopsy results. "It's more than that."

She stood, half listening, at the copier, printing out the photos of Marcus's autopsy report, which she'd downloaded from her digital camera.

"Whoever's incriminated in this notebook wants it found and—"

"I gathered that, René."

"*Non*, think out of the box. Look at it from a different angle. What if word leaked out about what was in the book?"

"Blackmail?" she said.

René shrugged. "Or maybe an insider takeover, someone looking for sensitive information to control the situation?"

"You're right," she said, scooping up the copies. "Martine needs the autopsy."

"Eh, did I miss something? How is Martine involved in any of this?"

Fizzing nervous energy filled her. "If Martine exposes the real autopsy findings, either the Hand or its rivals—"

"Will jump up and fight over the same bone." René looked worried. "This cover-up shows power. Power to murder, influence the police, and disappear an autopsy. I'm glad you're going hands off on this. Once you tell Martine, leave it alone."

Hands off? Not without knowing what the notebook said about her father.

"My father always said the flip side of power is fear. Fear of losing power."

WITH A WARNING in the header, she emailed Martine Marcus's gruesome photos, the toxicology results, and autopsy findings.

Put in an hour's work on her paying jobs. She hadn't even made a big dent in her client list.

Maxence entered with his jaunty John Lennon cap pulled over his Beatle bangs. A flesh-colored bandage on his cheek.

"How's your injury?" Aimée asked.

"That scratch? Healing fine." He slapped a file on her desk. "I found a little more about Léo Solomon's business license. Red flag here—he was working with a holding company in Luxembourg."

Hopeful, she read Léo's business history: accountant at the Gobelins office, under the Ministry of Culture, and accountant at a limited holding company registered in Luxembourg. The perfect place for a hidden nest egg for the Hand, beyond reach of the Ministry of Finance. His position had been terminated on the first of the previous month. Right before his death.

"Aimée, don't get ideas. Hacking into a Luxembourg-based company is no walk in the park." René shook his head. "For all you know, they've moved the money to the Caymans by now."

"*Alors*, if the notebook's history, how will this help?" asked Maxence, after she'd brought him up to speed.

"We don't know its history," she said. "But we know someone's desperate to find it. And that it's worth murdering two people to them. I think this notebook is the only proof."

She stared up at her list on the butcher paper. Stood, winced at her damn ankle, and added the names *Vauban* and *Dandin*, which had been mentioned in Morbier's email.

Who was she missing?

Cyril Cromach. As if she could forget who had gotten her time in a holding cell.

"Eyeball this for a minute, René," she said.

"Me, too?" Maxence said eagerly.

René looked up from his screens. "As long as you get the Y2K analytics in the hopper by four . . ."

Maxence set a file on his desk. "All done, René."

Amazing, this kid.

She shifted to her other foot. "*En effet*, someone, in the collective sense, has enough power to derail a murder investigation, hide the autopsy report, hire Cyril—a sleazy ex-*flic*—to snoop on Léo's tenure at les Gobelins and derail me by having me held at the *commissariat*."

René had turned in his ergonomic swivel chair to stare at the butcher paper. "Wouldn't whoever hired Cyril be in a report?"

"A Madame de Frontenac." She wrote the name under Cyril's. "Let's find this woman."

René hit SAVE. Nodded to Maxence. "Up for searching around?"

"Do bees like honey?" Maxence loved this kind of thing.

Aimée opened her Moleskine to the map she'd scribbled at the Gobelins dye works while talking to Madame Livarot. She remembered how her father used to moan that his toughest cases were the ones where the object hid in plain sight—the thing you were looking for often stared you smack in the face.

She copied the rough sketch of the Gobelins courtyard, adding the surrounding buildings onto the butcher paper. Made an X where Leo's apartment had been located.

"Léo and his wife, Marie, lived here for fifty years. The apartment was a perk for years of service—they were allowed to stay even after retirement. Madame Livarot said Léo had been back a few days before he died."

"To pick something up?" asked Maxence.

"Or to hide something?" René guessed.

"Not the notebook," said Maxence. "He gave that to Besson. So something else important?"

"Maybe a copy?" Aimée said. She'd wondered if Léo had kept a backup log; a meticulous accountant type would be likely to. "Or corroborating documents? Worth a look." She needed to get back to Gobelins to check. But when?

René shook his head. "A good accountant would use a secure place. Meaning a bank safety box."

Her phone trilled. A number she didn't recognize appeared. Deep in what she was doing, she let it go to voice mail. But the caller didn't leave a message. Then the phone rang again.

What if Serge was calling from the morgue? Maybe he'd found out something more? She couldn't ignore the call.

"*Oui?*" she said.

"You're like me, Aimée. *Zut*, never answer an unknown number." She recognized the Parisian accent of Xavier from the reception. "I've got good news—we have a new foundation sponsor. Can you tell René?"

"Fantastic." Her neck felt warm. Flushed. She wondered why he hadn't just called René himself. "Better yet, you tell him."

She handed her phone to René.

"Perfect, Xavier . . . What? I wish," said René. "We're on deadline . . . Aimée's the boss; invite her."

René handed her the phone back.

"I've got this incredible chance to sign on major sponsors," Xavier said. "It's what René and I discussed last night. René pooped out. Can you make it to lunch at Le Batofar, say one o'clock?"

His face floated in front of her vision, and she remembered how warm his hands had been when they gripped hers. She knew something stupid would come out of her mouth if she opened it.

Somehow she managed, "*Tant pis.* I'm on a project."

"You have to eat, *non*? If you come, we can secure their sponsorship today."

She looked at the clock. "Make it one-thirty." Hung up. "Xavier's got this hot foundation sponsor. But I have to go to lunch."

"I told you he gets things done. Go ahead. We'll cover the office." As she wrapped her foulard around her neck and double knotted it, René looked up. "You've got pink cheeks."

Blushing—when had that last happened?

"So warm in here." She hit the switch, and the overhead fan chugged to life. Grabbed her Hermès bag.

"I forgot, the concierge asked me to bring up the mail. It's on your desk," Maxence said to Aimée.

She swiped it into her bag. She'd read it later.

LE BATOFAR WAS moored on the Seine close to Bibliothèque François-Mitterrand. After opening the previous year, it had become a hot venue for *le clubbing*. Not that she'd ever gone—she was always so tired at night with a *bébé*.

The sun had come out, shining so brightly on the moving Seine she pulled out her Jackie O sunglasses. Aimée couldn't miss the red barge with its distinctive lighthouse. Or Xavier waving from the deck. Why did his crooked smile make her insides tingle and her neck flush?

His hands gripped hers. Warm as they'd been the night before. Then he pulled away, embarrassed. "*Desolé*, I'm like a kid, excited. I just need you to go over their website specs."

She chucked her bag under the table and sat down. The cool river breeze was tinged with the scent of algae. A world apart from the morgue and Marcus's remains, just a bridge away.

"*Fantastique,*" she said. "Who's the sponsor?"

By the time they'd ordered—salad Niçoise for her, steak tartare for him—he'd filled her in. She felt that connection from the previous night again—that fizz warming her blood. Le Batofar rocked in the wake of a long blue barge.

"*Parfait,*" she said. "René promised to squeeze time in today to get their name up on the website. But how did you manage this?"

"We're going to sponsor a contest at les Gobelins, a woven textile from a tag artist's design. Graffiti in silk—the melding of new art and ancient tradition."

Aimée was skeptical. Everything she'd seen of the tapestry

factory seemed closed off from the rest of the world—no outsiders. "Do you have an in there?"

"My stepfather knew a *fonctionnaire* there."

Aimée's hand stiffened on her fork. "Léo Solomon?" Too much of a coincidence?

"No idea. Never met him. It's my stepfather's friend of a friend." Xavier leaned back in the rattan chair, incurious. "You know how that goes, that old boys' thing."

"What do you mean?"

"Freemasons. Stupid secret handshake, hush-hush meetings, that kind of thing." He gave a knowing wink. "In reality, a bunch of old farts with money who like a bit of community service to their name."

He was talking about the tapestry factory, but he'd sparked another thought. Talk about an old boys' club—could the Hand be Freemasons?

"You do have a way with you," she said as Xavier poured her mineral water with a splash of rosé. She looked over the website contract paperwork he had set in front of her. "I'm just thrilled les Gobelins agreed."

He clinked his glass to hers and grinned.

After she studied the disclaimer, she grinned back. "Brilliant work." Took her pen and signed. "Happy we'll work together on this."

And then he'd enfolded her hand in his. Raised it to his lips and kissed it. "You're unique. *Alors*, my sommelier friend's sponsoring a wine tasting . . ."

Her hand burned. So he felt the connection, too.

Her phone vibrated. She wondered if that was Benoît, felt a tinge of guilt. But he'd never called her back.

Xavier's forehead had crinkled. "Done it again, sorry. I'm too eager—"

"I'd love to come," she said. "Just need to arrange a babysitter." Her phone vibrated again. "I've got to get back. Sorry, there's a crisis, *toujours*."

IT HAD BEEN Morbier calling her, but she hadn't felt comfortable taking the call in front of Xavier. Too bad.

Hurrying along the quai, she punched in Morbier's number.

A sea gull swooped and landed on the choppy Seine.

"You have to trust me, Leduc."

Trust him? She'd trusted him all her life only to discover he was involved in Papa's murder.

"To do what?" she asked.

A frustrated sigh. "Look, I'm worried about Chloé's safety with the Hand involved."

"By that, you mean you're worried about the fixer, an urban myth called Charles Siganne? That he's going to come after me and my baby? Or maybe Dandin, the one with the cauliflower ears I remember playing poker at our kitchen table? Or another one of your friends?"

Merde. She'd wanted to question him about this, not accuse him. If only she'd bitten her tongue.

Pause. "I'll ignore that for now. And I won't ask you where you got those names." His voice had gone dangerously calm. "*Alors,* I'm going to make a call to your mother."

Where did that come from? "*Quoi?* Why get her involved?"

"You know she wants to be part of Chloé's life. And yours."

"Funny way of showing it. She disappeared. Again."

"*Vraiment?* Didn't you two argue?"

She froze on the quai's uneven pavers. Her thoughts swirled. "Wait a minute. How do you know this?"

"You stomped out on her after her comment on your ratty trench coat." Pause. "So petty, Leduc."

Petty? She loved that vintage Sonia Rykiel. "As if she's got the right to dispense fashion advice?" Or anything else? "And what, she vanishes for two months but goes and complains to you behind my back? That's what you call wanting to be part of my life?"

"Don't let that rule out a chance of a relationship. She's trying . . . Okay, she's not well versed in the mother thing."

"Some women weren't meant to be mothers," she said.

"Sydney's feeling her way. Didn't you say you wished Chloé came with an instruction booklet?"

"So I should forgive her? Let her drop into my life after twenty years? She expects me to welcome her with open arms, after how she hurt Papa?"

"Have that conversation with her, not me. It's called working things out."

A sea gull waddled into her path. She shooed it away. "And you're the expert in relationships, Morbier?"

Pause. It hurt that her mother had confided in Morbier. Not her.

"Why didn't she talk to me?" she asked.

"Because I have no fashion sense?" Morbier expelled air over the phone. "*Zut alors!* I can't stop you from wanting to battle the Hand. So far she's the only one who's outwitted them."

"And why's that?"

"Ask her. Doesn't she owe you for helping her escape in Montparnasse?"

"Owe me, *non*. I don't keep score."

Impossible with someone who evaporated into thin air.

"It's that damned notebook, Morbier. I need to find it."

"Look, I'm in a wheelchair. If only I could—"

"And I put you there." Emotion took over. Guilt. Anger. Sadness.

"My ticker would have done it sooner or later. Right now . . .
You need to remember you're not Superwoman."

Something niggled in the back of her mind, jolted loose by her
speaking her thoughts. Her father had always believed in talking
things through. "*Attends*, you haven't answered me. What's so
interesting about Siganne and Dandin?"

But he'd hung up.

Thursday Afternoon

AIMÉE HEARD THE din of children's voices through the open doors of the *piscine* in Butte-aux-Cailles. The public pool, housed by an Art Nouveau redbrick building, was fed by hot ferruginous water from the local artesian well. Inside, flanking the rippling turquoise pool were *les bains-douches*, the public baths, to the left and, to the right, the staircase down to the showers and changing rooms.

The humid air was laced with chlorine. She couldn't avoid the traffic jam by the locker room with the *bébé* swim class ending, the junior swim team arriving, and the changing of lifeguard shifts.

"Babette?" she said.

Chloé's distinctive squeals came through the shouts and laughter and slapping of wet feet on the soapy tiled floor.

"In the shower," Babette called. "Noémi's toweling off the girls by the lockers."

Aimée found them—her Chloé in a dry sunsuit and Elodie nestled in a striped towel. Noémi's wet hair was pinned up. She smiled at Aimée. "Class ran late. Still want to take our little fishes to the park?"

"Just a quickie visit today. Got more meetings."

She planted kisses on Chloé's flushed cheeks, delighted by her daughter's clapping of her two pudgy hands. She'd learned to clap and did it all the time.

Aimée noticed that Elodie was shivering despite the hot moist air. *Mon Dieu.* There were goosebumps on her arms.

"Where's your *bébé* bag, Noémi?"

But Noémi had jumped in the shower to rinse off.

Aimée couldn't find Elodie's baby bag, so she pulled out the red hoodie Martin had given her for Chloé. The little girls were too cute—Aimée couldn't resist. With her palm-sized camera, she took a few shots to add to the hundreds she already had. These days she had to stop herself from being one of those *mamans* who forced people to look at dozens of digital pictures of their *bébés*. She didn't want to bore clients who'd politely inquired after her daughter. But *vraiment*, how adorable.

Aimée rubbed Elodie's arms to warm her up. The swim team stampeded by, splattering Aimée's silk blouse. Elodie wiggled out of Aimée's grasp and toddled through the crowd of little girls and their caretakers toward her own mother in the shower. Aimée scooped Chloé up in her arms to chase after Elodie, but the passing horde jammed them up against the wall. All Aimée saw was a sea of legs.

"Noémi!" Aimée called.

"I'm coming," said Noémi. "Be out in *une petite seconde.*"

Babette emerged, toweling off, with Noémi behind her. "Babette, have you seen my baby bag?" Noémi asked. Elodie was crawling toward her mother.

In Aimée's arms, Chloé hiccuped and clutched her bottle. Aimée couldn't wait to get out of the steamy heat. "It's too crowded down here," Aimée called. "We'll meet you upstairs."

OUTSIDE, IN PLACE Paul Verlaine across from the *piscine*, a few men played boules on the chalky earth. Aimée filled Chloé's bottle from the pure artesian water source, one of the few remaining in the city. She was capping the bottle when Babette arrived, backpack slung over her shoulder as she checked her phone.

"See you tomorrow," said Aimée.

Babette kissed Chloé. "Noémi couldn't find her baby bag," she said as she rose. "She'll be up in a minute. Now, where is that little escape artist?"

"Who?"

"Elodie."

"She's with Noémi."

"That's strange," Babette said, checking her phone. "I thought she said Elodie was with you. I'll go check in a minute."

Just then Chloé burped, spitting up all over Aimée's silk blouse. Thank God it was just water.

Mostly.

Reaching into her bag for a wipe, Aimée found the packet of mail she'd stuck in there without reading it this morning. Contracts, invoices—but what was this? A color photo. No envelope. She pulled it out of the pile: a playground and sandbox she recognized as part of Square Henri Galli down and across the river from Ile Saint-Louis, where she went almost every day. In the sandbox was Chloé wearing the red hoodie. The photo must have been taken that morning.

Her heart pounded as she tried to take this in.

On the other side, one line:

We're watching—hand it over.

Hand it over—the notebook? She didn't have it. But this was a threat to her *bébé*. Feeling sick to her stomach, she hugged Chloé tight and scanned the people near the pool.

Shouts came from the pool door as an attendant ran out.

"Stop him! Catch that man."

A piercing scream—a voice Aimée recognized.

Noémi stood, hair dripping, shirt inside out, shaking her fist in the face of the pool attendant, who had been pinned against the wall by an *égoutier*, a sewer worker in fluorescent green. The *égoutier* had a cigarette hanging from the side of his mouth.

"He stole my baby!" Noémi shrieked.

"Crazy. This woman's crazy." The attendant's face contorted in pain as the *égoutier* twisted his arm. "I work here."

"Steal, more like it." The burly *égoutier* turned the man's pockets inside out, and several cell phones and a wallet showered onto the stone pavement. "Call the *flics*," the *égoutier* said to a woman standing by watching the fracas. The woman took out her phone as the *égoutier* turned back to the restrained man. "Where's her baby?"

"Baby?" he said. "How the hell do I know?"

With Chloé in her arms, Aimée ran to the scene at the door, Babette close behind her.

"What's wrong?" Aimée said.

"Elodie's gone," Noémi sobbed.

Gone?

"But that's impossible. *Alors*, we'll find her." Aimée grabbed Noémi's elbow. "Don't panic. She's downstairs somewhere—"

"How do you know?" Noémi said. "I couldn't find her."

Aimée's confidence was evaporating. What about the photo?

She hesitated, then thrust Chloé into Babette's arms. "Don't let her out of your sight. Promise me, Babette."

Babette nodded, her eyes wide. "We'll stay right here. Find Elodie."

At the pool's reception desk, Aimée caught the attention of the manager, a young woman who was on the phone. "Please, lock the doors and exits."

"But, mademoiselle—"

"Now."

"On what authority?"

"A baby is missing. She could be in danger, crawling around open drains, the outdoor pool . . ." Aimée swiped her hair from her eye. "We need to find her before she's hurt. Page your staff; organize a search."

The manager, now galvanized into action, nodded. "It's not the first time a baby has gotten loose. We'll find her."

Noémi had come up behind Aimée at the desk. "Aimée, that man was rifling through the lockers. I saw him . . ."

Over the loudspeaker, the lockdown announcement came with a tinny reverb.

Aimée ran after Noémi down the stairs. She took off her heels and padded in her stockings over the wet tiles and puddles, asking everyone in the changing room and showers if they'd seen Elodie.

Only one mother from the *bébé* swim group was still in the changing room. *Oui*, she remembered Elodie but had last seen her in the shower with Noémi. None of the remaining lap swimmers remembered a baby in a red hoodie. No one had seen anything.

Panicked, Noémi opened the changing cubicles. "Elodie, Elodie?"

Aimée checked the open lockers. No baby. She even tapped on the ones that were locked. Leaned down, straining to hear an answering cry or sound. So difficult to differentiate noises with all the people calling out and the loudspeaker.

Now a girl from the swim team joined them, searching each steamy corner, all over the walkway, and the outdoor pool. The lifeguards blew whistles, and staff were searching the deck area and had asked swimmers to get out of the pool.

Aimée thought she heard a sound in the pool supply closet.

Was that a little moan, cooing? Or was she imagining it, hoping she heard something?

But the closet held poisonous chemicals . . . Good God. She yanked it open. Empty, apart from Chloé's red hoodie.

Aimée's insides churned.

Noémi had come behind Aimée as she picked it up. "Didn't you put this on Elodie . . . ?" The question ended in sobs.

Aimée put her arms around Noémi, nauseated by guilt. She'd thought Noémi had been watching Elodie—she never should have gone upstairs.

All of a sudden they were surrounded by a trio of blue uniforms. "We received a report of a theft and a missing baby. Do you recognize this man?"

There was the pool attendant, arms restrained behind his back by a young *flic*.

"Where's my baby?" Noémi screamed at him. "You locked her in this closet, and now she's gone!"

An older *flic* with grey sideburns put up his hand. "Hold on. Why do you say he locked her in the closet?"

Aimée held up the hoodie and explained. "Maybe it was prearranged. Someone hid the baby here and then took her out the back exit."

"We'll check. Meanwhile—"

"You're crazy!" The attendant was yelling.

"According to the *commissariat* report you've served time, Monsieur Arnault," the older *flic* said.

The attendant was bundled away.

"We need to call your husband and any family in the area to see if they have any information," said the *flic*, his notebook out.

"My ex?" Noémi paused, and her face turned white. "We're in a custody battle. Do you think he would . . . ?"

"Sit down. We don't know anything until we check. Let's get down his phone number, address, details about any of his family members nearby."

The *flic* turned his head to speak into a mic clipped to his collar, giving a callout for a unit response. Good, the *flics* were taking this seriously.

The second remaining *flic* motioned Aimée forward. "We need your statement, too."

"My nanny and I were both there by the showers. Let me show you."

While one *flic* took down Noémi's info, Aimée backtracked with the other.

"The girls were here on the floor," Aimée said. "Together by the lockers."

The *flic* jotted everything in his notebook as she detailed what she remembered, from the lap swimmers to the swim team.

"The last I saw her, she was wearing this." Aimée held up the hoodie. Her hands were shaking. She wanted to get out on the street and look for Elodie. Every minute was vital. How far could someone have taken her by now?

He pulled out an evidence bag for her to drop the hoodie in. "Can you tell me the precise timing?"

Not even fifteen minutes had passed.

By the time she'd rejoined Babette upstairs, Chloé needed a diaper change, and Babette was late for her class. Aimée clued her in.

"My friend will take notes for me," said Babette, her eyes full of worry. "I'm going down to give the *flics* a statement. I feel sick over this. Responsible."

So did Aimée. Responsible and guilty. The horrible idea that had been lurking at the edge of her mind overwhelmed her.

"Aimée, you've gone white," said Babette. "What's the matter?"

"What if Elodie wasn't the right baby?"

"What do you mean?"

Aimée showed Babette the photo. "She was wearing Chloé's hoodie. Chloé was the target."

Thursday Afternoon

THE POOL, THE small square, and the surrounding streets had been cordoned off. This was a kidnapping scene.

Aimée had called Melac, alerted him to the photo she'd received, relayed her suspicions, and made sure he would meet Babette at her apartment door. Only then had she sent Babette and Chloé home in a taxi.

Melac had confirmed their arrival. Thank God for that. Right now Chloé was safe.

Now all that mattered was finding Elodie.

Alive.

Inside the *piscine*, Aimée sat with a shaking Noémi near the *bains-douches*. She held Noémi's hand, wet and sticky from wiping tears. Antsy to join the search, Aimée checked her phone. No missed calls.

"Noémi, I want to help them look—"

"*Non, non*, please stay with me. Please."

Aimée didn't know what to do. She didn't want to leave poor Noémi alone, but she would be better used helping out with the search. Time was vital.

Two new *flics* joined her and Noémi on the bench.

More questioning? Aimée had already given a statement, and she distrusted the *flics*. Didn't the photo prove the Hand was behind this? Anyone in uniform could be involved. Yet how could

she not cooperate? Torn, she hesitated. If there was any chance
. . . There had to be someone she could trust.

"We've got a unit at your husband's apartment now," one
officer told Noémi. That was quick. With children involved, they
responded in record time. "Another one en route to your mother-
in-law—"

"Ex-mother-in-law," Noémi corrected. "She hates me. She's
the one who convinced Marc, my ex, to sue for custody. His girlfriend's in league with them."

Noémi had no idea of the danger Elodie was in. Noémi thought
it was her ex who was behind the kidnapping, not a hardened
criminal who might kill her baby. Guilty and agitated, Aimée had
to make her understand.

"Noémi, listen—"

"Try not to worry," interrupted the older *flic*, a weary look on
his long face. "Your *bébé* will be back any time now."

Easy to say, Aimée thought. To recite a platitudinous reassur-
ance to a distraught mother.

A squawk came from the microphone clipped to the older *flic*'s
shirt collar. Before Aimée could explain her suspicions that this
wasn't a custody kidnapping, that Elodie had not even been the
target, he'd stood and beckoned a few of his men.

Good news? Had they found Elodie?

The chlorine smell seeped in from the pool as the *flics* rushed
past.

Noémi clutched Aimée's sleeve. "How low can he stoop? But
why am I surprised? Remember when you came yesterday and I
was on the phone with him? More threats." Noémi gulped. "His
viper of a mother calls me unfit. But her son was already having
an affair when Elodie was born. I told you."

She had—a sad saga of a cheater. Her ex was a director at

the prestigious Mobilier National, the repository of the French state's historic furniture and tapestries. The office was not far from Noémi's studio, which made their breakup even more awkward.

But sad as that story was, Aimée didn't think it had anything to do with Elodie's disappearance.

"Noémi, I think it's a mistake."

"*Bien sûr*, it's a mistake." Noémi's hands were shaking. "A big mistake when my lawyer gets on this." She punched a number on her phone, listened for a moment, then hung up angrily. "Marc's not answering."

Aimée tried not to think the worst—but the possibilities roiled in her gut. Concentrate. She had to do anything she could to help. But her thoughts kept spinning and circling back.

"Elodie was wearing Chloé's hoodie," Aimée said.

Noémi checked her phone. Hit REDIAL. "*Et alors?*"

"Say the abductor's target was a *bébé* in a red hoodie. Chloé."

Before Aimée could pull out the photo, Noémi'd laid her hand on Aimée's. "I know you mean well, Aimée. But Marc's . . . This is just the kind of thing he'd do."

Aimée wished it were that simple. But it wasn't. Her hand trembled under Noémi's.

Officer Perrine had rejoined them and was listening with sharp interest. "What exactly are you trying to say, Mademoiselle"—the *flic* consulted his notes—"Leduc." His eyes flickered in recognition. Her name was mud these days with the *flics*.

"I think Elodie was abducted by accident," Aimée said. "I think my daughter was the target."

"Now, why would you say that?" Officer Perrine asked.

Not knowing which side he was on, she'd play this cautiously. "She was wearing my daughter's red hoodie." She pulled out the photo of Chloé in the sandbox. "Look. Someone sent me this at my office. This is a threat."

He looked at it. Turned it over. "Can I see the envelope it came in?"

"None."

"Who sent it?"

"I don't know."

"You obviously didn't take it seriously."

She bit back a retort. The *flics* had man power and resources at their disposal. Unlike her. Finding Elodie was all that mattered right then.

"Look, I'd stuffed the office mail in my bag, had no chance to read it this morning," Aimée said. "Then I found this photo. Please, I'm cooperating."

But Perrine had turned his attention to an officer who was beckoning him. He took Noémi's arm and escorted her to a huddled group of officers. Their voices echoed off the tiles, but Aimée couldn't catch anything.

News?

If this baby snatch was intended to get Aimée to cough up an old notebook she didn't have, how long until the abductor realized they'd bungled the job? Left little Elodie on a bench, tossed her into a dumpster . . . or worse?

The *flics* were already canvassing the area. Aimée tried to think objectively. Most Parisians regarded the thirteenth, with its rougher parts, as the end of the world. The new library was part of a plan for a revitalized Left Bank, a reclaiming of the rail yards, warehouses, silos, abandoned train tunnels, and hovels. Not that long ago, the arrondissement had been dotted by bidonvilles—shantytowns built from corrugated metal siding, *bidon*, and old pieces of the defensive wall.

As a little girl, Aimée had seen the smoke spiraling in winter from the hovels. She'd been surprised that people lived in them. She remembered the pounding machinery of the air compressor factory, a dull brick behemoth surrounded by dirty, crumbling stucco. A monster bellowing smoke in the night.

She drummed her damp stockinged feet on the tiles.

Every minute counted. Every second. *Bébés* attracted attention, *non?* They cried; they wet their diapers. A liability for a kidnapper. Anyone who kidnapped a baby wouldn't plan to keep it for long.

But a baby couldn't identify its abductor. Harming her would be more trouble than it was worth. Wouldn't it?

Why hadn't they found Elodie by now?

Noémi, now on the phone, paced back and forth, gesturing and shaking her head. The pool's chlorine smell was getting to Aimée. In a cubicle, she took off her stockings, dried her damp feet, and slipped on her ballet flats.

Emerging, she noticed another *flic*, in his late twenties and dressed in plain clothes. The new breed. She approached him.

"Have you worked in this quartier long?" she asked.

"You could say that," he said. "I've patrolled here for eight years."

He had to be good if he'd graduated that quick to undercover work.

"Does that include Chinatown?" she asked.

"Le Quartier Asiatique," he corrected. "That's *only* a slice of this arrondissement. Roughly thirty percent of the population."

Thirty percent legally registered. No statistics on the undocumented.

"Why do you ask?"

"What if it's a hired kidnapping?"

"We're investigating all possibilities, mademoiselle."

Translation: keep your mouth shut, and let us do our work.

"Look, I'm not sure everyone's seen this . . ." she said.

The *flic* took the photo she handed him. Turned it over. "What does this mean?"

"It's a threat. I think my baby was the target. The kidnapper made a mistake."

Interested, he pulled out his police notebook—the kind her father had used.

"Who do you think would send you this?" he asked.

"I don't know."

"Catch me up here, okay? I presume you showed this to the other officers."

She nodded. "They weren't interested."

"*S'il vous plaît.*" He gestured for her to sit on the locker room bench. Steam fogged the mirrors and turquoise tiles. "Did you receive this at home?"

"At my office. But this park's across the river from my apartment. My Chloé goes there almost every day."

"Did she go today, this morning?"

"After breakfast, Babette, her nanny, took her. See, she wore the same hoodie that Elodie was wearing when she was kidnapped."

"About what time?"

She told him. Gave him more details. He took notes and asked questions, taking her seriously.

"And where's her father?"

"Melac's ex–*brigade criminelle*. He's watching her now. He's in private security, lives in Brittany but works in Paris once a month."

"Why would someone threaten you? Can you think of any reason?"

Should she tell him? She hesitated.

"Can you think of a former caregiver, someone in your building with a grudge?" he tried. "Distant family?"

"I'm thinking," she said, buying time to decide if she trusted him.

"If you're saying your child was targeted—that this wasn't a random abduction—did you or your nanny notice anyone watching your baby?"

Hadn't Morbier warned her? Why hadn't she paid attention? Could she trust this *flic*?

Several *flics* had gathered. Perrine waved the young plain-clothes officer over to join him. *"Excusez-moi,"* the officer said, standing. "We're doing all we can."

Of course they were. Maybe they'd find Elodie. And maybe it would be too late.

Guilt and terror clawed at Aimée. Why hadn't she watched closer? Why hadn't she been more alert?

She watched as Noémi was led away by the police family liaison. She was useless here. She had to get out there and try to help.

Thursday Afternoon

VADDEY MANG SWEPT the cobblestone cracks in front of her aunt's handbag shop, dislodging the candy wrappers, damp leaves, and cigarette butts.

Filthy *barang*, as her auntie would have said, spitting behind the French colonials' backs. In the old days, her aunt had been a servant in Phnom Penh, until Pol Pot sent them both to the countryside and hunger. But life means change. Now Vaddey helped her aunt sell designer handbag copies, well-made imitations in soft pleather, to students and budget-conscious matrons.

As Vaddey was bending over to pick up a particularly stubborn cigarette butt, a blood-curdling scream came from the narrow passage beside their shop. Then a baby's cry.

That wife-beater again? Vaddey gripped her broom, her knuckles white with anger. Everyone turned a blind eye. No one wanted the Loo Frères gang on their back.

The screams kept on coming. Passersby with full shopping bags hurried by, eyes down. The mah-jongg players on the café terrace nearby melted away; people disappeared into their buildings. No one wanted to be witnessed witnessing.

Vaddey had come here to escape the violence—the Khmer Rouge soldiers raiding the village stores, stealing all the rice, bayoneting whole families and leaving them in the fields for the flies.

But today the shrieking cries brought back the nightmare she had fled.

Her hands trembled on the broom. If she waited, it would be taken care of. There were people who dealt with *problems*.

The baby's cries escalated.

The last scream faded into an eerie quiet.

Vaddey couldn't stop herself. She peeked around the wall in time to see a car peeling away. A young woman was sprawled on the cobbles. Unmoving.

There was a baby in a pool of blood. Its mother's blood or its own?

Vaddey couldn't just leave a baby. She couldn't pretend she hadn't seen it.

A horn honked. It was Alain with their delivery—he was trying to turn his truck into the alley.

A young man with short-cropped hair and gang tattoos on his neck had appeared at the alley mouth. He waved Alain away, motioned for him to park down the rue Nationale. Vaddey's insides churned. How could they hide this? But they would.

Back in the shop, her auntie barked, "Keep your eyes to yourself." She handed Vaddey a tray of Gucci-like wallets. "Special order."

Vaddey nodded. Another day, she would have obeyed her auntie. But today she stepped behind the stack of packing boxes, pulled out her cell phone, dialed seventeen, and whispered.

Thursday, Early Evening

"WHERE ARE YOU, René?" said Aimée.

"Going over details at the meeting with Xavier and Demy at la Maison des Cinq Sens," he said. "We signed up for the campaign, remember?"

She'd forgotten with everything that had happened. But at least he was close by. "Stay there. Turn on your police scanner. Elodie's been kidnapped."

"What?" She heard something drop in the background.

"They were trying to kidnap Chloé."

She hung up and took off, running through the narrow streets of Butte-aux-Cailles.

CRUNK . . . STATIC erupted, punctuated by voices, as René fiddled with the police scanner knobs under his Citroën's dashboard. In the falling dusk, she listened to the scanner from the car at the garden's edge. Twilight fell on la Maison des Cinq Sens and the wall sundial composed of different plants. She kept glancing at her phone.

She'd given René a quick rundown, shown him the photo.

"*Mon Dieu*," he said, frantic, "Chloé's in danger. You've got to send her away. Why not ask Melac to take her to Brittany? Forget your pride."

She hesitated. "Chloé's safe at home with Melac. I have to help with the search."

The last thing the *flics* wanted her to do.

"When the abductor realizes he's got the wrong *bébé*, you think Chloé will be safe?" René's voice rose. "Look at the photo; they've been watching her, won't stop at anything now."

She knew that and knew she had to stop them. Melac, ex–*brigade criminelle* and elite anti-terrorist squad. Right then he was, as Chloé's father, the only one she trusted.

Melac answered on the first ring.

"Chloé's fine, eating yogurt, though most of it's on her face," he said. "Don't worry."

Easy to say. "It's hard not to," she said.

"In these situations, you need to wait, Aimée. Not gut-react," he said in a calm voice. "From experience, believe me, it's better to give the *flics* room so when they catch him . . . *Alors*, it's a done deal—behind bars for life."

Finding Elodie right now—that was all that mattered.

"Take a deep breath," he said. "Keep calm for your friend's sake, okay? Update me when you know something."

She hung up, strained to listen to the police frequency.

"René, if I'd opened the mail this morning, we wouldn't be here."

"You don't know that," said René. "Why would they even think you had the notebook?"

"Someone must have reported that I was asking questions at the morgue; that's all I can think."

"Could Éric Besson have mentioned that you were involved in the search?"

"To whom?" She shook her head. "Not to the *flics*." Éric knew what was in the notebook—knew not to trust the *flics* farther than he could spit.

"Besson's not even paying you. Now he's fled the country, leaving you with the mess."

René fiddled with the dials, searching the frequencies.

"We gave statements—an endless waste of time. Babette missed her class." Aimée's throat tightened. "I can't believe I dragged my friend Noémi's baby into this."

Static and voices came from the police scanner. So far just back-and-forth as the *flics* widened the net over the quartier. Her sore ankle didn't help matters.

And then sirens whined, getting closer.

"They're crossing Pont de Tolbiac," said Aimée. "I can tell." The wind, cutting through the four towers of the *bibliothèque*, carried sound in a strange way.

René leaned toward the scanner. "Major incident reported off rue Nationale near Les Olympiades," he said.

"Who's responding, René?"

"At this point, who's not?" he said, a pained look on his face. "*Brigade des mineurs* reports they're stuck in traffic . . ."

Her heart jumped. "That's it."

JUST A KILOMETER away René pulled into the shadows of Les Olympiades, the seventies-era residential high-rises overlooking the Pagode shopping area on the esplanade between them. Karine had lived in one of these eyesores. The Asian shop fronts and noodle restaurants stood empty; the streets were quiet apart from arriving police cars and emergency vehicles. Deserted. Such a to-do and not a single gawking onlooker.

Aimée looked around for Noémi. Farther down, a knot of first responders and police photographers stood where the small passage, Impasse Bourgoin, hit rue Nationale. Aimée recognized the coroner's vehicle, the "dead van," in front of her.

Her pulse skittered.

"What's happened?" René caught her arm. He recognized the

dead van, too, and she felt his grip on her arm tighten. "We're in the way, Aimée. Leave this to the professionals." René pulled her arm harder. "Don't look. Please don't."

"Not until I see if the baby's . . ." *Non, non . . .*

On rue Nationale, a car pulled up. She saw Noémi getting out. She had to support Noémi, whatever scene awaited her. She was ridden with guilt. How could she ever make this right?

Aimée shook René off and ran, ignoring the driver's shouts, her throbbing ankle. Her steps halted as she saw the scene in the passage. A maroon web of blood veined the cobble cracks. Dear God. She turned away . . . couldn't look. Her eyes caught on a face in a window overlooking the narrow impasse. A young Asian woman. She was gone in a flash.

"The public's not allowed here, mademoiselle."

"Did . . . did you find a baby?" she gasped.

"Please step back. This is a crime scene."

A piercing scream echoed off the walls. The *flics* turned to look, and Aimée stepped between them. "Noémi . . . Noémi . . ."

She saw a woman's blood-covered body lying on a stretcher. Crime scene techs in white paper suits moved around her. Noémi huddled in the back of an ambulance, clutching a bundle wrapped in a foil shock blanket.

It couldn't, *non, non*, but there was so much blood . . . The air carried the copper smell of blood and rotting fruit. Aimée pushed closer. Was Noémi cradling her dead child, refusing to let go?

But over a shoulder Aimée saw the flushed face of Elodie, mouth open to empty her lungs. Alive—the baby was alive.

"*Calmez-vous, madame,*" a woman in a blue uniform was saying. "Your baby's all right. Please let the doctors run some tests . . ."

A *flic* waved Aimée away. "What are you doing here? I'll remove you physically if you don't . . ."

The body, now a mound under a blue foil cover, had been lifted onto a gurney. A tech stepped on a pedal, and the gurney jerked up. The woman's thin wrist flapped out over the railing. Her fingernails were broken, grimy and smudged with clotted blood.

Thursday Evening

AIMÉE STARED AT the photo of a woman's gaunt, bleached-out face, her bony shoulders poking up and making triangle dimples in the sheet. The body had been cleaned up for the autopsy slab photo.

The photo sat on the coffee table in the "situation" room—what had been the Pitié-Salpêtrière Hosptial surgery staff lounge until an hour before, when the *flics* took over. The surgeons' lounge, with its faded green walls and wooden benches, resembled a rural train station's second-class waiting room.

A middle-aged *flic* conducted the questioning, sweat stains under the arms of his short-sleeve shirt. Did Aimée recognize this woman? Had Aimée seen her at the pool?

"Is she the kidnapper, the woman found in the impasse?" Aimée asked.

"I ask the questions. You answer. Simple. So again, do you recognize her, Mademoiselle Leduc?"

Even if he was doing his job, his condescending tone rankled her.

"*Attendez un moment.*" She pulled out her digital camera.

"Didn't I ask if you recognize her? We're trying to establish her identity."

"*Attendez.*" She clicked through photos on her camera. Found one. "There. In the background. That looks like her, coming out of the *bain-douche*. I saw her for a quick minute."

He studied the photo. Made a notation in his notebook. "We'll compare the clothing. Anything else?"

Homeless used the public baths. But so did a lot of students who lived in *chambres de bonne* on the sixth floors of the surrounding apartment buildings, rooms once used for maids and with only a shared WC on the landing.

"So she stole Elodie?" Aimée asked.

He hesitated. "The body was next to the baby. We don't know more."

But you can add it up, she thought. Had she been a homeless woman using the baths? Aimée thought of her thin wrists, the ragged, dirty nails.

A pang hit her. Could she have gotten it wrong? She'd looked at the abduction only one way after seeing the photo of Chloé.

What if this had been random—a poor woman who desperately wanted a child to love grabbing an opportunity?

Had this woman slept in the park, in a doorway, a squat? How could she have cared for a baby?

What had she been thinking?

Or was it possible Noémi's ex had engineered this after all?

Aimée took back her camera and looked at the photo again. "Have you checked with the hospital?"

"I'm asking the questions, mademoiselle."

She pointed to the photo. Even at that distance, the band on the woman's thin wrist was visible—a hospital bracelet.

"See that?" Aimée said. "It might identify her if you can find it. Is it still on the body?"

His lips pursed. His round face was unpleasant. She was guessing they had not noticed a bracelet.

She heard voices passing in the hallway. ". . . inquiries door to door, every building, canvassing the area, the parks, court-yards . . ."

The voices faded. She wished this *flic* would give her something. "She's not Asian, so what was she doing in Chinatown? Hiding? Or does she have a connection? Was she working for someone? She was supposed to steal the baby and hand her off, maybe?"

He stared at his watch. "Anything else we should be aware of?"

She'd try one more time. "What if Elodie wasn't the baby she was supposed to kidnap? What if that's why she was killed, for taking the wrong baby?"

Concern filled his face. "I know it's scary for a mother to hear about something like this. But don't look for boogeymen around every corner."

"But Elodie was wearing my daughter's hoodie—what if my Chloé was the target?"

"Our investigation works on evidence, mademoiselle. Not sup-positions." The *flic* checked his watch again. "If that's all?"

"Are you a parent?" she said. "What would you do?"

"Take *vacances*."

He turned as a woman walked into the room, a cell phone to her ear, and slung a straw market bag onto the table. Parked her squeaking roller bag.

"Speaking of vacation," he said, "shouldn't you be halfway to . . . Barcelona?"

"Biarritz." She shrugged with the phone still to her ear. Took one look at Aimée. The woman's eyebrows rose and she hung up. An officer from *brigade des mineurs*, she wore a blue and white striped Breton *marinière* shirt, jeans, and the same espadrilles she'd worn the previous summer when she'd helped Aimée track down the man who'd abducted Zazie, the daughter of the owners of the café below Leduc Detective.

"We meet again, Mademoiselle Leduc." Madame Pelletier opened the file on the table. "Last time you had a bun in the oven."

"My daughter came out perfect," said Aimée. "But I'm a little biased."

Madame Pelletier turned to the round-faced *flic*. "She's a handful. I'll finish questioning her."

"About to go on holiday, like last time?" said Aimée.

Madame Pelletier nodded, pointed to the train ticket poking out of her straw bag. "Life gets in the way in my business." She sat on the edge of the staff coffee table and ran her fingers through her short blonde hair. She was attractive, blonder than before, with diamond studs in her ears and new lines parenthesizing her mouth. "How are you involved?"

"It's in my statement. There."

"Please tell me in your own words. Start at the beginning." She smiled. *"Je vous écoute."*

I'm listening. The standard professional line.

Well, she'd go through it for the fifth time.

So Aimée recounted the sequence of events. Again.

"I vaguely recall this woman," she said, showing the photo on her digital camera. "Look, in this photo, there's a tag on her wrist. You didn't find it on the body, right? Otherwise you'd know her identity."

"Who says we don't?"

"I'm not dense. Why did she take the baby to Chinatown?"

Madame Pelletier thumbed through the file on the desk. "Any number of reasons. Prearrangement to sell the baby—there's a market. This could link to one of our ongoing investigations."

A baby market?

"Or another common reason for abduction: a mentally unstable woman loses a baby—has a miscarriage or a stillbirth—and abducts someone else's as a replacement. The autopsy will tell us more."

At least Madame Pelletier knew her stuff. But things slipped through the cracks, especially with corrupt police.

"When they found the body, there was a woman watching from a window," Aimée said. "I know it doesn't mean she saw what happened—"

"*Mais oui*, someone called this in," said Madame Pelletier. Now Aimée had her attention. "We're working on tracing the caller." She pulled out a map. "Show me where you saw her."

Thursday Evening

"MY FIRST CRÈME brûlée," said Milo, a rookie *flic*.

The burned-out car reeked of burnt rubber and melted plastic upholstery. Fine pale soot, like confectioners' sugar, dusted the blackened interior. The doors had been blown open.

"Call it in," said Milo.

"A VIN number would help," said his partner.

Milo felt the hood. Warm, and the catch was fused shut. The techs at the garage would find the engine serial number. "Report a Renault Twingo, two door. Older model, from '92 or '93."

His uncle used to own one like this.

"You're professional, eh?" his partner said.

Was it joy-riding kids from the *banlieue*, a carjacking? Why go to the trouble? This *quartier* was a wasteland, his new chief said, a dumping ground for mistakes.

"There's a child's car seat in the back," Milo said.

His partner looked up, his expression blank. But Milo had caught his apprehension. "Anything in it?"

Milo donned latex gloves. Climbed in and over the chassis's protruding ribs. Ran his hands over and around the car seat. Its charred corners split like blackened banana peels.

The stink permeated his nostrils.

"Nothing," he said.

Sneezed. Sneezed again. Backing out, he ducked his head, and that's when he saw it.

"Just this." A plastic wrist tag from Pitié-Salpêtrière Hospital. He could read part of the lettering . . . a woman's name.

"Dumb luck that didn't fry," said his partner, furnishing an evidence bag.

Thursday Evening

THE HOSPITAL "SITUATION" room was stifling. A fan recycled hot air. Aimée felt a stream of perspiration between her shoulder blades. Madame Pelletier looked up from the notes in front of her as an officer knocked on the open door.

"Madame *le Commandant*, a moment, *s'il vous plaît*," the officer said.

"*J'arrive*," Madame Pelletier said, stepping out before Aimée could ask if they were done. Great. She had to get back to Chloé.

And René, where had he disappeared to?

Not even a call. So unlike him. She tried his number. His voice mail box was full.

She'd last seen him in the narrow street, as she'd been bundled off by the police . . .

She thought of that face in the window.

Thursday Evening

RENÉ HAD SEEN the young woman's face watching the scene below.

He'd overheard Aimée's altercation with the police, heard with relief that Elodie was alive, watched Aimée accompany Noémi in the ambulance.

While all the *flics* were distracted, he'd sneaked past the personnel barrier and ducked into a doorway overflowing with pots of ivy. He watched officers going building to building on rue Nationale. Would they find any witnesses?

There was a scraping noise as an anonymous-looking door opened across the passage. It was a shop's back door; René could see stacks of boxes within.

A young woman came out—petite but more than a head taller than him. The face in the window.

She looked both ways.

Took off down the street, away from the police.

"*Excusez-moi*," he said from the doorway.

She kept walking.

He followed. "Please, tell me what you saw." His short legs struggled to keep up. "Look, I'm not with the police. My friend's the baby's mother."

He'd met Noémi only once, but that counted.

The woman hesitated, her step faltering, then continued

toward the main artery of rue de Tolbiac. "Not here." He could just make out her low words.

"Where?"

She didn't pause again until she was by a bus shelter. She bent to whisper a meeting spot and then quickly boarded the arriving number 83 bus.

René reached in his linen jacket pocket, mindful of the stares of the Asians around him. Busied himself with his cell phone, which was dotted with bits of one of Chloé's stale teething biscuits. There must have been one in his pocket.

With showy nonchalance, he pretended to talk on his phone. By the time he'd reached his car, he knew where he had to go.

Thursday Evening

THE ATMOSPHERE IN the situation room had changed. Aimée could feel an increased sense of urgency among the *flics* who were bustling in and out, charging up and down the hallway.

Madame Pelletier was studying another file she'd brought in. "I'll need your camera's memory card."

"As long as I get it back and you tell me what's happening."

"I remember your determination." Madame Pelletier regarded her. "Are you always like this?"

"A character trait." Aimée grinned. "I've been called a pain in the derriere. Look, Noémi and I are friends, and I want to support her. Please, just tell me you don't think it's her ex or his family."

"That's under investigation now that we've tracked down her ex. Finally." Madame Pelletier's mouth pursed in anger. "Now, may I have the memory card?"

"If you fill me in on the latest."

"There's a tentative ID on the victim; that's all I can share. That's why I need to compare with your photo."

Aimée depressed the lever on the digital camera, slid the memory card out, and handed it to Madame Pelletier. "So you've found the hospital ID bracelet. Where?"

"Never give up, do you?"

"Wouldn't be good at my job if I did."

"But this isn't your job. It's mine. Now go home to your *bébé*."

Aimée wanted to shout in frustration. But acting pliant would get her further. "Look, I understand your process, but the crime feels so close . . . My child was the target."

"I've attached the photo to your statement, noted your opinion. For what it's worth . . . it looks like the kidnapper was a distraught homeless woman."

Aimée had caught a glimpse of the file Madame Pelletier was reading. Even looking at it upside down, Aimée had been able to make out the name of the shelter and the brief list of the victim's belongings.

"How does a homeless woman have two thousand francs stashed in a woman's shelter?" Aimée asked.

Madame Pelletier slapped the file shut. Her eyes were angry. "How do you think?"

"A bribe to abduct my baby," said Aimée, controlling a shiver with effort. "Between you and me, there's some kind of cover-up going on. Look at the park photo, read the threat on the back, put it together with the fact that Elodie was wearing my baby's hoodie when she was abducted . . . It's obvious. Stares you in the face." She caught her breath. "When they discovered it was the wrong baby, maybe got interrupted—I don't know—the woman was killed to prevent her from talking."

Madame Pelletier grimaced. Nodded. "I can understand your concern."

Trying to placate her? Condescending? *Mais non*, Aimée heard the truth in Madame Pelletier's voice.

"So what will you do about it?" Aimée asked.

"Call for you, Madame *le Commandant*, line three," said a voice from the hallway.

Businesslike now, Madame Pelletier indicated the door. "Mademoiselle Leduc, I suggest you let me do my job."

AIMÉE TOOK A taxi back. Her mind was unable to let the case go. This seemed sloppy for the Hand. A rush job? Interrupted?

She thought of Vauban dead under a bus. Shivered. Cyril Cromach snooping around. Didn't want to think of how the Hand would threaten her next.

She couldn't expect the *flics* who hated her to protect her. Nor would she want them to.

Her phone rang. Noémi. The guilt rose up again.

"Elodie's all right. She's asleep. Aimée, we're home finally . . ."

Relief filled her. "Thank God. You okay, Noémi?"

"Taking it minute by minute," she said.

"I'm so sorry. It's all my fault—"

"Stop it, Aimée. This is between me and my ex. The *flics* know. They always look at the family for a reason."

"But, Noémi—"

"Just listen, Aimée. I did ask them if Chloé could have been the target. Unlikely, they said. Almost all abductions are family. Not one *flic* had ever dealt with a random kidnapping by a woman who'd lost a child or a kidnapping for money."

Voices rose in the background. There was a high metallic scraping, like fingernails on a blackboard, the signature sound of Noémi's atelier's wrought iron gate.

"*Merde*, the *flics* came back." Noémi sucked in a breath. "More later."

Thursday Evening

RENÉ WEDGED INTO a parking space behind the gargantuan Italianate-style *mairie* of the thirteenth on Place d'Italie. He'd circled the horrendous roundabout several times.

The meeting place was a café in the arcade leading to a 1930s art house cinema. Covert and quiet. René found her at the last table at the far end of the black-tiled café.

He pulled himself up onto the seat. His short legs dangled.

"*Merci* for meeting me," he said.

"No trouble, *promittez?*" A soft accent hung on her French syllables.

"*Bien sûr.* Tell me what you saw."

She crossed her arms in front of her chest—defensive, René thought. And the nervous type, he noted from her bitten fingernails and ragged cuticles.

"*Desolé*, where have my manners gone? Would you like to order something?"

"I'm not hungry." She hesitated. "Look, monsieur, I heard screams; that's all. I don't know what else I can tell you."

"Just think back. Maybe there's a small detail, like a noise or someone you saw nearby," said René. The woman's expression was unsure. He was certain she had something to say and was just afraid to say it. He rummaged through his brain to find the right words. Something Aimée would say. "Please, if there's anything you remember, it will help to catch who did this."

Her eyes batted in fear.

"You're afraid. I won't put you in danger. Here, relax. Let me buy you a drink." René shoved a menu toward her.

She ignored it.

"You came here," he tried. "I think you want to help."

"No one talks," she said finally. "They keep silent, and it made me sick."

"What's your name?"

"Never mind my name."

"Okay, I'm René. But you saw my friend Aimée, big eyes, tall, *non?*"

She nodded.

"She's scared for her own baby, who was almost stolen instead of Elodie, the baby who got taken."

She glanced at her watch. Her mouth was set with worry; René could see she was trying to decide what to say.

"What did you see or hear? Please tell me. I won't talk to the *flics*."

"The gang makes sure no one talks."

René's ears perked up. "Which gang?"

For a moment, she looked at him in disbelief. Then she turned her head a fraction and scanned the empty café. "You don't understand how it works here."

"I'm getting that feeling. So tell me how."

"I heard the screams—I thought it was the man in the passage who beats his wife. But *non* . . . this car drove away. A Twingo."

"That's helpful." René nodded. "Did you notice what color?"

Her index finger made a circle in a wet spot on the table. "Green, I think."

Good, she noticed things.

"Do you remember if it was a two door, four door?"

"I don't know." She swallowed. "After that, I saw the woman lying there, all bloody." Then took a deep breath. "She wasn't Asian. I've never seen her before. And a baby. Then a Loo Frères gang member appeared and shooed our delivery driver away. That's all I know."

"Did you see the driver of the car?"

"How could I have? It had pulled away . . ." Her index finger paused on the table.

"You remember something?" Hopeful, René leaned forward.

"Maybe a flash of a black sleeve . . . like leather? But there's nothing else I can tell you, monsieur." She stood. "If you follow me or come around again, they'll know it was me who reported."

"How?"

She scanned the café again. Whispered: "I called the emergency number."

René pressed his card into her hand. "Trust me. Call anytime."

And then she'd gone. He reached for his phone and called Aimée. Busy.

"IT'S A FRONT, Aimée," said an excited Maxence over the phone. His rising voice almost squeaked.

"*Attends.*" She pulled her scooter over to the first place she could find. Smack in front of France's oldest labor movement organization, Friends of the 1871 Commune. Still a rowdy bunch who carried on *l'esprit des Communards* in a yearly block party.

"What's a front?" she said, wishing she had her damn earbuds.

"Madame de Frontenac runs a dry cleaner's on rue de Patay."

Aimée switched the scooter's ignition off. Covered her other ear with her left hand. "A money launderer?"

"I don't know. But her maiden name is Dandin. I remembered that name from what you wrote on the chart."

Dandin, the name from Morbier's email—the *flic* who'd retired, whom she'd found no records of. The *flic* with cauliflower ears who'd played poker at the kitchen table while she sat on her father's lap.

"Go on," she said.

"Madame de Frontenac lives by her business, which she co-owns with a brother, Charles."

"Brilliant, Maxence."

"I delved deeper. Found out Dandin does security part time at you'll never guess where."

She had no time for guessing games. Took a wild shot anyway. "At the Gobelins tapestry factory?"

"How did you know, Aimée?"

"I didn't."

Still, how did that figure in the whole story?

"So a Madame de Frontenac, co-owner of a business with Charles Dandin, who works at les Gobelins, hired Cyril Cromach to snoop around?" Aimée said.

"Funny, eh?" said Maxence. "Why couldn't her brother snoop around?"

Good question. "Tell me more, and how you found out where he works."

She grabbed her Moleskine. Took down the details. After a check-in with Melac—Chloé was safe and eating dinner—she headed to find out.

THE SLOPING ZINC roofs with their forests of chimney pots were barely discernable against a deepening indigo sky—*entre chien et loup*, the dim light in which one couldn't distinguish a dog from a wolf. Aimée watched Dandin, more years on him but recognizable, board the number 27 bus steps away from where he worked as a guard at the Gobelins tapestry factory.

No chance to visit Léo's old apartment—the complex had closed.

Thanks to Maxence's digging, she knew Dandin's part-time hours. The day she'd visited he'd been off—she remembered Olivia in the caretaker loge. But no connection to the slime Cyril Cromach.

But why? Her mind went to Morbier's email: *Tell Dandin. We've got to keep story straight.*

She looked up the bus route. One of its stops was on rue de Patay near the address Maxence had given her. Going home?

Aimée followed the bus on her scooter, alert to see where he got off. Eight stops later, he did. She skirted a nineteenth-century neoclassical church, breathing diesel exhaust fumes all through the quartier Jeanne d'Arc, and watched him cross the street. There she saw a low stone wall, crumbling in places, and a closed Bricostore cut-rate carpet store in what had once been a row of small shops. Behind a gate, she could see a compound: a four-story building with green shutters; to the right a small, run-down warehouse; on the left what looked like a pensione last remodeled in the thirties.

Dandin entered LAV-MAT, a well-lit dry cleaner's with a seventies storefront. Over the low hum of her scooter, she heard the bell on the door tinkle as she rode past. She parked her scooter under a plane tree, walked up, and peered in the window. Dandin was talking with an older woman—an argument, judging by the raised voices. And Aimée saw the woman's ears—a match for her brother's cauliflowers.

Maxence had said Dandin's sister had gotten chatty after he'd called and mentioned a sweepstakes prize. A boy after Aimée's own heart. Was Dandin upset that his sister had given Maxence information?

Aimée scooted into a doorway before Dandin exited, slamming the shop's door closed. He went through the gate next door.

She debated knocking. Would he remember her? But he'd remember her father. No lights went on behind any windows. Then she heard a put-putting sound of a moped. The gate creaked open . . .

Dandin had a phone to his ear. He clanged the gate shut. Then his moped shut off.

"*Non*, not you," he was saying into the phone. "*Attends*, I'm telling that two-bit . . . *Quoi? Oui.* To his face. He screwed up."

Her mind flew to Cyril. Screwed up the kidnapping? A murder?

She wanted Dandin to tell the Hand to lay off her. That she didn't have the notebook. But what proof of his connection to the Hand did she have?

Dandin hung up, put the phone in his pocket, paused. She made herself small in the doorway as he looked up the street.

Careful.

Better to follow and see where he went and whom he met.

He pedaled to restart his moped and turned into a side street. Only then did she get back on her scooter and turn her key in her ignition. There was little traffic at this time of the evening, so she stayed a block behind him in the haze of dimly lit streets, quiet apart from her thrumming scooter and the pounding of her heart.

He followed the steep rue Regnault in the direction of Maison-Blanche. Nearby lay the decrepit Panhard and Levassor car engine factory, commandeered by the Germans during the war to manufacture airplane engines for the Luftwaffe. On the other side, the cavernous la Petite Ceinture, the abandoned nineteenth-century rail line that had once belted Paris. Now overgrown, a deserted place where disoriented *cataphiles* emerged from the catacombs to find themselves with junkies and foxes. Parts of the Left Bank were wilderness, green where nature had rooted in the cracked stones. She loved the wild flowers sprouting on the tracks and the neighborhood groups that planted allotments of vegetables and kept rabbits.

Dandin wove through the small streets to Jardin du Moulin de la Pointe, a park where mills once harnessed the power of la Bièvre. Here the Petit Ceinture tracks led into a tunnel. He got off his bike. She parked, grabbed her jacket, and picked her way down to the tracks in her ballet flats along a winding path lined by bushes and trees.

Ahead she made out Dandin's figure keeping to the steep wall along the rail line. His flashlight beam bobbed on chunks of gravel as he made his way.

If she walked on the gravel, he'd hear her, as would anyone else. She kept to the wide-spaced wood ties, once the path of steam trains.

Graffitied train cars were parked in the tunnel. Farther down, at the end of the tunnel, a fire flickered; voices were raised; glass shattered. A party? She didn't see Dandin anymore. Figured he'd gone inside a train.

More glass shattered. Shouts that sounded like a drunken fight.

Chance going inside? She didn't relish waiting out here.

High steps led to an old-fashioned train car. Dank, mildewed air. Damp newspapers, garbage on the rotted floor.

Dandin's voice, and another man's. Cyril? But she couldn't tell.

Footsteps. Quick—she had to hide. But where in this narrow space?

She backtracked and jumped down the steps. Landed with a crunch. Winced at the twinge in her ankle. Nowhere to go without being seen.

She rolled under the train, crawled behind a rusted wheel, by the remnants of a soggy blanket. Something slimy on her hands as she scraped her knee. The least of her worries.

Had anyone seen her?

In the darkness, she saw silhouettes of shoes—what looked like Dandin's brogues and another pair hurrying away, crunching on the gravel.

Who had he met? What had they said?

Frustrated, she crawled under the train until her knees ached. She rolled out to see two men rounding the bushes ahead. Leaving.

"I'm no pushover. You owe me." Dandin's voice sounded clear in the night air before they disappeared.

She should have gotten René to act as backup—thought this out more. But she'd jumped at the chance of finding Dandin.

She needed to get back to Chloé and figure out her next move.

She hurried now in the cool night air. Damp leaves brushed her face. As she turned on the path, her foot hit something. A rock or tree stump. Pain lanced up her ankle . . . again.

Kneeling down to check her ankle, she realized she'd kicked a groaning man lying by the path.

Mon Dieu.

"*Desolée,*" she said.

A wheezing her only answer. He didn't move. Behind her, drunken shouts, yelling. Others were breaking off, running toward her.

Her fingers closed around the hard, rectangular shape of a flashlight.

"Are you all right?" Her fingers came back sticky with a sweetish smell. Had she stuck her hands in vomit?

She picked up the flashlight, flicked it on, and shone it. Dandin's glassy eyes blinked at the brightness. His pupils dilated, and his moans sputtered. His big ears stained with pink spatter. Blood oozed from a jagged slash in his neck. One bloodied hand held a shard of glass he must have pulled out. His other reaching for his neck.

Oh my God . . . Her stomach lurched. Bile rose in her throat. Like Karine.

She had to stop the bleeding. Apply pressure. His labored breaths trailed into gurgling. *Mon Dieu,* if she couldn't prevent the carotid bleeding out . . .

And then she was grabbed from behind. Gloved hands around her throat. A cold shard of sharp glass pressing into her neck. Her hands flailed as she tried to get loose. Screaming, she was screaming. Somehow one of her flailing hands still gripped the flashlight, its beam jerking all over the place.

This was it . . . her life flashing in front of her, her *bébe* Chloé's face. Only a choked-up cry was coming from her as she tried to push the man off.

Shouts. Summoning her strength, she swung back. Connected with something hard like a skull. Then swung again. Heard an ouf. The hands released her neck; the glass shard fell, tinkling on the stones.

Her chest heaved as she struggled to catch her breath. He'd taken off. Still on her knees, she made her hand reach for Dandin's pulse. Ragged but beating. She balled up his shirt collar over the wound and applied pressure. Leaned down to his ear. Smelled the coppery tang of blood.

"Dandin, I'm Jean-Claude's daughter. You remember Jean-Claude Leduc."

His breath came in shallow rasps.

"I know the Hand's behind this . . ."

Pinkish froth bubbled from his lips. A hoarse grunt.

"Here's your chance to tell me, Dandin." She kept the pressure steady. "I'm calling an ambulance." She tried reaching for her phone.

His raspy grunts rose. Like a rattling in his chest, the death rattle . . . *Mon dieu.* He was trying to say something. Gurgling. Choking, and she couldn't make out the words. His bloody hand caught her head, gripped so tight she felt hair ripped from her scalp, and jerked her close.

His breath was like mold.

"*Moi?* I'm Aimée. You remember me when I was little, *non?* Playing cards in our kitchen . . . Remember?"

Anything to keep him with her. Get him to focus.

His eyes showed a dull recognition. "That's right. Of course you remember Jean-Claude, my papa. Your colleague. You can tell me, Dandin. Who's behind the Hand?"

His eyelids fluttered. Not looking good.

"Stay with me . . . please . . ."

Garbled noises. She was losing him.

"Who, Dandin? You can tell me."

She leaned closer and heard rasping breaths. "Son . . . fixer."

A lingering gurgle. His eyes glazed. She felt his pulse. Gone. *Merde.*

Several of the drunks had come up on the path.

"What's with him?" A man in a worn leather jacket grabbed at her to steady himself. "No more party in him. But plenty in you, *chérie.*"

Horrified, she realized from the man's glazed, stoned look how out of it he was. And his friend, who chugged from a wine bottle.

"*Tant pis*, this poor man's dead. Murdered by the *mec* who ran off." She picked up her bag, struggled to her feet.

But the man in the leather jacket caught her wrist, his grip like iron. "Come party with us."

"*Mon Dieu*, he's been murdered." How could she get away? Yet she needed to know what they'd seen. "You must have seen who he met at the train. Didn't you?"

"Largo, it's not cool . . . Let's go," said the other stepping back, sniffing.

Her voice rose. "Don't you understand the murderer—"

Aimée heard crunching on the gravel and almost reached for her knife. But it was a younger man. "*Merde*, that's the old *flic*," he said.

"Shut up, Brice."

"You know him?" she asked. "What about the man who waited for him on the train?"

"You gonna party or not?" the man called Largo asked.

He hadn't let go. She kicked him in the balls as she'd been wanting to do.

Several pairs of headlights illuminated the building façades on the street. A roar of motorcycles. "*Merde . . . les Chinois . . .*" She noticed the wild-eyed fear in the one called Brice.

"Tell me, Brice," she said.

They scattered. Left her with blood on her hands, glass shards.

With shaking hands, she felt inside Dandin's jacket pockets. She checked for his wallet. Gone. Pockets picked clean except for an old centime wedged in one of the creases. Where was the phone? Had the killer taken it?

Now voices speaking Chinese. Joined by more, echoing off the buildings. She had seconds.

One last try. She scraped her hands over the dirt.

Found the phone. Smashed to bits. *Merde*.

She checked everything she'd touched. Wiped off what she could with her scarf. Then she got the hell out of there.

Thursday, Late Evening

BY THE TIME Aimée unlocked her apartment door on Ile Saint-Louis, her neck muscles throbbed with built-up tension, and her damp blouse clung to her shoulder blades. She was ready to drop with exhaustion. She needed to cuddle her *bébé* and soak in a steaming hot bath. In that order. Then she'd figure out what to do.

Miles Davis's pink tongue licked her ankles. She leaned down, stroked his silky back. "Missed you, fur ball," she said.

"Aimée?" Melac stepped out from the kitchen into the hallway. Chloé's biological father, a former officer on the *brigade criminelle*, had a diaper in his hand. He was slim hipped and muscular as ever, and concern filled those grey-blue eyes, so like Chloé's.

And he still wore his rose gold serpent wedding ring.

"You all right?" he asked.

She'd witnessed a murder, been attacked, escaped a bunch of winos and a Chinese gang—all in an evening's work.

"Tired," she said.

"My contact at *brigade criminelle* says they've found the abduction vehicle, IDed the woman."

"I know," said Aimée. She plopped her bag on the hall secretaire, toed off her ballet flats. Sat down and rubbed her ankle. Tried to ignore the stinging scrape on her neck. She was glad she'd already cleaned off Dandin's blood; she didn't want to have to explain to Melac.

From the baby monitor propped on the table came Chloé's sleeping whistles. Thank God.

Melac set down the diaper. "How's little Elodie?"

Aimée's shoulders drooped with fatigue. "She's home. Safe."

"Nine times out of ten, it's the family, but . . ."

"I know, and you know, that's not the case. Chloé's in danger. I'm making a plan—"

"I've got a plan, Aimée." He sat down and leaned close. Took her hand. His musky lime vetiver scent clung to her skin. "She's my daughter, too."

Tired, so tired. Dandin had been a dead end. Like the man himself. And she'd put herself in danger.

"You look worn out," Melac said.

What did Melac have up his sleeve? He'd joined a private security firm. His year off after the death of his older daughter hadn't diminished the demand for his skills.

Maybe it would be safest to go into full flight mode. Bundle up Chloé and walk out the door with what was on their backs. Escape like Besson. Work remotely. René would help; she'd manage her business. Somehow.

Her eye went to her coatrack, the secondhand Hermès carryall, Chloé's pile of diapers. She'd only have to slip the passports and laptop into her bag, grab Chloé, leave Miles Davis with her concierge, and call a taxi. Decide the destination en route.

Melac followed her gaze and read her thoughts. "Get real, Aimée," he said. "You're not thinking of trying to run, are you?"

"It crossed my mind."

"Listen to me. Let me take Chloé to Brittany. Donatine's working in Lille this month, but I'll manage."

Melac lived in Brittany on a farm with his wife. Wife—why did Aimée always have a hard time saying that in her mind? His wife lived completely organically, spun wool from their own sheep, and couldn't conceive. She was desperate to have a baby—or custody of Chloé.

"Well, wherever your wife is working, it feels awkward."

"Why?" Melac took her arm. "You're in danger. I know you'll do anything to keep Chloé safe."

True. Suddenly, Miles Davis growled. His tail stuck up straight as an arrow, and he ran barking to the door.

The hair rose on the back of her neck.

"Melac, open the spoon drawer."

"Spoon drawer?"

"My Beretta's in there."

"You won't need your Beretta," Melac said. "It's not what you think."

"And what would I think? *Alors*, I've had enough surprises tonight."

The door swung open, and a woman appeared, swathed in black and slender, with shoulder-grazing white-blonde hair, designer tortoiseshell glasses. A sophisticated Parisian grandmother wearing a hint of muguet scent.

And carmine-red lipstick.

For a moment, the salon faded and Aimée was a little girl at the mansard window, staring down at the quai, hoping to see her— just once. The hurt had never gone away.

Light-headed, Aimée couldn't believe the woman who'd abandoned her when she was eight years old stood in her apartment. Her American mother, Sydney Leduc. Clutching a roller bag and Chloé's baby bag.

"What are you doing here?" It had been two months since the woman had last tried to intrude on Aimée's life. Their one attempt at lunch had been a disaster.

"Morbier called me," her mother said. "Evidently you agreed."
She had?

"You want Chloé safe," said her mother. That accent, that ach-ingly familiar tone. "She's my granddaughter. Please let me help."

"I should trust you?"

"Right now, I'm your best option. I do what I do very well, Amy."

That American way she said Aimée's name brought back memories. Lonely ones.

"Disappear?" Aimée said.

"That's the only way with the Hand," her mother said.

"You're the last person I'd trust."

"If you could hear how naïve you sound. Forget thinking you can control the situation. It's about playing the right hand and figuring out what to do if you don't have the right hand."

Pragmatic, as before. All the things Aimée had wanted to ask stuck in her throat. The craving for connection that battled with her anger.

Anger she couldn't harness. When they had tried to have a late-summer lunch together, Sydney had criticized Aimée's wardrobe, causing Aimée to stomp out of the resto. Stupid. Embarrassing. And Sydney's parting shot: *You're acting childish . . . When Chloé's your age, do you want her to act this way?*

How she'd deserved that but would die before she'd admit it.

"My driver's waiting on the backstreet," her mother said. "We'll make Brittany in under four hours."

Disbelief rippled her insides. "You think . . . *mon Dieu*, that I'll let you walk out of here with my child?"

"Aimée, I can't change what I did in the past."

And then she couldn't help herself. The feelings welled up, and she was eight years old. "Why did you leave?"

Melac averted his eyes. She'd rarely seen him look uncomfortable. But he looked that way right then.

"Why wouldn't Papa ever talk about you?" Aimée asked.

Sydney's lipsticked mouth quivered. "I hurt him. You. But it's now that's important, Amy. Chloé's in danger. You think they'll stop with one kidnapping?"

Melac met her gaze. "I could have taken Chloé and left," he said. "She's my daughter, too, and her safety is everything. But I wanted you to understand and agree."

Should she?

A sudden strident ringing came from a phone on the dining table. Melac pointed to it. "It's a burner phone I found on your doorstep an hour ago."

"You're being watched," Sydney said.

Aimée's heart jumped. "Have you answered it?"

"Think I'm stupid?" He handed her a digital recorder. "Put it on speaker. Record it."

The burner phone almost slipped out of her sweaty hands.

"*Oui?*" she said.

Canned music—a children's nursery song—played in the background. "Next time there won't be a mistake," said a robotic voice. "We don't want to hurt your little girl. We only want one thing."

The notebook.

"It's gone, destroyed," she said.

"Not at all. We're counting on you to find it."

The call went dead.

Shaking, Aimée clicked the recorder off. Looked up to see Melac holding a sleeping Chloé, bundled in a blanket.

She couldn't leave Chloé, abandon her like—

"I know it's hard for you to trust us, but this will be keeping her safe," said Melac.

"We've only been apart once . . ." Aimée's throat caught.

"Come with us," said Sydney.

And lead the Hand to her *bébé?* Did she have a choice? "*Non,* I've got to take care of the problem. This won't be over until I find the notebook."

Shaking, Aimée took a sleepy Chloé in her arms, kissed her, inhaling that sweet baby smell. Chloé's tiny, warm fingers clasped Aimée's thumb. "I love you, *ma puce.*"

And then she was following them down the worn marble steps to the courtyard, behind the carriage house, to the narrow walkway to the next street.

"All contact goes through Morbier," said Melac.

Had she really agreed to do this?

She put Chloé in his arms.

Her mother put out her warm hand, caressing Aimée's cheek and making her stomach churn. "You might hear lies about me. Stories. Only half are true."

A green plumber's van had pulled up.

A minute later they'd piled in, and Aimée watched the van go down narrow rue Saint-Louis en l'Ile. Her heart went with it. She felt as if she'd made a deal with the devil.

WITHIN EIGHT MINUTES, she'd bundled up her life essentials—lipstick, Chanel No. 5, a wig, her laptop—and was speeding in a taxi across the Left Bank with Miles Davis in her lap. She was still wearing the same silk blouse she'd had on all day.

Three taxi changes later she sat sipping espresso in l'Institut Culturel Italien's garden, swathed in the shushing sounds of the linden tree branches. The night clung, dark and damp; tiny white lights winked in a ring around the old garden walls. Miles Davis chased a moth. Next to her, Martine scanned Marcus's homicide report and the copy of his autopsy report that she'd printed and laid out on her Italian grammar textbook.

"I delivered, Martine," Aimée said. "Your turn."

"They tortured this poor boy? We're not in Angola."

"Things can turn dicey anywhere, especially in the center of Paris." Martine blew a puff of smoke. "The people you know, Aimée."

"Know? He's *your* relative. That's how I got pulled into this."

"A distant relation and only by marriage."

"*Écoutes.*" She brought Martine up to date.

"Your mother is back?" Martine's demitasse clattered to the saucer. "Even after your 'anger management issues'?"

"And disappeared again, Martine, but this time with Chloé."

"I need to interview your mother."

Aimée's jaw dropped. "That's all you can say?"

"She's fascinating. On the World Watch List, hunted, labeled a terrorist. She is the modern *femme d'espionnage.*"

"She's got my daughter, Martine."

"A masterstroke. Who else could handle this? A spook."

"A spook?"

"She's a CIA spy. And she's got an agenda."

"Agenda to abandon my daughter like she abandoned me?"

"Get over it. She didn't abandon you. She left to keep you safe." Martine took a drag, deep in thought. "It only makes sense, Aimée."

"What?"

"She *must* be a spy. Think about it," said Martine. "Forget your emotions a minute—easy for me to say—but . . . what if her terrorist persona's a cover? *Parfait* for a double agent."

"That's sick, Martine."

"Sick? *C'est brilliant, Aimée.*" She stabbed out her cigarette. Gave Aimée a knowing look. "You two need a tête-à-tête."

Their last had ended in a fiasco.

"*Alors*, now focus on your strategy. Find this notebook, and blow the Hand sky-high." Martine lit another cigarette. "Or did you plan to sit here twiddling your thumbs and pining for a cigarette?"

Aimée was stung. "I never expected that from you."

"Did you expect your friend's baby would be kidnapped? That two more people would be murdered? The Hand's all business, Aimée. Get on your scooter, and ride it to the end."

Marcus's and Karine's murders, the autopsy cover-up, the dodgy police investigation, Elodie's kidnapping, that poor homeless woman, Dandin, the call on the burner phone . . .

"If I don't find the notebook—" Aimée began.

"You better," Martine interrupted, "before they do. Get it into the right hands. I've got a story here."

Aimée's phone vibrated. René. She ignored it for now. "You'll write it?"

"I'll skip Italian conversation class tomorrow, make some visits. You know what we say in my business—climb the stairs. I'll shoot for the weekend supplement, an exposé. And you'll let me interview your mother." Martine pulled a biscotti from her bag, waved it at Miles Davis. "Oh, and I get to dog-sit."

Aimée leaned down and tried to pet Miles Davis, but he was more interested in the biscotti. Her hands were shaking. This was all going too fast.

"I'm on the run, Martine. Scared."

"Scared of not finding this notebook? Or of finding it and learning what your father did?"

She bit her lip. "Both. And losing Chloé."

Martine stubbed out her cigarette on the Ricard ashtray. "Remember what you told me once? Scared keeps you alert, on your toes. Less prone to mistakes."

"My father used to say that," she said.

Martine was right. Time Aimée got on her toes. Then worried about keeping on them.

SHE TOOK THE Métro a few stops, then a taxi, then another before she'd hit the bright lights of the Champs-Élysées. Her phone vibrated. René. He related how he had tracked down the woman in the window.

"Brilliant. Did she intimate it was a gang murder?" Aimée asked, expelling a plume of smoke in the night air. "A hired hit by the Loo Frères gang?"

"*Pas de tout,*" said René.

She'd cadged a Gauloise from an orderly outside the Pitié-Salpêtrière Hospital ambulance bay. Right now she willed the nicotine jolt to calm her nerves. Guiltily, she savored what she'd been missing for eighteen months, three days, four hours.

Counting, who was counting?

"What's that sound?" René said. "Don't tell me you're smoking again."

Suddenly she wanted to throw up. Tossed the cigarette into the nearby geranium pot.

"No way," she said. "Tell me more about this young Cambodian woman and why she thinks it's a gang thing."

"Did I say that?" said René. "Now, if you just listen . . ." Horns honked. "*Alors,* I'm driving. Let me put you on speakerphone."

Aimée paced back and forth, oblivious to the wind shimmying the plane-tree leaves and the lights shimmering on the rain-spattered pavement. "So does this woman know anything? Did she witness what happened . . . the murder?"

"She heard screams, saw a green Twingo drive off. Then found the woman. One of Loo Frères gang appeared, covered the scene in minutes. She's more afraid of them than anything else."

"So the Loo Frères got involved?"

"She didn't say that."

"Maybe they were contracted by the Hand. Or . . . René, there's a fixer."

"Fixer?"

Her nerves jittered. "Listen, Chloé's gone to Brittany with Melac." She left out her mother.

"I know. Thank God for that."

"How do you know?"

"Melac called and filled me in about the burner phone," he said. "Maxence and I are working on the spirit catcher."

"Spirit catcher? It's me who should be drinking, René, not you."

"Just hear me out. It's a device to trace the burner phone. We retrieved it from your place half an hour ago. Lots of watchers out front."

Her heart skipped. "You left out the back?"

"*Bien sûr*. We've taken over an office at the *bibliothèque*. No one cares at night. We'll camp out here."

"Did something happen at the office?"

Pause. "An envelope came with a photo of Babette unlocking your apartment door with Chloé in her arms."

Another one.

Hating to admit it, she felt relieved that Chloé had been spirited out of town.

She recounted how Maxence had led her to Dandin. His dying words.

"The Hand's getting close, Aimée."

"Tell me about it."

The blue-coated doorman tipped his hat to her and swept Le Drugstore's double door open.

"Got to go," she said.

Madame Pelletier's words rang in her head—the ongoing investigation into a kidnapping ring, a baby market. But it didn't make sense for a gang running a baby ring to send threatening photographs. What was the Chinatown connection? Maybe the gang was working on contract.

And what about les Gobelins? Why had Cyril been sniffing around? Dandin had worked there, too. What role had he played?

Martin should have answers.

He sat in his "office," the last banquette in the back dining room. He was conferring with a "client" wearing a pinstripe suit, blue shirt, and red tie—the man looked ministry all over. He rose, shook Martin's hand. Was gone out the back door.

"Ah, Mademoiselle Aimée," said Martin, beckoning her over. He kissed her on both cheeks, summoned the waiter. "Her usual." He lit a cigarette. "You quit?"

"I'm always quitting," she said, longing for a drag. Even thinking of the last one made her sick. "*Alors*, any info on the babynapping and murder in—"

"You're stealing my thunder, little that I've got," interrupted Martin.

The black-haired waiter brought her *chocolat chaud*. Sometimes she thought he was mute. The windows overlooking the side street were speckled with raindrops.

Martin waited until she'd taken a sip.

"I heard Loo Frères were on the scene," she prompted him.

"*Mais non*, this is how rumors start." He tsked, exhaling a plume of smoke. "Loo Frères issued a total denial. Expressed horror that their patch was used as a dumping site. This brought unwanted attention to the quartier. They don't tolerate outsiders on their turf. They'd be the first to turn the culprits over."

"You believe them, Martin?"

A nod. She hated when his large glasses reflected the light and she couldn't see his eyes.

"I know someone from the Hand's calling the shots. My friend's baby was abducted when she was wearing the wonderful hoodie you gave Chloé."

Expressionless, Martin took a drag. "You think it's to do with *l'hoodie?*"

"They knew Chloé had one, Martin," she said. She waited, but he didn't respond. "You live by a code, honor your word; that's what Papa said. But there must be something you can tell me."

His voice low, Martin said, "There's a whisper in the wind about a contract out on you, Mademoiselle Aimée."

Her heart jumped. "Does it have anything to do with a former *flic*, Dandin? Or the fixer?"

With a quick sleight of hand, he'd slipped his Gauloise packet into her bag, which was sitting on the banquette.

"Ah, my next appointment's here, Mademoiselle Aimée."

The signal to leave.

Martin nodded goodbye. "Go outside with my friend the taxi driver."

Thursday, Midnight

IN HER OFFICE at *brigade des mineurs*, Madame Nadine Pelletier donned her readers and studied the latest updates. As a recent grandmother at the ripe old age of forty-five, she felt this case already getting under her skin and a worming sense of dread.

Nothing could or should be allowed to dull her edge. She breathed her work, loved what she did. Her boss had offered to recommend her for a high admin post. She'd toyed with that idea for all of two seconds.

She took a moment now to inhale, gathered that analytical part of her brain and her essential optimism to focus on the bright side. The baby had been found—she was alive and well. In the heartbreaking world of crimes against children, this was a success.

Yet something didn't add up. She flicked through the statements again. Almost against her will, her fingers went to her neck, to the spot where she'd had to have a mole removed. A terrible habit, picking it like a scab when trouble knocked on her door. Like now, as her boss stepped into her office, tossing tinfoil from Nicorette gum into the bin. He half smiled and chewed furiously.

"What's with the rumors flying around?" he asked.

Not even an acknowledgement she'd postponed her *vacances*. "Rumors?"

"Marc Durand, the hotshot *fonctionnaire*, is being accused of kidnapping his *bébé* from his ex?"

She shook her head. "You know, and I know, it's too early—"

He interrupted her. "I need this cleaned up fast. He's breathing down my neck."

"How's that possible?" she asked, surprised. "We're questioning him right now. His ex-wife, Noémi, says he threatened her."

"My phone won't stop ringing. His family—"

"He's connected, eh?"

"More than connected. He's in the ministry, for God's sake."

She'd jumped off a train to grab an investigative handle that got greasier and greasier by the minute. "I'm reviewing each statement carefully." She looked pointedly at the wall clock. "I hope to finish sometime tonight."

Her boss chewed, looking out her window onto the quai de Gesvres, at the soot-stained Conciergerie's walls and the silver mercury of the Seine under storm clouds.

"What have you got so far?" he asked.

She picked up a file. "We've identified the victim as Ria Girond, twenty-four, no fixed address. The hospital intake nurse confirmed she'd been referred by Emmaus. The hospital accepted her right away since she was in a program. She'd suffered from complications after a recent D&C."

Her boss paused. "So a botched abortion? Postpartum?"

Weren't back-alley abortions a thing of the past? Clinics offered safe and sanitary conditions. "It's more complicated than that."

"Chemical addictions?"

"Alcohol. Suspected fetal alcohol syndrome."

"How do you make that leap?"

"Officers interviewed several women in the shelter's dormitory. No grass under their feet, sir." She handed her boss the evidence bag with franc notes inside. "Discovered under Ria Girond's bunk bed mattress. I'm sending them to the lab to see if they're counterfeit."

Payment for a snatch and grab, to her thinking. But she'd let her boss put it together. Let him think it was his idea.

"Interesting." Her boss seemed lost in thought. "What about the Twingo?"

"So far we've identified the vehicle owner, a Paul Vitry, who works as a legal documents messenger."

An entry-level job often given to parolees.

"We're checking his latest movements," she said. "If he was on parole and stayed at the men's shelter. We'll find him."

He unwrapped another Nicorette gum. "What's the ground status report?"

She read from her checklist. "So far we've got officers checking a squat, interviewing more late-shift staff at the women's shelter. Got a unit canvassing the streets, another collating door-to-door reports by the homicide site. My team's on overtime questioning the mothers from *bébé* swim, the swim team, lifeguards."

"Or," said her boss said, spitting his gum into a trash can, "we'll catch the murderer the way we usually do—while he's running a red light or committing some other crime."

Since when had he gotten so jaded?

Her boss's phone rang. He glanced at it. "I've got to take this."

After he left there was a knock on her open door. A tech with even more reports.

"Just in from the lab, Madame *le Commandant.*"

The one she'd been waiting for.

Madame Pelletier compared the half-melted hospital ID bracelet to the high-resolution magnified photo from the memory card from Aimée's camera.

"A match," she said, "good job." She looked up at the *brigade des mineurs* tech and smiled in approval. Next to him stood a young *flic*, thin and dark haired.

"Milo Barres, Madame *le Commandant*," he said. "From the *commissariat* at Place d'Italie. You wanted to see me?"

The rookie *flic* rocked on his heels. Nervous. Not much older than her daughter. He could be her son. She'd beaten the cobbles like him once.

"*Merci* for coming," she said. He was the one who'd found the burned-out Twingo. "I read your file."

Alarm fluttered in his eyes.

She assumed a motherly expression. "I read the files of everyone who works on my investigations. Do we know anything more about the Twingo's torching?"

"*Oui, Madame le Commandant.*"

Eager, he pulled out his notebook. Her team were trained pros, but she knew from experience it always paid to involve the local *flics*. Observant *flics* who knew their *terroir*—the habitués, repeat offenders, junkies, who'd talk.

"The concierge at 51 rue de Domrémy, in the quartier Jeanne d'Arc, smelled smoke and noticed flames at five-fifteen," he said. "She called the fire department. But according to bystanders—"

"Bystanders?" she interrupted.

"A Paul Anglin and his younger brother Mathieu, who live down the street."

"Go on."

"They noticed the Twingo there as they were coming home from school. Putting it there approximately twenty minutes before."

She nodded to give him encouragement. "You trust those boys?"

He shrugged. "I know their grandmother. They're good kids."

"So let me pick your brain since it's your patch. You grew up there, didn't you?"

He rocked again on his heels, which made a rubbery sound on her floor. "My cousin did," he said. "But I know it like the back of my hand. My aunt watched me after school. Now I live near Bastille because I don't shit where I eat." He looked down. "*Excusez-moi* for the language."

"Sounds like you know where crime happens. Why don't you show me on the map?"

He grew voluble now. Pointed to a spot on her map of the thirteenth. "Crimewise, it's mainly burglaries here near the abduction site and around Butte-aux-Cailles." He ran his finger down to the Periphérique. "Around Porte d'Ivry, it's lowlifes running scams. Over in the section surrounding Porte d'Italie, we're called to purse snatchings. By rue Watt, it's a homicide dumping ground. Here by Place Nationale, it's small-time drug dealing." His finger stopped. "But Chinatown's quiet; they police their own."

"Can you come up with a scenario? You know, thoughts about where this victim could have been headed?"

"You're asking, where would I go if I kidnapped a baby?"

"Wouldn't the kidnapper, in theory, need a place to hide, to lay low?"

"My bet's the abandoned rail tracks and tunnels of la Petite Ceinture."

"Show me."

He pointed to a spot on the map. "You could hide a baby there, if you knew where you were going. There are down-and-outers who live there. They keep to themselves."

She studied the map, concentrated on la Petite Ceinture, the abandoned rail track and its tunnels. Wouldn't it make sense to pull a unit to search there for Ria Girond's accomplice—assuming it was Paul Vitry, the Twingo driver?

Again, that unease overtook her. She looked at the copy of

the photo Aimée Leduc had given her, the baby playing in the sandbox in a red hoodie.

Had they picked up the wrong baby, botched the job? Had Paul Vitry murdered Ria Girond to keep her mouth shut?

Who the hell had hired them?

"*Merci, Barres,*" she said, in dismissal.

He turned to go. Paused at the door. "Madame, my partner took the statement from the young woman who called the incident in."

"Ah yes, Vaddey Mang. I read her statement."

"The woman refuses to leave. She's afraid."

Madame Pelletier thumbed through the reports on her desk. "Afraid of whom?"

"She wouldn't say."

Of course not.

"Look where she lives," Madame Pelletier said. "It's right here in her statement. I hope you know what to do."

He looked nonplussed. "Escort her home?"

She tsked, shook her head. Talk about wet behind the ears. But ripe with potential.

"In your file, Barres, it spoke of your future aspirations to make detective in the *brigade criminelle.*"

His shoulders straightened. "*Oui, Madame le Commandant.*"

"Then here's an early Christmas present." She handed him Vaddey Mang's folder. He blinked. "*Et alors,* turn Vaddey Mang into your informant. She's come this far. Risked giving a statement. This is your chance; use it. Wouldn't you like to be *the only flic* with a Chinatown informer? A real connection?"

He stood at attention, understanding in his eyes. "Should I give her a burner phone and send her home in a taxi?"

"*Et voilà,* now you're thinking," she said with a little smile. "Gain her trust. Cultivate a relationship. Start by signing her up for an evening class. Get her a student card, and go back to school with her. That's where you can meet, and no one's the wiser. It gives her an excuse and cover. Start there, and think long term."

His face glowed. She could almost hear the wheels turning in his brain.

"For incidentals," she said, palming him a hundred-franc note. "Repay me when you make *le crim.*"

"*Merci, Madame le Commandant.*"

Her boss entered and motioned the rookie out.

After Barres had left, he closed the door.

Never a good sign.

"We're going quiet on this," he said.

Startled, she paused by the map. "I don't understand."

"I think you do. The homicide victim, a homeless alcoholic, suffered complications from a D&C, was released from the hospital, and snatched a baby. Her boyfriend, a Paul Vitry, whose body we discovered in the morgue half an hour ago, owned a Twingo, which they used to get away."

Where had this come from? "Half an hour ago?" She shuffled through her files. "Why wasn't I informed?" Her pulse raced. "How does that solve who killed Ria Girond? Or this Vitry, for that matter? Who hired them to abduct a baby?"

"Back-burner time. Refer to this as an ongoing investigation . . . the usual."

Anger boiled inside her. "My job's to investigate an abduction of a juvenile—"

"Your job's to conclude the active investigation. Word's come down, and that's the way this ball rolls. *Comprends?*"

Her shoulders tensed. "Who's rolling this ball?"

"Higher pay grades than either of us."

Thursday, After Midnight

TRUE TO MARTIN'S word, a G7 Taxi waited outside, parking lights on, engine purring. Puddles glimmered on the Champs-Élysée's pavement under the fingernail moon. The air was clear and biting, freshened by the storm.

"You're Monsieur Martin's client, *c'est ça?*" said the taxi driver, a young woman wearing a headscarf.

"That's right," Aimée said, checking her phone. No word from Melac. "Where are we going?"

"I believe you have information that explains." She smiled. A warm, crooked grin. "Please sit back and enjoy the ride."

In other words, shut up, and read whatever Martin had slipped in the Gauloise packet. She pulled out a red ticket stub. On the back was written, *Always forgive your enemies—nothing annoys them so much.*

An Oscar Wilde quote—what did that mean?

Under it a string of alphanumeric script. A code.

Curiouser and curiouser.

The taxi let her off in front of an arching black wrought-iron gate, VILLA DE PORT-ROYAL lettered on top. She entered the alphanumeric code as the red lights of the taxi faded in the night. The small, rain-streaked door on the right buzzed open. She found herself in a narrow, damp passage opening to a court-yard redolent with night-blooming jasmine. As quiet as a grave, she thought. She shuddered.

A diffuse yellow glow showed behind the etched glass double doors of a townhouse. A knock brought a broad-shouldered, white-uniformed nurse to the door.

"He's tired tonight," she said without any greeting. She was middle-aged, with wide-set eyes. "Please keep it short." She spoke in an even tone with an accent. "This way."

Unsure where she was headed, Aimée followed her into a ground floor corridor and then into a master suite. A cloying warmth came from portable heaters running at full blast.

Another nurse, young and blonde, checked the IV drip of an ancient man lying in a hospital bed. His sunken face, flecked with brown age spots, didn't diminish the twinkle in his eyes. Aimée watched his long fingers reaching out to pinch the young nurse's bottom.

"Behave, Monsieur Chopard," she said in a bored tone. German, based on the roll of the r's.

Maybe she was paid to ignore. Maybe he was harmless.

Aimée doubted the latter. She committed Chopard's name to memory.

The nurse pulled up a chair for Aimée, then with quiet steps exited and shut the door. A click. Antiseptic odors mingled with the old-man smell in the baroque-style suite.

"You're not a nurse," he said. His voice came out dry, rasping, and caked by years of nicotine.

"True," she said. "You're up late."

"Sleep? I'm lucky to get three hours."

"Martin sent me. I'm Aimée Leduc."

The blue irises of his eyes, clear for his age, bored into her. A scrutiny that made her squirm.

"Ah, such an unfortunate series of events," he said at last.

She looked at this shrunken old man and knew the truth. Her

stomach churned. "You're part of the Hand," she said in what came out a whisper.

He didn't deny it. Smiled. Reached up to moisten his lips with a damp washcloth. She noticed his thick-ridged fingernails.

"Do you have it?" he asked. "*Non*, of course you don't. Not yet. But you want Léo Solomon's silly notebook as much as I do."

The old man's crepe-lidded eyes, piercing and sunken in his face, studied her. A thin nest of silver hair crowned his skull.

"You're going to find it. A matter of time." His sigh rattled in his throat. "Don't screw it up with a high body count."

She'd play along. "Like the others have?" She slid her hand into her bag, and her fingers closed around her makeup compact.

"If only people listened to me . . ." Another rattling sigh. "*Alors*, I don't handle day-to-day operations now. I'm ninety-one, had to quit that last year."

Quit running the empire he and his cohorts had built, which would keep functioning as long as others did the dirty work. She'd had enough.

"Call me stubborn," she said, "but if I take the chances, I do it my way."

Choking sounds; then a fit of coughing overtook him. Good God, was he going to choke to death in front of her? Couldn't she wring his neck first? But the hideous sounds subsided into laughter.

"Mademoiselle Leduc, such a chip off the old block. But ancient history doesn't concern me."

She snorted. "*Au contraire*. Léo Solomon's notebook seems so juicy and incriminating you're killing for it."

A cocktail of drugs and painkillers sat on his bedside table next to rubbing alcohol and lanolin lotion for bedsores.

"Prove it," he said.

"If I find it, what's in it for me?"

"We're very generous. Your father understood."

"I don't think so. You murdered him."

"Crossed wires. An accident. So regrettable."

That was all he could say?

"Seems you don't like loose ends," she said.

"Please, mademoiselle, don't take this the wrong way."

"You tried to kidnap my child."

No one got away with that.

"A mistake," he said. "We want to work with you."

Like she believed that? Once he had the notebook, she'd be the one with a pair of scissors in her neck.

But she had to understand how it all connected.

"You were in the POW camp with Léo and Pierre," she said. "That's the bond among all of you."

"Ah, we radicalized behind barbwire before it became fashionable. Kids today think they're the first."

Radicalized?

"We struggled to survive in the stalag, returned home to no jobs, rationing. So we used the skills we learned in the camp; the Nazis were good teachers. We vowed never to go hungry or so cold again, stuck together, and survived."

That was how he justified cheating, lying, and extorting money. But for once, she'd act smart. Grit her teeth.

"I'm a realist, Monsieur Chopard. What's generous to you?"

"Ah, très efficace, mademoiselle. Who has time to haggle?"

He didn't have much, judging by the cardiac monitor's erratic blips.

"Name your price," said Chopard. "Want to supervise the ministry's computer security division? Or do you prefer the private sector? And I'll throw in stocks, a seat on our board, as we like to call it—a shareholder position."

She cringed inside. So that was how he enticed the next generation, infused new blood. Money was the universal language. This shrunken old relic had hired troops, signed checks. The old man's life was ebbing, so he'd farmed out the evil. A withered root whose tree branched and flowered. She wanted the names of the foot soldiers and brains of the next generation.

"Why me?" she asked.

"You get results, mademoiselle. Better we're on the same side."

"Same side?"

"It's business."

That was what he called it? She wanted to spit. "I don't play well with others and make a point of knowing who I do business with."

"Furnish the notebook, and I'll introduce you to the board."

As if that would happen. Lying, cheating, stealing, murder, all in the course of a working day. For two centimes, she'd pour the bottle of rubbing alcohol into his IV.

Instead, she leaned forward and looked him in the eye. "I want your goons called off." As she spoke, she surreptitiously took René's latest toy, a centime-sized listening bug, from her makeup case and stuck it on the metal bar under his hospital bed.

"*D'accord.* You'll receive an envelope on your way out. And *picaillons* for your pocket."

The old country term for chump change. She hadn't heard anyone use it since her grandfather. And she didn't come cheap. This man couldn't afford her.

She stood. So hot—she couldn't stand this suffocating heat.

Another rattling sigh. The old man reached for the needle in his wrist where the IV dripped.

"Don't scratch," she said.

"Call the nurse."

So he could grope her?

"Morphine. More morphine."

Aimée nodded. "It's time to forget the past. Move on. So I'm forgiving you."

"I don't want your forgiveness." He grimaced in pain as if a knife were gutting him.

"It's included in our agreement."

A lie, but she enjoyed his discomposure.

"*Il fait un froid de canard*," he said. It's as cold as a duck. She'd heard the expression—it was used for the weather at the onset of duck hunting season.

"No, monsieur, you're too early," she said to him. "Hunting season doesn't start until the ice freezes."

"Ah, *mais oui*, your *bébé*'s with her *grand-mère* in Brittany. For me, the season's started. It always pays to keep game in one's crosshairs."

Aimée stiffened. "What do you mean?"

"Your mother, *la terroriste*, sings for the highest bidder."

Had Sydney taken Chloé to make sure Aimée would hand over the notebook? Ensure she'd cooperate with the Hand? No, there was no way. Even after everything her mother had done, she would never hurt Chloé.

Hadn't Sydney said Aimée would hear lies? Her insides twisted.

"I don't believe you," she said.

"It's insurance. Bring me the notebook."

The door opened. A man in a green loden jacket beckoned her. As she was ushered out, someone else was ushered into the room behind her. The door was shut before she could catch a glimpse of who it was.

Her knees trembled.

In the entryway the green-jacketed man handed her an

envelope. "Perform your duty." He had a thick German accent. "We'll be watching."

He gripped her arm—no way for her to double back and spy. He hit the buzzer, escorted her to the sidewalk. Disappeared back into the Villa de Port-Royal.

The fear she'd been holding at bay invaded her mind. She thought of Chloé's sweet face, a blind panic settling over her senses. Breathing hard, she punched in Melac's number.

A recording answered saying that the number had been disconnected.

What could she do? Chopard had her *bébé*, wherever she was, in his sights. The Hand's tentacles spread like a choking net.

Answers. She needed answers. Punched in Morbier's number.

She wanted him to tell her it wasn't true. That her mother wouldn't work for the highest bidder—that Chloé was safe.

"I want to know where Chloé is, Morbier."

"Why would you think . . . ? Isn't she home with you?"

Clicking sounds.

His line was bugged.

She hung up. No doubt she was being watched.

Hurrying, she ducked into a bistro several doors down, pretended to be waiting for a friend. Checked the time and activated the listening bug by pressing the button in her makeup kit. Counted to three and dropped a fifty-franc note from the envelope she'd been given on the mosaic tiled floor. A moment later she motioned to the waiter. "I think someone at that table dropped this."

"*Merci, mademoiselle*," he said, picking it up.

Clutching the note, he asked clients at a large table if it was theirs, and soon other gazes were attracted to the note. When heads were turned, she took the nearest trench coat off the coatrack without being noticed.

In the small space behind the velvet draft curtains ringing the door, she slid her arms into the coat. An Isabel Marant, chic, only a wine stain on the cuff. Found a knit cap in the pocket. Seconds later, with a new look, she glided out and dipped into the Métro. Ran and caught the last train of the night.

Friday Morning

AN INSISTENT BUZZING pulled Aimée from a nightmare of chasing a stroller down a long dark corridor . . . only to find the stroller empty, Chloé gone. She sat bolt upright. Her face was wet, her hair damp and matted. She'd been crying in her sleep.

No Chloé, a strange apartment, a cold fear filling her. Was her baby safe? She hated being apart from her this long.

She tried to remember where she was. Dawn light filtered through balcony doors over the white couch she'd slept on, the hanging plants, the Moroccan rugs, the high ceiling, and the carved woodwork.

Then she remembered the previous night. Remembered coming here to Martine's colleague's apartment on Boulevard Auguste Blanqui. Tossing and turning all night.

Her phone was buzzing.

René's number.

"Delivery."

The apartment overlooked an L-shaped courtyard full of linden trees with their yellow-green flush of autumn coloring. Below, a watchmaker, one of the few left in the quartier, stood in his leather apron behind his shop, smoking.

She opened the door to René and Maxence, who was carrying a large bag. Aimée smelled coffee and buttery brioches. René cleared space on the table.

"Not bad," said René, surveying the high-ceilinged nineteenth-century Haussmannian interior. "Martine's friend's an aristo?"

"Journalist at *Le Monde diplo*, René," she said.

"So you're watering the plants for *une bobo* with a trust fund."

"Did anyone follow you?" She tore a warm nub of a brioche, cupped her palm to catch flaking crust before it fell on her laptop. She hadn't realized how hungry she was.

"We had the taxi circle the block twice," said Maxence, "got out behind the garbage truck." He crinkled his nose. "Fragrant, too."

"I hope you got everything I asked for," she said.

René nodded, opening the lid of a coffee cup. "Even the uniform, and don't ask me how," he said.

From the corner of her eye, she saw René swallow a pill with his coffee. She felt a guilty pang. She'd been so caught up, so selfish, she'd forgotten about his appointment with the heart specialist, the one he'd lied to her about.

"What's wrong, René?" she asked.

"What's wrong with what?"

"I mean, why are you hiding your visit to the cardiologist?"

Maxence looked up in surprise.

"Since when is that your business?" Angry, René slapped down the coffee cup, spilling hot brown foam. He used his monogrammed handkerchief to swipe up the mess.

"Since you're my best friend," she said, her eyes brimming. "And I don't know what I'd do without you."

"Chloé's who you need to concentrate on. To keep safe."

"Answer my question, René."

"I'll say it once. No more. Every few years my ticker acts up due to the rheumatic fever I had as a child. Medicine controls it." He pulled out his laptop. "Now can we get to your wild-goose chase of a plan?"

She and Maxence shared a look. Discussion closed.

She had to focus, concentrate. Believe Chloé was safe.

Trust. Trust her mother for now. Trust Melac.

Otherwise she'd fall apart. Be no good to her daughter.

Now for the plan she'd concocted with René. He clucked his tongue, shook his head.

"Won't know until I try," she said.

"*Alors*, tell me more about this Chopard 'hiring' you to bring him the notebook," René said.

"That vampire? Cut off his head, and he'd grow three more." Her fingers drummed the table. "He says my . . . mother . . ." It still felt strange to say. "That he's paying her off to keep Chloé as insurance."

"I wouldn't put it past her," said René, handing her a telegram. "But this came from Melac."

Arrived safe.

She sighed with relief.

"I like Martine's theory that she's CIA," said Maxence, occupied with hooking up the phone line and router. There was humming, intermittent beeps. Maxence set down sheets of paper covered by numbers and small red stars.

What in the world?

She watched as Maxence organized the sheets and taped them together. On his knees, he removed a bulky black-and-silver box that reminded her of an old radio transceiver from the bag. Maxence slid open the window facing the courtyard. Reached on his tiptoes in his scuffed Beatle boots and set an antenna in a flowerpot of red geraniums.

"*Voilà*," he said, coming back to the table. What a geek he was. And only eighteen. Like poor Marcus.

"Tell me how it works," Aimée said.

Maxence swiped his bangs from his forehead. "I tapped the

throwaway mobile. Used a base station emulator," he said, his Québécois accent more pronounced in his earnestness.

"A spirit catcher," René chimed in.

"They're expensive," Maxence said. "I borrowed my friend's uncle's. This spoofs the cell tower operations, so the *flics* can gather any private data they want without a warrant or you even knowing it . . ."

"Aah, an IMSI-catcher," Aimée said. "Do those ever work?"

"If used correctly." Maxence shrugged. "It pretends to be a legitimate base station on the mobile phone network and tricks the phone into routing its call via the base station emulator, where the data can be decrypted."

"Meanwhile, the IMSI-catcher passes the call on to the network, so the suspect has no idea they're being monitored." Maxence studied the sheets. "Given the time of the calls to the burner phone, the caller was . . ." He paused and superimposed a map of Paris on transparent tracing paper over the sheets. Drew a circle. "In the thirteenth arrondissement between the quai d'Austerlitz and the quai François Mauriac."

"Amazing. But that was yesterday," she said. "Wouldn't the caller keep switching phones?"

"*Bien sûr*," Maxence said. "But as long as you're contacted on the same burner, the system works. It operates on the same principal, RDF—radio direction finding—that the Nazis used to find clandestine radio operators in Paris. That was passive, though— they could only listen. But base station emulators can manipulate."

The stuff this kid knew.

"How does this get us closer to the notebook?" she asked.

But Aimée never heard the answer. The burner phone delivered to her apartment the previous night rang. Maxence adjusted the antenna, nodded for her to answer.

"*Oui?*"

"The person you visited died last night," said the robotic voice.

"You mean Chopard?"

"Naughty girl, installing a bug. But the deal remains the same."

Stupid. Last night no signal had ever been emitted—it had been found right away.

Maxence motioned for her to keep talking.

"Wait—" she started to say.

The phone went dead.

Maxence fiddled with the machine. "I've got to regraph and decipher coordinates."

How long would that take? An hour? Two? She didn't have time to wait.

She had to find the notebook. Where could she even begin looking?

And then she saw a voice mail. It was from Gaëlle, Besson's assistant. Why hadn't she noticed it the night before?

"Meet me at the office."

With Maxence busy with equations and René on their project, she jumped in the shower. Toweling off, she scanned Martine's friend's bursting armoire. The journalist favored vintage and classic, a woman after Aimée's own heart. And size.

Slipping into a man's crisp white shirt and a vintage Ungaro black silk-lined pantsuit, she packed up what René had brought. Donned the chic trench. One her mother would approve of—silly how that bothered her.

Two minutes later she was out the door.

IT WAS MARKET day on Boulevard Auguste Blanqui. Shoppers with string bags bustled among booths of seasonal vegetables and the Reinette apples Chloé loved, just in season; a fishmonger shouted, "*Moules* by the kilo!" and the cheese seller's apron was stained with runny yellow Brie. Aimée wove between crowded market stalls, alert in case she had a tail. Satisfied, for now, that no one was following her, she hurried up the two long blocks to Besson's office on Boulevard Arago.

When Aimée arrived, Gaëlle was in deep conversation with another partner, all allure and innocence, fawning on the partner until he'd disappeared into the next office and closed the door.

She turned to Aimée, her black eyes hard and red lips tight.

"Éric's not coming back," she said, almost spitting the words. "He's left me to close up his office, transfer clients. But that's not why I called you. There was a message for you on the office voice mail."

"A message?"

"Marcus stashed the item."

She already knew that. "Where?"

"She didn't say. That was the whole message she left on the answering machine."

Aimée wanted to scream with frustration. It had been weeks—no doubt the notebook was long gone by now anyway. "Wait, she who?"

"A girl."

What girl? "Karine?"

"I don't know. She didn't leave a name."

"Why didn't you tell me before?"

A shrug. "I only heard the message last night."

Lili.

"She had a little bit of an accent. She said the hiding place was mysterious, but she didn't say where it was. She said, 'Tell the detective,' that you'd understand."

She would? She hadn't even known Marcus or anything about him. What was she supposed to understand?

"Do you still have the message?" Aimée asked. "Can I hear the exact words?"

Gaëlle, efficient as always, found the message in no time and played it for Aimée.

Lili's voice: "Marcus stashed the item. Tell the detective the hiding place is mystic. She will understand."

"The hiding place is mystic," Aimée repeated. "Not mysterious." Could she mean Miss Tyk, the graffiti artist?

Aimée would find out.

"Marcus lived upstairs, correct?" she said. "I need the keys."

Gaëlle found them on an old-fashioned key ring. "No one's touched the apartment since the *flics*, but I'm having movers come in today. Donating everything."

"What about his mother?"

"I told you before she's unstable. *Et alors*, that's Éric's job. After she was hospitalized, Marcus was alone. Éric tried to help him, but I wouldn't call Éric father material. Or nominate him as a role model."

From her expression, it looked as if she knew from experience.

Surprised, Aimée said, "What do you mean?" Éric had always seemed like the overachiever, detail oriented and conscientious.

"This office looks impressive, *non*? But he's leveraged his assets to the hilt."

Before Aimée could ask if that was related to the divorce, Gaëlle answered the ringing phone.

The back servant's stairs, narrow and winding, led to a converted attic room with a sloping ceiling and a mansard window overlooking rooftops. Faded, old-fashioned blue floral wallpaper; mismatched chairs; a mattress on the floor; dirty socks cluttering the duvet; posters on the walls; and a shelf of thin graphic novels—a typical adolescent boy's room. Except the posters, she realized, were high-end prints by tag artists who showed in galleries. Expensive.

Like the ones at Demy's foundation award ceremony.

She recognized one, a busty Parisienne in biker leathers—she'd seen others in the same vein painted on walls all over the quartier in Butte-aux-Cailles. Miss Tyk had a signature style, a black stenciled figure paired with a line of *poésie* or a pun.

She punched in Demy's number.

"Aimée, is everything okay? Xavier has been asking about you."

Heat rose to her cheeks. She'd never gotten back to him about the wine tasting.

"Busy, like always, working on your website," she said, stretching the truth. "Off the top of your head, where are the Miss Tyk creations painted?"

She jotted their locations down in her red Moleskine. On the opposite page was her grocery list, and tears welled in her eyes when she saw *formula* and *diapers*. How she missed Chloé.

No time for that now. She had a notebook to find.

"*Merci, Demy.*"

She took the Miss Tyk print off the faded wallpaper, which tore. She rolled up the print. Time to track down the original.

DRESSED IN A black wig, glasses, and a crisp nurse's uniform, complete with white cap, she knocked on the front door.

"*Entrez.* It's open."

Careless again.

Morbier looked up from his wheelchair in the kitchen, motioned toward the ceiling with a disgusted expression. Warning her the house was bugged.

"It's time for some outdoor therapy, monsieur."

She released the wheelchair's brakes and rolled him over the stylish hardwood. She handed him a pair of sunglasses and a cloth cap, then pushed him out of the house.

"Talk about gaining weight, Morbier," she muttered in his ear.

"Kidnapping me, Leduc?"

She was huffing and puffing. Pushing him up the hill was harder work than she had expected. "Your phone's bugged."

Morbier nodded. "My house, too. Where's Chloé?"

"Remember telegrams? Melac sent me one this morning. They arrived, but I don't know where."

He put his hand up to ward off questions. "It's better you don't know."

Better she didn't know? She bit back a reply.

"Who's the Hand's fixer?"

"I would have taken care of him if I knew . . ." He left the rest unsaid.

"*Mais alors*, you mean he's a hired assassin," she said, taking a guess. "Is someone using the dead petty thief Charles Siganne's persona?"

"That urban myth?"

"Dandin, the retired *flic* with big ears, mentioned someone's son."

"Dandin got snuffed out last night."

"I know. Those were his last words."

Morbier expelled air. "How in God's name did you get involved?"

"I'll get uninvolved when I find this damn notebook."

Morbier scanned the street. Pointed to a corner in the shade of a plane tree. She pushed him under the dappled shadow and set the brake.

"As a *flic*, I learned to leave something alone if word came down, keep certain things to myself."

Aimée scratched her neck. Wished she'd worn a different black wig. "Why does this sound like the beginning of an excuse?"

"Leduc, it's like any job. You have to know whom to trust."

"Don't *flics* trust each other, have each other's backs?"

"You trust your partner. That's a bond for life. *Alors*, like any place, it can be a minefield if you don't know who wields power, who gets things done for you . . ."

"Politics," she said, pulled out a Gauloise from Martin's pack and toyed with it. If ever she needed a smoke it was now. "What are you trying to say, Morbier?"

"Your papa and I were told to turn a blind eye, ignore a report, put a suspect on the X list to use or turn them later. We weren't the only ones—the ambitious ones made it up the ladder, got the promotion. You couldn't ever really leave."

She didn't want to hear this. "Papa tried." It sounded feeble even to her.

Morbier's eyes were distant. Somewhere else. "Your father had one last job; he'd told them that was it. They weren't going to let him leave. I couldn't stop them from doing what they did. I was too late. That's why I couldn't face you for a long time."

Could she believe him?

"In the past ten years, the Hand's gone deep, spawned a new generation. They assumed this ancient history got destroyed."

Aimée released the hand brake. "I gathered that. Politicians, judges, all the people who've had dealings with them, taken bribes, pushed legislation their way—they don't want it coming out."

"An octogenarian's scribbled notes won't bring them down."

From the get-go, he'd wanted her to give this up. Afraid of what she'd discover about him? Or did he think that even if she found the damn thing it wouldn't make any difference? Right then she didn't care. She needed his help.

"Funny, last night Chopard attempted to hire me to find it."

"That old bastard?" She could count on one hand how many times she'd seen Morbier surprised. This was one of them.

"Chopard suggested Sydney, my own mother, had taken Chloé as a hostage until I complied."

"Sydney's not in his pocket, Leduc." He shook his head. "I can't believe that bastard's still alive."

"He was until this morning," she said. "The notebook bothered the Hand enough that they tortured a teenage boy to death to get it and then killed his girlfriend when she had no information. Then they made an abduction attempt on Chloé." She handed him the print. "Unroll it. We're looking for the original some-where on rue des Cinq Diamants."

"So we're on an art walk to look at the same graffiti I used to nail kids for spraying on the walls?"

"C'est ça."

"Why? How will this connect to the notebook?"

"Go with the program, Morbier. Keep your eyes peeled."

En route, puffing up the rue du Moulin des Prés, which stretched down to la Petite Ceinture, she caught him up on her meeting with the vampire Chopard.

"But you knew Chopard, non?" she said.

"By reputation. Met him once; that was enough."

She breathed hard as she pushed the wheelchair up the steep cobbled streets of the quartier of Butte-aux-Cailles, where street art decorated walls, nooks, and unsuspecting crannies. On the low wall opposite the hotel, she saw it—the Miss Tyk graffiti of a busty Parisi-enne, a life-sized spray-painted figure surrounded by hanging plants. The ingenious artwork even incorporated the ventilation grate.

She remembered seeing this from the hotel room where Marcus had died.

"*Et alors*, now what?" Morbier asked.

"Imagine you're eighteen years old and your girlfriend is waiting under the duvet in that hotel room." She pointed at the hotel on Cinq Diamants. "You want to get under that duvet, but first you've got a hot potato to hide." She realized they weren't alone—a dark-complected bearded man was standing at the corner, an orange scarf knotted around his neck. "There's a *mec* watching us."

To her surprise, Morbier waved. "Ahmed, you lying raccoon, you said you'd visit me."

One of Morbier's old friends or informants?

"As Allah is my witness, I tried, but your battle-ax of a nurse shooed me away." Ahmed smiled. "Who is this beautiful mademoiselle?"

"Got any mint tea on the boil?" Morbier asked.

"*Bien sûr*," he said.

A moment later they were in the back of Ahmed's small shop by a heater with an enamel pot of water boiling on top.

"You like my sister-in-law's manicure?" said Ahmed, pointing to Aimée's lacquered nails.

Aimée blinked.

He laughed at her expression as he poured mint tea into tiny gold filigree glasses. "In our quartier, everyone knows everything. We watch out for each other. Help our neighbors."

Then maybe he could help with Miss Tyk.

"Ahmed's grandfather ran this shop and the hotel before the war," said Morbier, growing voluble over the sweet mint tea. "The family still does." He turned to Ahmed. "He's still working, your *grand-père*?"

"Retired like you."

"Types like us never retire; we just fade away."

Fat chance.

"What are you looking for?" asked Ahmed.

"A hiding place close to Miss Tyk," Aimée said. "Somewhere you could stash something on the fly."

"Why didn't you say so? But we'll need a screwdriver."

Aimée pulled a miniscrewdriver from her Swiss Army knife.

"Who carries a screwdriver besides a handyman?"

"*Moi.*"

Morbier watched the street as Aimée and Ahmed crossed to the graffitied wall. Aimée unscrewed the metal grate covering the stilettos on Miss Tyk's creation. Searched inside the small duct space.

Nothing.

"Do you know specifically what you are seeking?" asked Ahmed.

Aimée shook her head. "Not exactly. A notebook, a sheaf of papers, a journal. Something that would fit in a backpack easily."

"Ah, if that's what you're looking for . . ." He reached up and felt behind a rectangular planter. Nothing.

He motioned for the screwdriver and started unscrewing a plaque next to the planter . . . which fell off onto the pavement. He reached inside and pulled.

Handed her a plastic Monoprix bag containing a notebook bound up with twine.

Friday Morning

TWO FIGURES STOOD in the bronze morning light in front of the mausoleum in Cimetière de Gentilly. Their conversation was nearly inaudible over the constant traffic from the Périphérique, the highway ringing Paris built on the site of the nineteenth-century defensive wall.

The tall man held yellow chrysanthemums, the de rigueur bouquet for the dead. A depressing place, Éric thought, desolate, abandoned houses of the dead, the stones weathered and worn. Here and there, a tomb displayed a photo on enamel, a face long forgotten and the grave unkempt. The bust of the famous Zouave soldier glowed dully from atop his grave.

Desolate, Éric thought, but peaceful, apart from the hideous, never-ending traffic. Downhill the eyesore high-rises poked up from near Place d'Italie. The land in between was scarred by derelict warehouses, manufacturers, and rail yards spreading from Gare d'Austerlitz. A no-go zone until the recent renovation projects.

"You know what to do," said the man holding the flowers. "You need to shut her up."

"Too late," said Éric. "Everything's spun out of control. You were supposed to scare Marcus. Not hurt him. Not kill him." Éric's throat caught. If only the kid had answered his phone. Éric had called him as soon as Léo had left the office; he'd tried to tell Marcus to bring the notebook back. Telling him to deliver the notebook was only supposed to have been for show so the old man would buzz off and Éric could make the handoff.

"You know what they say about the best-laid plans . . ."

"You botched it with the poor girl, who knew nothing." Pause. "I can't do this anymore. I'm out."

The other man kneeled and set the chrysanthemums in front of the mausoleum. Bowed his head.

"You say that like you have a choice. You don't, Éric. You tried to get out of your commitments once. Didn't work out well, did it?"

Éric had pulled out last year, lived clean until his divorce and debts crippled him.

"Don't tell me what I can or can't do," said Éric.

The tall man stood and smiled. "Unless you'd like to stay here."

"I'm your attorney," Éric said with more bravado than he felt. "You can't threaten me." Not in broad daylight with a hearse and funeral not far off. He wouldn't dare.

"I think I just did." He brushed the chalky dirt off his knees. "Your Normandy farmhouse, the pied-à-terre in London, those expensive gaming gadgets, your ex-wife's Yves Saint Laurent account, and her alimony," he said. "We pay that price for your cooperation. Do you want it all to go away?"

Éric's shoulders tightened. "The judge in the Brussels case refused to cooperate. So I offered him what you suggested."

"And were persuasive, I'm sure."

"*Alors*, I told him the consequences, but . . ."

The hearse was pulling away. The mourners were gone. Éric couldn't stop the shaking of his hand. But he was safe. They needed him too much.

A sigh. "Now you're a loose end."

Éric stepped back. "Loose end? There's only so much the judge can cover up within legal parameters."

Éric gasped when the blow came, at the sharpness tearing his insides. His eyes watered. This couldn't be happening. He tried to scream, but nothing came out. His lung was collapsing as blood filled his chest cavity. Pain radiated up his chest; he couldn't breathe; the gravestones before him clouded and spun.

Once the grilled door of the mausoleum was locked again, Éric's body inside, the fixer rearranged the chrysanthemums. Glanced at his vibrating phone. "Only one more loose end to take care of."

Friday, Late Morning

AIMÉE PERCHED ON the wobbly stool by the old printing press in the cellar of Ahmed's shop. Ahmed had told her that in this very cellar the Resistance had printed clandestine tracts encouraging sabotage against the Germans. Judging by the look of the press, she wouldn't have been surprised if the story was true, but then, a lot of places grew Resistance history over the years.

Regardless, it was an ideal location to pore over and interpret the old accountant's notebook. No one but a few old-timers knew of the existence of the cellar, accessible only by a ramp in the shop's backyard and with only a peach tabby the wiser.

The twine knotted around the old-fashioned blue notebook yielded, and Aimée donned latex gloves to turn the pages. Pasted with stiff yellowed glue to the inside cover was a black-and-white photo of a group of gaunt young men in ragged French army uniforms behind barbed wire. Over a hole in the ground by the ice-frosted fence was a sign: FLUCHT VERBOTEN; next to it, a smiling Wehrmacht *Kommandant* held a basket of spoons.

SHE'D PLANNED TO scan each page using the portable scanner Ahmed had lent her and then, only then, read it.

But Léo's confession, in small, concise handwriting in blue ink, intrigued her. What debt had he owed this Pierre? How did he rationalize the lifelong promise?

Frostbite and black toes landed me next to Pierre in the stalag's infirmary—if you could call it that—a few cots, Red Cross blankets, and dried mud sealing the window cracks against the howling sleet. Stale bread and turnips if we were lucky. All I ever thought about was Marie, mon cœur, and, if the war ever ended, how I'd put a ring on her finger. C'est fou, when I look back, but it was my idea to dig below Pierre's cot—to tunnel out and escape beyond the barbed wire. Eight of us dug for weeks with spoons, the only things we had. We had to be so careful. The Germans counted the spoons each night.

This was early in 1945, and the Soviets were approaching, but we didn't know that. I miscalculated—such an idiot. Our tunnel fell half a meter short of the fence—me, good with numbers, all my fault. The camp Kommandant knew Pierre was the stooge, demanded to know who was involved. Pierre said it was his idea, he'd put all of us up to it. Suspecting, the Kommandant chose me to make an example of—told me to run, so he could shoot me escaping, in accordance with the Geneva conventions. That's when Pierre insisted on taking the blame. L'amour trumped everything, he said; I must survive to go home to Marie. Demanded to be shot in my place. And he would have been the next morning but for the Soviet tanks. In the morning, the Wehrmacht were gone, only us POWs in the snow.

Pierre would have died to save me. I owed him my life. In Paris some years later, he asked me for a favor—to hide dirty money. That's how it started. Every so often he'd re-appear, like a bad centime, and ask a favor, then another. It made me sick, but he'd remind me of the stalag, that I'd come home to my Marie because of him. So true.

I've kept on paying for the rest of my life. Ma chère Marie knew nothing. She was innocent. An angel to put up with me. I felt too ashamed to tell her. I used to think Pierre changed after the war, but then I realized the war had changed him. Changed me. Changed all of us. After Pierre passed, my debt was paid. In full. Here are the records I made of the illegal transactions I and others made. I am guilty. So are these people. I only hope it's not too late for what I hid in guilt and shame to bring about a form of justice. I will find my justice in the next life, and I take full responsibility for all my actions. Léo Solomon

Sad and horrific. She'd seen her grandfather's reluctance to speak of the war and "dark times," heard his nightmares. That generation had survived. At a cost.

"I've hooked up the scanner," said Morbier. "Ready?"

The columned entries dated from 1950. Forty-nine years of entries. Léo Solomon's accounting system was methodical, with entries cross-referenced by name.

Later, she'd read and decipher this later. For now, compartmentalize. They needed to scan this whole thing and get it to *la Proc.*

But this was a payment log alone. There was no documentation to back it up. No invoices, check stubs—the proof was missing. Where in God's name was it?

For an hour and a half, she scanned entries. In the meantime, Morbier downloaded the scanned images onto his laptop, made backups.

Done. Finally she let herself look for her father's name, her heart trembling, her pulse speeding. Took a deep breath. Would this prove his guilt?

Leduc, Jean-Claude. Entries with amounts in 1974, 1978, 1981. The last entry was from November 11, 1989, the day he died in the bomb explosion in Place Vendôme. Ten thousand francs in the payee column but a zero in the recd column.

"*Voilà*," Morbier said. "I told you, Leduc. It's only old Léo's word, and half these people have kicked the bucket. You need tangible evidence to take anyone to court, any ordinary person, never mind ministers and police *préfets*."

Léo, the accountant, had known this. Had to have.

Then it hit her. Of course. "Léo's clever. It's a two-parter."

"*Quoi?*" Morbier rolled his wheelchair over.

"You don't keep your PIN number and bank card together, do you?" She tied the notebook back up with the old twine. Knotted it. "The proof's ready and waiting, Morbier."

"Figured it out, have you?"

She nodded. "Léo was guilt ridden for years. After his dear Marie dies, he wants do the right thing, expose the corruption—can't summon courage until Pierre kicks the bucket. But meanwhile, he's dying."

She stuck the notebook back in the Monoprix bag.

"Léo's old school, detail oriented, a precise accountant, as we see," she said. "He'd have kept the actual invoices, bank statements, receipts—I don't know what—separate. He'd have backed up his entries and confession."

"Safest place is a bank. To keep it secure in a vault, *non?* An accountant would do that."

"True, he would have hidden this proof. But think of his generation, his experience. This was a man who survived a POW camp, the type who tried to escape. He would have picked someplace basic, elemental. A place someone could find without a key, a place you wouldn't need a password for . . ."

"*Alors*, Leduc, so where are the bank statements and receipts for his entries?"

"Maybe he didn't have time . . . was trying to . . ." She remembered Madame Livarot saying Léo came back to the Gobelins before he died. Aimée had been meaning to get back there and poke around. What had happened to that idea?

Getting locked up by the *flics*, Elodie's kidnapping, the burner phone threats—*zut*—that's what had happened.

Merde. She should have carved out the time.

Somehow.

Paging through Leo's confession, Morbier snorted. "*Moi*, I could have written this fiction, a cheap novella sob story without meat on the bone."

Aimée released the wheelchair's brake, gritted her teeth.

"We need spoons," she said.

René grunted as he piled Morbier's wheelchair in the back seat of his car. His trunk was jam packed with computer equipment. Aimée paced in the tiny courtyard behind Ahmed's shop, waiting for *la Proc* to answer her phone. Ring . . . ring . . . Then a series of clicks as her call transferred.

In as few words as possible, she summed up her request.

"You're asking me to meet you on a Friday, my day off, Mademoiselle Leduc?" said Madame *la Procureure*, Edith Mesnard. In the background the clang of a pot, the metal flick as *la Proc* lit a cigarette, an inhale. "I'm not on call. Refer this to the duty procurer."

"But I trust you, Madame *la Proc*. Plus you like adventure," she said.

"Doing your best to intrigue me, mademoiselle?"

"I hope it's working. This will rock *la république*."

"My grandson's coming for family lunch. That's enough to rock my world today."

Great.

"The on-call procurers wouldn't be Lederer, Finchot, or Masile?" Aimée asked.

She heard a door close in the background. Quiet.

"How do you happen to have those names, mademoiselle?"

"If any of them are on duty, that's a problem."

"Quit the vague innuendos. What problem, and why?"

"The Hand."

"Not all this again. Didn't you wreak enough havoc?"

"I hate disturbing your day off, but you need to see this, Madame *la Proc.*"

"Sounds *un peu dramatique.*"

Aimée had to make her understand. "A young man died attempting to get this into your hands. Long story, but I have something that was meant for you. For your safekeeping."

A pause. "Deliver whatever it is to me at le Tribunal's intake office. Thirty minutes." She paused. "Not my office."

MORBIER SIGHED. "YOU'RE sure about this, Leduc?"

She'd set the Monoprix bag with Léo's notebook in it on his lap. He sat in René's front seat, a blanket over his legs.

"Got any other ideas?" She looked at her Tintin watch. "You need to hurry. You know what to say."

A cell phone in his hand began to ring. "It's Melac with some-thing to tell you," Morbier said after answering.

Her pulse jumped. "Has something happened?"

Forget wasting breath on recriminations; she needed to hear Chloé. She grabbed the phone.

"Melac, what's happened?" she said into it. "Where's Chloé?"

"Chloé's happy," said Melac before she could get more questions in. "Loves the garden here, entranced by the butterflies. She needs a diaper change."

The sounds of splashing water—a fountain? And then the dulcet baby tones she would have recognized anywhere. Her heart juddered. "Let me talk to her."

Melac laughed. "It's *Maman*, Chloé."

"*Bonjour, ma puce,*" she said, trying to keep calm.

Gurgling noises. Chloé's soft, sweet laugh. Relief flooded through Aimée.

Safe. Her baby was safe. "*Maman's* taking care of one more thing. Then—"

Melac's voice cut in. "You found the damn thing, Aimée. Let the people whose job it is do what they should have been doing all along."

"Can I talk to my . . . mother?" It still felt strange to say that. How her tongue stuck to the roof of her mouth. But she needed to apologize. To take the first step and start to deal with this ghost in her psyche.

Pause. "Sydney's out. She'll call you back."

Gone. Again.

"Take the train up here . . . Join us."

He thought her part was over.

But it wasn't.

"I've got one more thing to do," she said.

She handed Morbier back the phone. "No room for me, so I'll take a taxi and meet you at le Tribunal," she said. René turned the key in the ignition. She followed Ahmed as he opened the shop's back courtyard gates to the street and guided René out of the narrow space.

Watched as René pulled out.

She could do this, couldn't she? Had to do this. No choice.

SHE HAILED A taxi and, instead of following them to le Tribunal, told the driver, "Les Gobelins, the back entrance at rue
Berbier du Mets." On the way, she pulled off the wig and unbut-
toned the nurse's uniform. "Keep your eyes on the road," she told
the taxi driver watching her in the rearview mirror, "or forget
your tip."

BEYOND THE HIGH wall at the Gobelins's back door, she
could hear the gardeners' rakes and warbling birdsong. The sun's
rays warmed the back of her neck. She passed the place where
she'd shoved Cyril against the wall, where the *flics* had shown up
and taken her to the *commissariat*. Now she pictured the small
garden, the hedged path where she'd chased Cyril, the dye works
and chapel behind.

"*Excusez-moi, messieurs,*" she shouted through the back door.
After several attempts, she finally got one of the gardeners' attention. The metal back door scraped open.

"This is not an entrance, mademoiselle. Go around to the front
for the museum."

She smiled. Determined to make her concocted story work.
Showing a bit of leg wouldn't hurt.

"My friend Olivia, the weaver, forgot a silk thread pattern," she
began, borrowing the name of the crying girl from the concierge
loge. She promised to be in and out in five minutes—Olivia
was desperate, blah blah—and finally promised to meet the gar-
dener for an *apéro* later, traded phone numbers, assured him how
thankful Olivia would be. And *voilà*, she found herself inside by
the chapel.

The atelier complex hummed. She peeked inside the glinting windows of the weaving studio, then entered. Again, that smell of linen, the shushing sounds of wooden bobbins trailing silk threads through the heddle strands, the little clacks of the ivory-handled combs tamping down the warp. Weavers concentrated on the glowing colors on their massive looms. Madame Livarot's work desk was vacant.

"Looking for Madame Livarot again?"

The woman who'd pinned her hair up with a chopstick sat at a high-warp loom.

"*Oui*, have I missed her?"

"Retired."

"Just like that?"

A shrug. "She's a funny one."

"*Zut*, but of course she left instructions for me," said Aimée, making it up as she went along. "The information regarding Léo Solomon's bequest in his wife Marie's name."

Another shrug. "At the office, maybe?"

She made a show of consulting her Moleskine, thumbing the pages. "Ah no, it's about Léo Solomon's old apartment. She'd arranged for me to view it. We're planning a photo shoot, getting some history for the bequest."

"No idea, *desolée*. His old apartment's getting remodeled. See." She pointed a wooden bobbin. "There's someone going in the door of that building. Check with her."

Aimée recognized Olivia, the crying young woman with love troubles from the *gardien* loge.

"*Merci.*"

Aimée crossed the cobbles again, her ankle starting to throb. Olivia had disappeared. Aimée remembered Léo's apartment was on the third floor. Thick plastic sheeting covered the doorway and the old stone pavers of the landing. Inside, she found buckets of plaster half-dry, mixing sticks at half-mast. Old wood beams were stacked against the window, and everything smelled like paint. The rooms were gutted to the dark timbers and stone. The oak floorboards had been ripped up, exposing the crossbeams.

Nothing here.

Where had Olivia gone? She knew Madame Livarot and could shed some light, couldn't she?

Aimée passed the plaster buckets and made her way downstairs, following the cool flagstones of the corridor to the cellar door. A wooden door pitted with age stood under a delicate Gothic-style lintel festooned with carved stone leaves.

A damp chill assailed her as she picked her way down the stone steps to the cellar. She took out her penlight and shone it. Rat turds.

She shivered, avoiding them and keeping close to the wall.

The corridor was half stone, half packed dirt—a huge underground storage space of vaulted stone with boxes upon boxes piled high. Aimée scanned the boxes for any kind of labels. In the rear, she saw old wooden ones marked with black writing.

"What are you doing here?"

Olivia stood loading boxes onto a hand truck. Dim socket lights hung from metal hooks, giving the cellar an eerie glow.

"Madame Livarot directed me to locate Léo Solomon's documents," she said. "It's important to find them. Something to do with his wife's bequest; I'm not sure of the details." Not a complete lie. "I'm so glad you're here. I don't know where to start."

"Wait, you were here the other day," said Olivia, a sheen of perspiration on her upper lip. "But who are you?"

Aimée pulled out a card from her collection. "Aimée Leduc. My firm's handling Léo Solomon's legal matters. I'm here to pick up his documents—"

"Madame Livarot never told me anything about you or this," Olivia interrupted.

"Forgot? Other things on her mind? Didn't she just retire?" Aimée sensed something else going on here.

"Why would she send you and me both?" Olivia said suspiciously.

She was hiding something. Aiming for casual, Aimée smoothed down her pantsuit jacket. "Where did Madame Livarot tell you to look, Olivia?"

"How do you know my name?"

Stupid. "I'm not checking up on you."

"Sounds like it. Sounds like you're snooping around in things that don't concern you."

"Can you help me, Olivia?"

"I'm calling security."

Not this again. She needed to enlist Olivia's aid. "I'm here to fulfill Léo Solomon's promise to his wife—Madame Livarot's dear friend. Didn't Madame Livarot keep his things hidden because of her loyalty to Marie?"

"I don't know what you're talking about."

Aimée saw it now. The old wooden wine box with faded black letters. She could just make out STALAG III-C.

Before Olivia could stop her, Aimée hurried over and moved the boxes on top of it to the packed-earth floor. Musty scents filled her nose.

"What are you doing?" Olivia asked.

Aimée started to pry the old hinges off with her Swiss Army knife so she could move the wooden lid.

"Olivia, Léo Solomon wanted his papers in the right hands. He wanted to do the right thing. Those were his last wishes."

"You're lying!"

"Madame Livarot cared for Léo. Wouldn't she want his last wishes carried out? To make sure the truth comes out?"

"What truth?"

Aimée wedged the lid off. More musty scents.

She shone her penlight.

Empty.

Dismayed, she shook her head. No proof.

"See, you're crazy," Olivia said.

"I'm too late." Aimée's shoulders sagged in disappointment.

Olivia joined her. Sniffed. "That's so bizarre. All the boxes I found were empty, too."

Empty. Aimée wanted to kick something.

"Poor Madame Livarot," said Olivia. "She called me this morning and said she'd retired. Just like that. Asked me to bring up the old boxes. She was so positive Marie's things would be down here. There's nothing."

The timing of Madame Livarot's sudden retirement, sending Olivia for "Marie's things"—this meant something.

"The bequest isn't even here," Olivia said. "Old Léo was so adamant about it. It was all so weird . . . He came a few days before he died and begged Madame Livarot to take care of the donation."

"Donation of what, Olivia?"

"Why, the spoons; he wanted her to donate his collection of spoons," said Olivia. "I thought he'd lost his marbles."

Aimée shoved each of the other wooden boxes with her foot. All empty except the last one. A metallic shaking.

She knelt down in the dirt and pried the lid off. The box

emitted a smell of oxidized metal. Inside were twenty or thirty dented aluminum spoons, rusted with age. Léo's memory box.

She imagined how the POWs had moved earth spoonful by spoonful in the freezing camp.

How Pierre had saved Leo's skin, and Léo had paid for it the rest of his life. Now even in death, Pierre and the Hand won.

She shined her penlight wildly around the area, flashing it left and right, up and down. That was when she noticed the dirt. Reddish and packed in a distinct square under where the box had been.

She grabbed a rusting spoon, the flakes coming off in her hand, and started digging.

"What's the matter with you?" Olivia asked.

"Grab a spoon, Olivia. Please help me."

"You're as crazy as the old man."

"Léo's secret's buried here."

Aimée's phone trilled. She hit the ANSWER button, put it on speakerphone so she could keep digging.

Maxence's voice sounded far away. "Where are you, Aimée?"

Winded, she took a breath. Fine reddish dirt powdered the cuffs of her shirt, trailing up the jacket's silk-lined sleeves. "Underneath Gobelins."

"The burner phone rang. Should I answer?"

"Only if you can pinpoint where it's coming from."

"I'm trying. Hang up. I'll call back."

Olivia, now curious, joined in digging. The spoons scraped the dirt slowly into a mound. Deeper and deeper, small progress with each scoop. Aimée's spoon hit something hard, and the handle broke off.

"I heard that," said Olivia. "There's something there."

"Careful," Aimée said, now scooping the dirt up with her bare hands. Dust rose in the close air.

Her fingers felt the outlines of a box. Breathing hard, she pulled, maneuvering it as Olivia scraped away the excess dirt.

Again, Aimée's phone rang. She wiped her brow, hit SPEAKER-PHONE.

"Any luck, Maxence?" she said, keeping to her efforts with Olivia, tugging and pulling. Sweat dripped down her back. Finally they pulled out a grey metal file box.

"You're by rue de Croulebarbe?" Maxence's voice sounded tinny.

She tried jimmying the file's lock, which had rusted shut, with her knifepoint. Tried again. Not a budge.

Then stood and kicked it.

"Did you hear me, Aimée?" Maxence said.

The rusted lock gave way and sagged.

"Could you trace it, Maxence?" she asked.

Garbled noises.

Aimée lifted the lid to a plethora of documents neatly ordered by file tabs: BANK ACCOUNTS, INVESTMENTS, TRUST MANAGE-MENT, EMPLOYEES, RECEIPTS, ANNUAL FEES, OFFSHORE. Thick sections for each.

She opened the employee file. Scanned the beginning of the alphabet. Saw Éric Besson's firm. Her jaw dropped.

"Aimée . . . there's a problem," Maxence said.

"I'll say there's a problem," Aimée said. "Besson's—"

"The caller's near you," interrupted Maxence.

She stiffened. Reached for her Swiss Army knife with her free hand. "Olivia?" She'd been so intent on reading the file she'd forgotten about Olivia.

No answer.

Aimée slapped the file back inside the box, had almost made it to her feet when an arm encircled her neck in a choke lock. She gasped, trying to breathe. Trying to jab at the attacker with her knife.

Her hands were grabbed, her wrists flex-cuffed behind her. Plastic bit into her skin. Her knife was whisked out of her hand, and she found herself unceremoniously plopped on the dirt. Dust swirling over the borrowed Ungaro pantsuit.

Her chin quivered as she looked up. Her eyes brimmed with tears. "You? And you let me do all the work."

Xavier shrugged, grinding her cell phone to bits with his heel. "Not a gentlemanly thing to do. Apologies."

"Where's Olivia?"

"Unconscious. She'll live, if you behave."

It all made sense now. He'd cozied up to René, who'd sung his praises. *Brilliant. Gets things done. A fixer.* The puzzle pieces fit. A perverted puzzle.

"Doubt it," Aimée said. "The fixer leaves no traces."

"You're smart, Aimée." He didn't deny it. "That's why it's hard for me—"

"Hard for you?" She knew what he was about to say but feigned ignorance. "You won. The Hand keeps control again."

He hefted the file box. All her proof snatched out of her grasp. He brushed the dirt off his hands.

"That old Léo," he said. "He really stymied me; I admit it. Couldn't figure him out."

"He had what's called loyalty. Old fashioned, misguided, but he kept his word."

"But you, Aimée, you're good. Really smart. I ignored the spoons, thought they were a box of garbage. But clever you put it together and knew what they were for."

Keep him talking. Keep him engaged. Think of something.

"You know, Xavier, I have the worst taste in men. Stupid as

usual, but I like . . . liked you. Did you feel something? Was I wrong?"

He stared. A laser focus that unnerved her even more than her knife in his hands. "Non, you're right. We connected. Nothing like that since . . . But you and me, that wasn't in the plan."

So she should feel good?

"Plan?" she said. "You, bound by a plan? Never read you like that."

She'd sparked his interest. He was a narcissist at heart.

"How did you read me?" he asked.

"Brilliant. Wounded. Thirsty for something real. Like me."

How long could she keep this up? When would a security guard come?

But why would anyone come down here and check?

"I don't know why, Xavier, but something about you made me feel that no one had listened to you before. You'd struggled. Still struggle."

Xavier glanced at his watch. *Merde*.

"But I don't get why Éric would want me to find Léo's notebook if he was involved in the first place. Why did he get Marcus killed?"

"Doesn't matter now."

"He's dead?" She swallowed, trying to buy time. Took a stab in the dark, hearing the urgency in her own voice. "Éric worked for the Hand and got in over his head?"

"You could say that." Xavier shrugged. "Divorces are expensive."

She grabbed at a straw, remembering Dandin's dying words: *Son . . . fixer.* "Was it your father?"

"My father? What do you know about that?"

"That's right," she said frantically, remembering what he'd told her about his childhood over lunch. "I mean your stepfather."

Something in his eyes changed. "You met him. So you'd know."

She felt sick with the realization: Xavier must have been the one coming into Chopard's room as she left.

"Chopard was your stepfather, *c'est ça?* The notebook incriminated him, the organization he'd built, you, everything. He grew obsessed with finding it."

Xavier didn't disagree. She thought back to Marcus's cell phone log. The two unanswered calls from his uncle.

"Did Éric want to pull out after realizing the notebook's importance. Did he try calling Marcus to tell him to bring it back but—"

"Éric had the notebook right there in his hands. All he had to do was be a little tougher with the old man. Instead he made a charade out of sending it to *la Proc*, created a huge mess. The kid hid it, refused to give it up. *Comme d'habitude*, I had to fix things myself."

The fixer.

"You didn't have to kill him," she said. "Or Karine."

The flex-cuffs stung, cutting into her wrists. Her fingertips scrabbled in the dirt—trying to find a nail, something.

Damn manicure. Ruined.

"In business one always ties up loose ends," he said. His tone made her shiver.

"Was the homeless woman a loose end, too? And Dandin?"

"Sloppy job. I contracted out to an ex-*flic*, a friend of yours. My mistake."

Cyril. It made her sick. "No friend of mine."

He checked his watch again. What was he waiting for? Was someone coming to join him?

She had to make something happen. Open a nerve.

"How did your face really get that way?" she asked. "What happened?"

His expression changed. He hadn't expected that. Good. Keep him off kilter.

"It wasn't an accident, was it? I bet one of your victims fought back."

His eyes hardened. "No accident. My stepfather taught me a lesson. He'd learned from the best—the Nazis who tortured him in the stalag."

She sucked in her breath. Horrific. The war was a gift that kept on giving.

"But he's gone now, Xavier," she pleaded. "You don't have to keep his secrets anymore. You don't have to do his dirty work. Break away."

"He always said I wasn't good enough," said Xavier. "Never good enough. Neither was my mother. Chopard treated her like a whore. He never stopped saying, if you want this business, you do it yourself. You work harder than everyone else. Do things no one else would do; instill fear. That's the only way to power."

His voice had changed. Grown softer, sadder.

"I understand," she said.

"Do you?" he said, sarcastic. He'd come closer, squatted by her in the dirt, playing with her knife. Her pulse raced. "I think you'd say anything right now."

"I would. But I met your vampire of a stepfather and wouldn't wish him on anyone."

Xavier laughed. "Then you do understand. Forgive me."

That was when she knew she'd die. There on a dirt floor under a seventeenth-century tapestry factory, her baby far away, in a futile attempt to take down the Hand, which had murdered her father. She'd done what she'd promised she'd never do, leave her baby, like her mother.

But Aimée hadn't been able to help it. She'd been wired this way, and her wiring was off. Maybe René would explain it to Chloé someday.

"Your child, I'll take care of her."

A ripple of fear ran up Aimée's spine—and then fury. "The hell you will."

Xavier moved closer. "Someday I'll take your advice and break away."

"Prove it now, Xavier. You don't need . . ." She lowered her voice so he leaned closer. It was all or nothing.

With every bit of strength she had, she propelled herself off the wall behind her and head-butted him. A crack so hard her head felt as if it had split open. Lights danced in her eyes. She panicked, screamed in pain.

He'd been caught off-balance. She heard an ouf, flailing in the dirt. Blindly, she kicked out her legs, tried to stomp whatever body part she could reach. Grunts, crunching.

The haze in her vision cleared.

Xavier sprawled next to her. Blood dripped from his gaping neck and into the dirt. Her head throbbed; her eyes spun. She had to be seeing things.

Sydney had wiped off the Swiss Army knife, was cutting the flex-cuffs from Aimée's wrists.

"So handy, these knives," Sydney was saying. "Can use them for everything."

Her mother was helping her up.

"So you finally ditched the trench coat," Sydney said.

"What . . . ? How can you still . . . ?" The lights faded.

"Stay awake. Don't sleep."

So hazy. Aimée's eyes couldn't focus.

"You're concussed. You have to stay awake . . . Amy, you can do it . . ."

That was the last thing she remembered as the lights faded.

You can do it.

Saturday Morning

A SEPIA AUTUMN light fell across the starched hospital sheets. Aimée's head ached; her vision clouded and cleared. The needle drip in her arm stung. Her dry throat was scratchy.

Water. If only she could drink water without throwing up.

Were those brown things outside the window falling leaves or birds?

"Can't keep out of trouble, eh, Leduc?" Morbier sat in his wheelchair by the hospital bed. Put down his *Cuisine Actuelle* magazine. "If it's not one thing, it's something else."

"Did you"—her parched throat made it hard to raise her voice beyond a whisper—"get it to *la Proc*? All of it?"

Morbier nodded. "We kept the fanfare to a minimum, but *oui*, *la Proc*'s doing her job. Heads are rolling, as they say."

He was implicated, too. "So proud of you, Morbier."

"*Moi?*" He shrugged. "Small fry. The big fish interest them more."

The doctor came in, consulted a chart. Made tsk sounds. "Nasty concussion, mademoiselle. A bit of a scare with your optic nerve, which was damaged before, according to the X-rays . . . But with complete rest and quiet, you'll recover."

"Rest?" she said. "I've got a business to run. It's the Y2K millennium countdown."

"Look at the bright side," the doctor said. "Camus said autumn is a second spring when every leaf is a flower."

She tried propping herself up on her elbow. Slipped. "Where's Chloé? Where's my baby?"

The doctor checked her IV. Glanced at Morbier.

"Why, she's outside waiting with your mother to see you," said the doctor. "Now, remember, you need complete rest. Your family has informed me they have it all covered."

"My family? I don't understand."

"Her grandmother, her father, her godfather, your business partner." He checked his watch. "They assured me your care would be under control."

Her head spun, and it wasn't from the concussion.

"Keep up the recovery, and I'll discharge you tomorrow." He smiled. "Up to seeing your family? Ready?"

Was she?

"Oh, she's ready, Doctor," said Morbier.

The hospital room door opened.

Acknowledgments

I HAVE SO many people to thank for their kindness, amazing generosity, and incredible help: Dr. Terri Haddix, a font of medical knowledge; the talented weavers; Tricia Goldberg; Micala, Chris and Jean Pierre Larochette; Jean Satzer, cat *maman* and reader extraordinaire; my accomplice in crime, Libby Fischer Hellmann; and Robin Stuart for the spirit catcher.

In Paris: dear Ingrid *et les filles*, who helped me avoid *fausses pistes*; the brothers Arakel and Haïgo of Chez Trassoudine; *haute-lissier* Olivia for sharing her time and expertise. Helpful beyond measure were Blandine de Brier Manoncourt and Dr. Christian de Brier; those walks with Huguette Allard and Julie McDonald. Above and beyond thanks to Arnaud Baleste, the sweetest *l'horloger* on Boulevard Auguste Blanqui; *toujours* Benoît Pastisson and Gilles Thomas, Heather Stimmler-Hall, Elke, Cathy Nolan, Carla Chemouni-Bach, always Anne-Françoise and Cathy Etile, *policier* Dede13. To Léo Malet and Tardi for inspiration; les Temps des Cerises in Butte-aux-Cailles; *ancien résistant* Naftali Skrobek and Lidia, plotmeister James N. Frey; the wonderful Soho family: Bronwen, Paul, Rudy, Abby, Rachel, Janine, Amara, Monica *et toutes*; dear Katherine Fausset; and my editor extraordinaire, for her insight and putting up with me, Juliet Grames. But nothing would happen without Tate and Jun.